**Bo**



*Blackwater Crossing*

*The Death Dealers*

*Without Redemption*

*Brothers of the Blood*

**The Freedom Series**

*Free to Run*

# Free to Run

## Book One In The Freedom Series

David Griffith

THIS BOOK IS A WORK of fiction. Names, characters, places, and incidents are the product of the author's imagination or are used fictitiously. Any resemblance to actual events, locales, or persons, living or dead, is coincidental.



Cover Artist: Katrianna Anderson

www.artstation.com/katrianna[1]



First edition November 2018

1. http://www.artstation.com/katrianna

# Prologue

I would have been content to leave my earlier years a distant memory, but after some pressure I allowed my part in this chronicle to be included. The story takes the reader to a prior time when I was more certain the world had no end of opportunity. In one's youth, a person makes decisions that are often life changing. I fell in love with a beautiful woman, which set in motion a train of events I could have never foreseen.

Dina came into my life some years before I reached the peak of my career with Stirling Associates. During that time, I recruited several dozen intelligence agents, some of them exceptional. You may have seen reports, or possibly have read Lonnie Bower's accounts regarding his years with our company. He remains one of the best, and though he is reticent to embark on new missions into the dark places of Mexico and Central America, we are still in contact on a regular basis.

The early death of my parents resulted in a boyhood move to America to live with a grandmother I'd never met. Gram gave me love, and a home for which I'll always be grateful, and that is where my part of the story begins. Dina, the great love of my life tells her own story. She is, and will always be an exceptional woman.

Best Wishes,

Frederick Roseman

# Chapter 1

When the silver BMW pulled onto the white gravel driveway of our Sonora ranch, I had no reason to suspect trouble. It was only Eduardo, though I'd no idea where he'd found the money for *that* car. Regardless, it was no concern of mine, and I had no intention of going to the house—at least not yet. Chiquita danced sideways, her ears pointed forward like tiny brown homing pigeons. The electronic timer flashed the red milliseconds as we crossed the line, driving for a record, running as only she could. She powered around the first barrel, every muscle working in perfect time, her body flexed, reaching for more speed as she came out of the turn. At the second, she barely broke stride, her lead change so smooth I hardly felt it happen. Then she was flying again, looking for the third barrel in the cloverleaf pattern. My knee whispered against it, and then she leveled out and scampered for home, her mane whipping against my hands. Even before I glanced at the clock, I knew it had been another exceptional run. We were ready.

Chiquita, the best horse I'd ever ridden, was the offspring of an Easy Jet stallion Papa had bought at a sale in Fort Worth. She had all the ability and breeding to be a barrel racing sensation. More important, she had the attitude it took to be a winner. That combination was as rare as water on our vast desert property.

After the mare's breathing returned to normal, I stepped off and walked under the shade awning to unsaddle her. The paperwork had already been processed. We were America bound. We would cross the border and find a place to call home, far from the furtive intrigue that surrounded my father. I still hadn't decided where, or how I was going to make it happen, but my future would be different.

I brushed Chiquita down, then scuffed my way to the house, wondering why Eduardo Garcia had picked this inopportune time for a visit. I didn't dislike him. We'd known each other forever. The problem was my family. They seemed to think he was the perfect catch for their only daughter.

The Garcia ranch made our few thousand acres look like a city lot. If I married Eduardo, my future would be assured. And my parents? They certainly didn't need an in-law corner on the Garcia money, but maybe that didn't matter. The suspicion that his family wealth and status might be the real reason for his welcome made my face burn. Surely Mama wouldn't . . .

I pushed open the side door that led into the kitchen of our adobe rancher and opened the fridge to pour a glass of water from the pitcher inside. Mama's voice, unusually nervous, carried through from the *sala*. As I trudged through the dining room my eyes darted to the ever-present crucifix above the arched doorway. Mama's next words sent a wave of anger and panic to the tips of my fingers. "Eduardo, you have our blessing. Your father and Bernardina's have discussed the matter." My mother's use of my full name didn't add to my good humor. I hated my clunky birth name. Everybody at school, including Eduardo knew me as Dina, pronounced as if there were two long e's. My mother, I think, used it whenever anger or frustration ratcheted the volume in her voice. She rattled on with her best attempt to seal my fate. "Bernardina is still very young, but that is the best time to marry."

A garbled, angry novena fell from my lips like boiling drops of acid as I stared at the crucifix. "We fly to thy patronage, O holy Mother . . . our petitions . . . deliver us from all dangers," . . . especially this one! Me forever linked to Eduardo Garcia? My hands balled into fists. This wasn't the 1900's. People didn't arrange for their children to marry the best catch in the neighborhood. I mean, my parents were old fashioned and probably the strictest Catholics in the whole of Mexico, but this was loco crazy. Caution stopped me from bursting angrily into the room. I didn't want to be disrespectful, but marrying Eduardo was *so* not going to happen. Sure, I'd gone out with him a few times. Both of us had attended the same American high school in Douglas, so we had naturally been thrown together during social occasions. Apparently, that was enough to seal my fate.

My eyes dropped to my brown roper boots. I forced the right one forward. The other had to follow, and that's how I made it into the room. Conversation instantly ceased. Eduardo sat on the middle cushion of the tan leather couch. He stood and stepped hesitantly toward me. His eyes held a hopeful glint, one I had no wish to see. I avoided his gaze and glared at my father. Papa stared at my mother, who gawked at Eduardo, then at me.

"How good to see you, Dina." Eduardo held out his hand. I took the tips of his fingers and did the phony little head tip that Mexican girls of my supposed station were expected to do—in 1923. It pleased my mother, but Eduardo's face fell. He'd executed the handshake number to impress my parents. He certainly wouldn't have done that if we had met elsewhere.

"It's a pleasure to see you as well, Eduardo." He didn't miss the hint of sarcasm in my voice, even if it was intended for Mama. He shifted his feet, now uncomfortable and self-conscious.

"Please, sit." I motioned toward the seat he'd left.

"Thank you." He retreated to the sofa.

I took another sip of water, then gingerly perched at the farthest end of the couch, prepared for whatever this ambush might hold. I hadn't long to wait. Mama started with her usual frontal assault.

"Eduardo has asked your father for your hand in marriage. Of course, we are aware things have changed in the world and that it is customary for young people to choose whomever they want to marry. We would have it no other way, but your father and I believe you are well-suited to each other, and of course you obviously have mutual interests, so . . ."

"So what, Mama?" I set my glass on the side table and clenched my trembling hands in my lap.

"You will marry. We will have a large wedding with five bridesmaids and—"

"I am not doing that."

"What do you mean? Why would you not get married?"

"No Mama, and what's more—I am leaving Mexico."

"Leaving Mexico? Where are you going?" Papa asked timidly.

"To Nevada—to college." Truthfully, I hadn't a clue where to go, so I picked the first state that came to mind. Both my parents stared at me, shock written across their faces. I might as well have said I was abandoning the Catholic faith, or that I had decided to become a prostitute.

I glanced sideways. Eduardo sat quietly, rubbing his long thin fingers together. He met my eyes. "I should leave," he whispered. He nodded a silent farewell to my parents. I stood and walked with him to the front door. Both of us stuttered an apology. Whatever camaraderie we had enjoyed in the past was gone, instantly skewered by unspoken accusations of betrayal. I felt he had overstepped the bounds of close friendship. Sure, we had been out a few times, but I'd never given him any reason to think I wanted more than a casual relationship. The resentment in his eyes as we walked outside was proof enough I had misled him. The silver sports car spun out of the yard, scattering gravel over the carefully tended east lawn. There was not so much as a backward glance from the angry and humiliated Eduardo—which wasn't my fault.

I returned to the *sala* to face my parent's wrath. Secretly, I was elated. I'd spoken the words that burned inside me. I wanted to leave, to search for opportunities that our country could never give me. Even without my parent's money, I would find a way to get into school. College rodeo would give Chiquita and me time to gain valuable experience before we broke into the tougher professional circuit. Inside my heart, I determined this was the time to make the final break from the cloying protection of parents who would never let go.

The recriminations started the moment I entered the room.

"Why do you want to leave, and go to the United States, like some—some penniless immigrant?" Mama now stood in the middle of the floor, her hands beseeching heaven and all the saints and angels for wisdom with her rebellious daughter.

Papa sank further into the wicker back of his chair, unwilling as always to run afoul of Mama's temper.

"Perhaps a vacation is what Dina needs." My father's quiet voice was a welcome contrast to Mama's harangue. He laid a hand on my shoulder. "After that, you could attend university in Guadalajara or Mexico City."

I fidgeted on the couch. University anywhere in Mexico wasn't going to further my goals. Mama paced around the room, then stopped in front of the big window, eyeing me as if I were an opposing chess queen that would require three of her most valuable players to capture. How could I ever explain my deep need to succeed to my mother? I needed to follow my heart toward a dream that had always been beyond reach—until Chiquita. With her, the dream could become reality. She would take me to a scholarship, maybe even to the National Finals. I had the opportunity to be the best barrel racer in the world with that unbelievably fast mare. My name would be right up there with all the champions. Nothing would stop me.

"I am not going to *any* university in Mexico. I'm going to the United States—with Chiquita."

My father shrugged. "She is *your* horse."

"Rodeos—and barrel racing. That is all you ever think about." Again, Mama threw her hands in the air, calling for heaven's help.

I admit I did the same as Mama, though I hoped with fewer theatrics. I suspected God wasn't inclined to help either of us in this mess, so he just left us to battle it out.

"What is wrong with doing all that here?" Mama lowered her voice. "If God had intended for you to follow rodeos all over America, you would have been born there. Don't we have enough horse events in our country?"

"Actually, we don't, Mama. Besides, Chiquita's breeding makes her a barrel racing horse. She is not a *charreada* horse. Neither am I suited for any of the fine opportunities a woman *so* doesn't have in our country."

Mama's lips compressed to a rigid line. "If you do this, it will be on your own. There will be no money or help from us."

I glanced at Papa. He avoided my eyes and stared at the floor. Further discussion would only fan Mama's anger, and Papa would never stand against Mama in this battle, or any other for that matter. Panic coursed through my veins. It was all very well to sit here and say I was leaving; that I would go north to make my way in the world. But how would I survive, and take care of Chiquita? I had only a few hundred dollars. I'd never needed any of my own money. All I had to do was tell Papa what I wanted, and it was provided. How would I make it through four years of school without their assistance? Neither my grades nor my unproven rodeo abilities would attract any immediate help with tuition. There was no chance of success without my parent's money. Nevertheless, foolish pride and stubbornness made me stand and walk out of the room.

The next morning, I loaded Chiquita in my rickety old single horse trailer and prepared to drive the short distance north to the border. I'd planned well. The necessary health papers for Chiquita would already be waiting for me at U.S. Customs. At the last moment, Mama came outside and hugged me, then huffed her way back into the house, or so it seemed. Papa stood beside my pickup, which was at least a bit newer than the trailer. He walked around the rig, kicked at the tires and peered at the hitch, trying to put off the last moment of farewell, but eventually there were no more mechanical things to check. We hugged, neither of us uttering anything of importance, but Papa told me he loved me and to go with God.

I drove out of our yard, my lips set in a firm line, my hands white-knuckled on the wheel to keep them from trembling. In the rearview mirror, Papa stood with his hands stuffed in the pockets of his jeans, his shoulders slumped forward, eyes staring at the red Mexican soil. Once he waved, and I forced myself to stick my hand out the window in a desultory farewell. After all, he was at least part of the reason I was leaving. It was then I saw the white envelope on the seat. Papa must have slipped it into the cab when I wasn't looking. It held a few hundred American dollars, enough to get me to wherever I was going.

# Chapter 2

By the time my pickup tires rolled onto the northbound highway to the border, tears threatened to blur my vision. My future beckoned. Somehow, even without my parent's money, with Chiquita, I would survive.

The familiar border crossing into Arizona appeared, the same one I'd crossed every day for the last three years to go to school in Douglas. All I needed to do was pick up the paperwork for Chiquita, a simple formality, certainly nothing to worry about. For any horse to travel to the United States, a clean Coggin's test was a necessity.

I parked the pickup and trailer in the appropriate spot near U.S. Customs and walked inside the building. This was familiar territory for me. I knew most of the agents on both sides of the border, so when I stopped at the desk to pick up the paperwork, it was a surprise to see a strange face. The tag on his right shirt pocket spelled out his last name. Agent Higgins sorted through a file cabinet and pulled out a document. He scrutinized them for a moment.

"Miss Rodriguez, usually we would go out and match these to the horse you have in your trailer. However, this time it won't be necessary."

I smiled and held out my hand for the papers. "Thank you, Sir." I was used to getting preferred treatment here.

He pointed at the bottom section on the first page. "You misunderstood me. You are not crossing the border, not with *this* mare."

I felt the blood rush to my face. "What's wrong? No—I don't understand."

His lips formed a hard line as he handed me the documents. "She failed. She is a carrier for Infectious Equine Anemia. Her Coggins Test came back with a positive reading—twice."

My hand trembled as I stared at the damning evidence that would change everything in my life. One little checkmark had shattered all my dreams. I stared at the pen mark on the white paper. A black blot in the box indicated that Chiquita, though she had no signs of the disease, was a dreaded carrier of the virus. The horse that carried all my hopes on her scampering fast legs would never enter America.

I looked up at Agent Higgins. He shrugged. "I'm sorry. Those are the regulations. Nothing I can do."

I stumbled outside, my vision blurred and watery. My throat tightened, but I didn't cry. Leaving Chiquita was too life-shattering for mere tears. Those were stored for later, when I led her into the deserted pen and unfastened the halter. When I gazed into her intelligent, liquid brown eyes, the storm broke. We had spent so many days and hours together. I might never see her again.

Eventually, I walked out of that dusty corral. She would eventually die from the disease. Bidding farewell to Chiquita carried all the trauma of the death of a loved one. At the pickup, I speed-dialed the number of our *Segundo*, Raul. The answering machine at the horse barn picked up the call. I left a terse message asking him to pick up the mare and take her home. He would understand. That, I didn't have to spell out.

The raw pain diminished as the miles fell away. I didn't have a destination, or how I was going to get there, but hunger and the need for gas forced me to pull into a truck stop near Phoenix. I topped up the tank, parked the pickup and empty trailer, then walked into the restaurant. Truck drivers and tourists filled the booths, people with a purpose, all of them headed somewhere. Where was I going with my empty horse trailer? What goal did I have now? Chiquita had been more than just a ticket to the pay window. She had been my life. For years, she had been my first thought in the morning, and most times my last before sleep claimed my tired body.

I stirred cream into the black cup of coffee the waitress set in front of me. Bitterness overwhelmed me, and I again wiped at stinging tears of anger. Why had this happened? The odds of a horse having that dreaded disease were one in several hundred, maybe a thousand. It could have been any of our dozens of other ranch horses. Why the beautiful, talented Chiquita?

The waitress brought the quesadillas I had ordered. Under different circumstances, they would have been fine, but today they tasted like scorched dirt. Slathered with sour cream and imitation salsa, they became chewable. Two women in the booth behind me chattered non-stop, lamenting over irascible husbands and wandering, ungrateful children. Someday those might be my worries. For now, I needed to find a way to carve my own niche in this land I would try to make mine.

Stopping would mean I would have to pay for a motel. Besides, anger and sadness still overwhelmed me. The open highway would be preferable to tossing on a cheap mattress until dawn. I might as well drive—but to where? Anywhere in Arizona was too close to home. How about Washington or Oregon? I'd never been there, but I'd seen pictures. They looked cold and rainy.

I slid out of the booth and walked to the counter to pay for my food. As I waited for the waitress to bring my bill, I thumbed through the tourist brochures on a rack beside the cash register. Most were about the Grand Canyon or other Arizona sites of interest. One of the pamphlets had an outline of a bucking horse and a barrel racer on the front. Idly, I leafed through the pictures and script advertising the glories of a small town in Montana. The place had everything I needed: rodeo, a college, and best of all, it was a long way from Mexico. I wanted to be where the name Dina Rodriguez was neither synonymous with wealth, nor a hindrance to my goals. Now that I didn't have Chiquita, my objectives were all scrambled, but whatever they were, I would reach them on my own.

I stuck the pickup in gear and pointed it toward Montana. Surely there couldn't be any Mexicans as far north as Miles City.

# Chapter 3

Two days later, the late afternoon sun lit the first Miles City exit. The same bucking horse statue I'd seen on the brochure back in Phoenix graced a parched strip of grass on the right side of the median. The rock-strewn hills garnished with sagebrush reminded me of home, only our hills were even rockier, and in Sonora we had saltbush and greasewood rather than sagebrush. Weariness, and a touch of homesickness might have colored my first impression of what I hoped might be my new home. Bars slouched back from the street, beckoning sinfully to unwary travelers. I averted my eyes when a drunken cowboy staggered onto the sidewalk. Overhead, a neon buffalo advertised the establishment below. My shoulders slumped. I'd made a mistake. Farther down Main Street, a turn of the century hotel reached for the sky, but of course it was next to one more saloon. It looked old enough to be in my price range. I drove around the block, then pulled onto a side street to find a parking spot. A small sign toward the back of the hotel announced to the world that Viva Mexico offered fine Mexican dining." A touch of resentment tightened my hands on the wheel. Mexicans came this far north? It didn't matter. If I went any further, I would be in Canada. No, this would have to do.

My eyes darted across the lobby as I trudged toward the girl at the counter. "I would like a room, please—if you have one?"

"Sure." She was blond, pretty, and popped her bubble-gum at twenty-second intervals. I avoided her inquisitive stare as she shoved a registration form in front of me.

While I filled out the card, she tapped her fingers on the counter in time with whatever music played into her right ear from her headset.

I hesitated over the home address. I didn't live in Sonora anymore, but I had no other residence, so I left the line blank.

"Where you headed?" the girl asked in an attempt to be friendly.

I looked up and pushed the card toward her. "Here."

Her head snapped up. "Oh-h?"

"I'm going to enroll at the college this fall."

"What course? That will be sixty-nine dollars."

I opened my wallet and fished out four twenties. "Equine Studies." I had no idea how I would use a two-year degree in Equine Studies. I loved horses, but how would that translate into an income? I shoved the money across the counter.

"We can't take cash. I need a credit card."

"Uh," I stuttered, "I don't have one." Suddenly, all the weary miles I'd driven, and the grief of losing Chiquita overwhelmed me. All I wanted was a hot shower and a good night's sleep. After that, I'd decide how to start my life two thousand miles from home.

"Then I need a hundred-dollar deposit."

Grudgingly, I dug into my wallet for five more twenties from my dwindling supply.

"I'm sorry. I just do what they tell me." The blond girl looked at me sympathetically. "Are you going to live in Pioneer Hall or the Quads?"

"I'm not sure. For now, I'm looking for a place to rent—and a job."

"Hmm, jobs aren't easy to come by in this backward dump. This fall, I'm moving to Billings. I'm out of here."

I nodded, uncomfortable with her vehement criticism.

She slapped a tiny folder with a key card on the counter. "Room two eleven."

"Thank you." I clutched the folder as if it were a pass to the Pearly Gates, then escaped into the gathering dusk to my dusty pickup. An overnight bag and a change of clothes were all I needed. After locking the doors, I clumped through the lobby and up the stairs to my room. Before I passed out from exhaustion, I would eat at the restaurant. Surely, a Mexican eating place couldn't be too expensive.

My hotel experiences were limited to Guadalajara and Mexico City, where Mama made sure we stayed at only the best lodgings. I dropped my bag on the bed and surveyed the room. A couple of cheap Frederick Remington reproductions decorated the walls. I didn't care. The bed looked wonderful. A single night-stand and battered desk were a several income grades from the hand carved wood I was used to, but they were more than adequate. Mama would have been mortified that her daughter was staying in a place like the Stockman's Hotel. A half-grin creased my tired lips because nothing in Miles City would have pleased my mother, and I didn't care. This town suited me just fine.

For a few moments, I collapsed on the bed, glad to have a refuge away from the world. Then I showered, walked downstairs and through the lobby to the restaurant. The waiter's face, like mine, was darker than most folks on this street, so we spoke Spanish. To fall into my mother tongue was comforting, but I vowed to avoid the place. I wanted to fit in, to be an American, and most Americans don't speak Spanish.

I ordered enchiladas, and when the waiter set them in front of me, I furtively glanced to both sides then bowed my head. A couple at the next table cast sidelong glances at me while I muttered the same prayer we always said at home before a meal. Even if they thought I was weird, it didn't seem a great time to ditch the God of my childhood.

The food, authentic and superb reminded me of home, but I ate too quickly to enjoy it. Then, in the gathering darkness I took the stairs to my room and crawled into the queen-sized bed. Tomorrow I would find a place to live, then a job. I pulled the sheet up around my neck as possible employment possibilities kaleidoscoped through my weary brain. A niggling doubt rose to the surface before I lost consciousness. What skills could I offer an employer? Most of my friends had worked after-school jobs in Agua Prieta or Douglas, but my family's wealth had insulated me from that necessity. Instead, I'd spent every spare minute with Raul and the horses. The only work experience I had would be of little use in town. And college? That could come later—if I found a job.

My eyes opened before the morning sun illuminated the street outside my window. I wanted nothing more than to roll over and go back to sleep, but that didn't seem wise. I was nearly out of money, so I threw off the covers and stumbled toward the shower. A half-hour later, I tiptoed downstairs. The Mexican restaurant wasn't open, so I walked a couple of blocks to a small café sandwiched between two bars. Toast and orange juice were all I could afford. While I ate, I scanned the local newspaper for a cheap apartment. There was little to be had, especially in my price range. Nevertheless, I skipped up the stairs to my room and started dialing. The first call, there was no answer. A man who seemed interested picked up the second call on the first ring. That lasted until I told him I was going to school in the fall.

His voice was gruff. "We don't take students."

There didn't seem any sense in arguing. The third call sounded promising, a furnished basement suite on the edge of town. A woman answered. Her voice crackled with age.

I took a deep breath. "Hello. I'm calling about the basement suite you had advertised. Is it still available?"

"Yes?" The voice hesitated.

"May I look at it this morning?"

"This is for yourself?"

"Yes."

"Good. Only one single woman is allowed. No one else."

"That will be fine. I'm starting school here in September."

A short silence ensued while the woman digested this. I had said the wrong thing. She wouldn't allow any students either.

"I am not a person who parties. I won't—"

"Okay." She interrupted me. "You can come at ten o'clock. The address is 2160 North 7th Street."

"Thank you. I'll be there." I hung up the phone and high-fived . . . God I guess, because no other person graced my humble room.

After retrieving my hundred-dollar deposit and settling my bill, I walked across the street to my pickup. I had an hour before I needed to meet what I hoped would be my new landlady. I set my bag inside and walked up one side of Main Street and down the other scrutinizing each business for a "Help Wanted" sign. My funds were already dangerously low. Even if I started work today, I would run out of money before I cashed my first paycheck.

Fear stirred inside me. What if I didn't find a job? Two blocks later I spotted a sign tucked into the corner of a window. I stepped back and surveyed the premises. Overhead a red neon sign with a bucking horse motif shouted to the world that this was the Spur Bar. No, I would never work in a place like that. Nervously, I peered ahead to the buffalo sign down the street. How well I remembered the cowboy who yesterday had staggered onto the sidewalk. I could never serve whiskey to drunken cowboys. Something would show up. Even cleaning stalls would be better than that.

I squared my shoulders and timidly walked farther up the street, then back down the other side, hoping for anything that would provide a paycheck. There was nothing, and I returned to my pickup, thoroughly defeated. I would look later. Now, it was time to go meet the lady with the basement suite.

I found the right street, then idled north toward the edge of town, peering at each house number. On the edge of the open prairie, a single-story yellow bungalow sat on a small acreage. The yard appeared unkempt, much in need of Alberto, our gardener. But the thought of Alberto made me homesick, enough that I wanted to turn my pickup around and drive all the way back to Mexico. Instead, I pulled into the driveway and knocked on the door. Immediately, the same cracked voice I'd heard on the phone, answered.

"Come in."

Timidly, I turned the knob and stepped inside. An old woman struggled to a standing position from a big leather recliner, then toddled forward behind a wheeled walker. Her hair was snow-white, her shriveled body hunched with age. Indignant eyes peered malevolently at me.

"So, who are you? You're one of those Mexicans, aren't you?"

"No, I—"

"Well then, where did you get the brown face? You look Mexican to me." She tottered toward me.

"I am an American." I tried to make my five-foot-four frame an inch taller.

"Sure you are. Do you have a job? Probably not. How are you going to pay the rent? Not that I've decided to rent to you."

"I have a job," I lied.

"Where at?"

"I will be working at the Spur Bar." Another lie, and not even a good one. My face flushed with embarrassment, but she didn't seem to notice.

"If I rent to you, there are no men allowed. I'll have no men sleeping over, so if you have loose morals, go elsewhere."

The woman's eyes flashed daggers at me as I shook my head. "No, I am not, I don't have—" Anger and caution clamped my jaws together. I needed a place.

"Alright. You might as well look at it." She thrust a key at me. "Go down the stairs, around the side of the house. If it's suitable, well . . . I may take a chance on you. Mind you, no monkey business. I may be old, but I'm not dumb."

I nodded my head, took the key and escaped. How I wanted to tell her I'd changed my mind, that I didn't have to take her miserable suite, that I had other options—but I didn't. Carefully, I sidestepped down the frost-heaved concrete stairs and unlocked the weathered and warped door. I pulled. It refused to budge. I gripped the rusty knob with both hands and wrenched it open. The hinges screeched like a backyard tomcat. The noise would undoubtedly give that sharp-tongued old woman an exact schedule of my movements.

Only three burners worked on the stove, the cupboards were one step above cardboard, and I had to flush the toilet twice to make anything happen. I tiptoed over the stained lime-green Berber that passed for a living room carpet and tried to avoid breathing in the musty smell. It was ghastly and had its own civil war with the ancient yellow linoleum in the kitchen. I shrugged. There wasn't a choice. Gingerly, I navigated the stairs, accepted Mrs. Riddler's long list of verbal conditions, and filled out her rental contract. After I'd plunked down the first month's rent and damage deposit, thirty-seven dollars kept the left side of my wallet from meeting the right, and it wasn't likely I'd get any help from God after the two lies I'd told.

# Chapter 4

After I'd extricated myself from Mrs. Riddler's dire warnings if I came within a mile of breaking her rules, I backed the empty horse trailer into a corner of the driveway and unloaded my pickup. That took all of five minutes. The apartment had been advertised as furnished. That meant it had a garage sale table, two mismatched chairs and a rickety bed. I wanted nothing more than to just get settled, kick back and let a good movie temporarily mask the harsh reality of my new life. However, I had no T.V. and I still had no job. Also, there were no blankets on the bed, and if I were going to eat, I could spare no money to buy any. My few clothes easily fit into the door-less bedroom closet. I spread the thin blanket I'd taken from my bedroom at home onto the bed. Though the thin layer would do little to ward off the night-time chill, I had nothing else.

I surveyed my new digs. They weren't great. No, actually it was a dump, but I wouldn't dwell on that. I would be thankful for a place to sleep. Quickly, I ran a brush through my hair, walked out to the pickup, and headed for town. After today, there would be no money for gas. Whatever job I acquired had to be within walking distance. An assortment of motels had a love affair with the interstate. I checked at every one, but none seemed to want housekeeping help, certainly not from a girl with no work experience of any kind.

After the fifth rejection, I trudged away discouraged and angry. A week ago, I would never have considered walking into such a place. Now, I was begging to clean their rooms. My stomach rumbled with hunger. It had been a long time since the toast and orange juice but eating would have to wait. Tonight, I would buy food at a grocery store, something that didn't cost much like rice and beans, because after today, I could not afford to eat more than once a day. My thirty-seven dollars would have to stretch until my first paycheck.

By five o'clock, I'd trudged every street in town that had any kind of business. At the end of the last block, a help-wanted sign hung from a string in a dry cleaner's window. I straightened my shoulders and opened the glass door. A stocky, balding man worked behind the counter. He turned, inspected my face, and gave me "the look." My face is brown. I know "the look."

"May I help you?" His eyes flickered over my face, then moved downward.

"I'm inquiring about a job." I pointed to the sign in the window. "Do you have an application I can fill out?" I tried to smile, but where his eyes rested, he wouldn't have seen that.

"Oh . . . of course." His eyes moved up a foot to my face. Whatever he saw there changed his mind. "Actually no, the job is already filled."

"Then why is the sign still in the window?" I snapped. Angry tears filled my eyes. Before he saw them, I whirled and marched out the door. After all, it was his business, but for a moment, an unreasonable resentment washed over me. To him, I was just another illegal Mexican. I was too discouraged to look any further, but as I drove down Main Street, I glanced over at the Spur Bar and the help wanted sign. Quickly, I turned away. Anything but that. Surely tomorrow I would find something.

After a stop at the grocery store, I pulled into the driveway. Mrs. Riddler peeked through the curtains. Pretending I didn't notice her surveillance, I grabbed the small grocery bag, walked down the steps, and unlocked my squeaky door. At the last moment, I'd decided I would savor the American diet. And tomorrow. And the next day. I emptied the bag. Either macaroni and cheese or Chinese noodles. I chose the noodles, but they didn't make me less homesick. Even our gardener ate better than this.

Later, prayer beads in hand, I sat on the bed and listlessly recited the familiar prayer. "In the name of the Father and of the Son . . ." What did it mean? As the words I'd recited so often rolled off my tongue, I wondered if they had ever actually meant anything. *"I believe in the Holy Spirit, the forgiveness of sins . . . ."* The forgiveness of sins? Today I'd lied to Mrs. Riddler, and I had been angry at the revolting man in the dry cleaners. I tried to continue the prayer, but nothing more would come. The words stopped at the ceiling, and I ground the beads together in frustration. Hopelessness overwhelmed me, adding more burdens to the homesickness.

Eventually, I gave up, threw the beads on the corner table and undressed. An old sweater served as a pillow. Most of the night I shivered under the single blanket, but somewhere near dawn I must have slept because the sun was well up when I awoke.

Mrs. Riddler's basement suite was situated so I had to walk right by her living room window to get to the driveway. Every time I came or went, she would know, and that first morning she was waiting for me.

"Young lady." She hobbled behind her walker to the front door.

"Yes, Mrs. Riddler?"

"What time do you go to work? Obviously, it isn't early, as you stay in bed until almost noon."

My face burned. How did she know I'd slept so late this morning?

"Well, speak up." Once again, her flashing eyes telegraphed her disdain for me, my heritage, and my future.

"Uh-h, I'm not sure what my hours will be. And yes, I did sleep in. I may have to work late." Now she would discover I'd lied to her, and I would have to find another place to live.

"You young people today don't know how to work. Why, when I was . . . oh never mind." A contemptuous wave of her bony hand was my dismissal. "As long as you pay the rent." She shuffled back inside, and I escaped to walk to what I hoped would not be my new job at the Spur Bar. My rumbling stomach and the lies I'd told gave me little choice.

Every step along the side of the pavement brought a new and unique fear of what it would be like working in a bar. The drunks with leering eyes and pawing hands were something with which I had no experience. How did one serve drinks? How did those girls slip sideways through a crowd of dancers with a tray full of glasses without spilling them all over the floor? That wasn't me. I would muck out stalls, scrub floors, clean toilets in public bathrooms . . . anything but the Spur Bar.

My steps slowed as I approached the downtown area. There must be a job mucking out stalls? What about the public toilets? Lots of big-hatted cowboys idled by on Main Street. Some even looked genuine enough to have stalls to clean, but none of them stopped to offer me a job, and I didn't know where to go to find out if they needed help. Once more, I walked every street in the business district. No new "help wanted" signs filled any windows.

When I got to the Spur Bar, my feet were dragging. How I hoped the sign would be gone. Even if it wasn't, surely they would want someone with experience. My stomach growled. I should have eaten some of the noodles for breakfast.

The covered entry had no glass to look through, nothing with which to prepare me for whatever lay inside. I took a deep breath and pulled at one of the massive wooden doors. The logs and western décor were at least in my eyes dwarfed by the massive dining area. Way at the front of the room, a cash register and counter with bar stools stood empty except for two cowboys eating breakfast. A fortyish man in a white apron polished glasses behind the bar. He looked up and smiled.

"Welcome. Y'all come on in." He dropped the towel, grabbed a menu, and walked toward me. His gray-flecked hair was thinning, and over the welcoming smile was the biggest handlebar mustache in the world.

"You look like you could use some breakfast. Would this be okay?" He gestured toward a nearby table.

"No—no, I wanted to talk to you about the sign you have outside—the one saying you need help?" I clutched at my purse with both hands, so he wouldn't notice my trembling fingers.

"Oh, that. You're interested?"

I forced myself to nod, though everything inside me screamed a silent denial of any desire to work here.

"Well, come and sit at the bar while I dry these glasses." His eyes drifted up and down my body, but it wasn't a leer, and it didn't make me feel uncomfortable. "I'm Trent Pearson. And you are . . .?"

"Dina Rodriguez. I've never done this kind of work, but I would try very hard, and—"

He held up a hand to stop me. "I know you would," he said kindly. "Sit here." He pulled out the bar stool at the end of the counter.

I perched on the edge of the stool, convinced this would be a short interview. "I would learn quickly, and I wouldn't quit, except . . . I would like to attend classes at the college this fall."

"You're new in town?"

"Yes."

"Where are you from?"

"I'm American."

Trent's eyebrows arched at my belligerent response. I hadn't meant it to sound like that. His voice softened. "That's not what I asked."

I shrugged and dropped my eyes away from his piercing gray ones. "Mexico." That was all he would need to know. There would be no job here.

"Where?"

"Sonora—Agua Prieta."

"Hmm . . . I'm somewhat familiar with that country. Have a good friend down there."

I looked at him suspiciously. "Perhaps I have met him."

"Probably not. Raul Altamirez. An absolute genius with horses. He hangs out on a big ranch a few miles south of town."

The man went back to rubbing at a speck on a glass, so he didn't see the stunned look on my face. Raul was not just one of our employees. He was my friend and mentor. Raul had taught me everything I knew about horses.

Trent set the glass on a shelf behind the counter and grabbed another. "So, Dina, how old are you?"

"Twenty." I straightened on the stool in a self-conscious effort to appear more mature and capable.

"What makes you think you want to be a waitress?"

Answers flipped through my mind like flung horseshoes, except none of them sounded lucky. The last thing in the world I wanted to be was a waitress, and I didn't dare try any phony responses on this man with the steel-gray eyes. I pictured myself confessing my sin of lying for the second night in a row. Who knows what misery God would send my way if I lied again? I clasped my hands together to still their nervous tremble.

"I guess I don't want to be a waitress—but I need a job." There, I'd said it. Now he would say thank you very much for coming in and there's the door. But he didn't. He just threw his towel toward the sink, then propped an elbow on the counter.

"So, what would you like to do?" The two cowboys sauntered toward the till to pay for their meal. Trent stepped to the cash register, apparently well acquainted with them. The cowboys bantered back and forth with Trent as they waited for change, then clomped to the door.

Trent returned and picked up his dishtowel. "So, back to my question. What would you like to do?" I searched his face, wondering if there was an agenda I wasn't seeing.

"Train horses—and barrel race."

"You have some experience with horses?"

I nodded.

"Tell me."

"I worked with an excellent trainer—of horses and people—from the time I was old enough to ride a horse. He taught me much." I shrugged. "I would like to use that knowledge, and someday pass it on to others."

Trent looked at me warily. "And the trainer was . . ."

My eyes rose from the cherry wood counter to his face. "Raul."

He stared at me, his left jaw muscle twitching in the silence. Suddenly, he chuckled. "You are *that* Rodriguez? And you want a job?"

My face colored. "Yes. I had no idea that anyone here would know Raul or my family." I slipped off the stool. "Thank you, Mr. Pearson. I won't take any more of your time." Before I reached the door to the street, his voice stopped me.

"Dina, you were looking for a job, weren't you? I need people I can depend on."

Desperation made me turn and walk back. "Yes, I need a job, but I want to do it on my own, not because of my family."

The handlebar mustache twitched at one end. "Fair enough. When could you start?"

The thought of more noodles followed by a single threadbare blanket made my decision. "Now."

Trent grinned and stuck out his hand. "Let's give it a try. Don't worry. If you don't work out, I'll fire you—despite Raul and your family."

I reached across the counter and we shook hands. He told me how much he would pay me to start, but I promptly forgot that with his next announcement. "We like to think we serve the best prime rib in Montana. We cater to town folk and ranchers who come in for a special meal. This isn't a place for drunks. You'll do okay, because we'll help you. Oh, and along with the wage we always allow our staff to eat here. Any time on your shift when you have a break, you can order whatever you want."

Tears stung my eyes. I had no money for food. Even the noodles and macaroni wouldn't last until a paycheck arrived.

I turned away to cover the tears. Meanwhile I pretended to study the neatly appointed tables. Out of the corner of my eye, I saw him rubbing away at another speck on one of the glasses before he arranged them on the shelves at the back of the bar. I swallowed the lump in my throat and quickly composed myself.

After he'd placed the glasses, he turned, his eyes flickering over my face. The handlebar mustache widened, exposing teeth stained from chewing tobacco that didn't in any way take away from the spreading grin. "So, you can start this afternoon?"

I nodded.

"Mandy and Susan work that shift. You can meet them, and they'll show you what you need to do."

"Sure. That would be great."

"Good to have you on the team, Dina." Trent threw his apron on the end of the counter and walked me to the door.

I hope you'll like working here, even if it is a bar."

My face reddened. He had known all along how much I didn't want to work here, yet he'd given me a job. I determined he would not be sorry.

# Chapter 5

Promptly at five minutes to three, I pushed the door open and entered the Spur. I would work to eleven, the same hours as Susan. Mandy didn't come until later, but she worked until closing time, which for the Spur was around midnight.

A red-haired, fortyish woman glanced up from the table she was clearing when I walked inside. Her lips pursed as her eyes flitted from my face, down to the fresh green uniform blouse, then to my jeans and chocolate-brown roper boots.

"Let me guess. You're Dina?"

I smiled and nodded.

She jerked her head for me to follow her as she headed for the kitchen with her armful of dishes. The plates slid effortlessly onto the massive stainless-steel counter before she turned to me. "I'm Susan. I'm sorry. I'm not *real* happy to see you. Trent is always hiring some waif off the street who hasn't a clue."

My face fell. "If you would just give me a little help to get started—"

"I will, but you have to pull your weight."

"Okay." My head bobbed up and down like a stressed-out prairie gopher. "Tell me what to do. I'll do it."

"Don't worry, I will." Susan grimaced. "Tonight, you are responsible for tables fifteen through twenty." She steered me through the batwing doors that led from the kitchen out to the seating area. "Those are yours." She pointed to the vast expanse of tables to the right. "Don't get behind, because if you do, you'll never catch up. Oh, and you might want to come with more practical shoes than those." She gestured toward my boots.

"Okay." Again, my head bobbed though I hadn't a clue how I would buy this new footwear she recommended.

From three o'clock to five, the dinner traffic was light. Even though Susan resented having to train a new waitress, she had taken responsibility for ten tables to my six. I nervously took orders to Trent in the kitchen, then wobbled my first two platters to table seventeen. Susan breezed by me with three or four at a time. By six o'clock, the place was packed, but by then Mandy had arrived. She took over some of Susan's tables and two of mine, so we could keep up with the constant stream of new customers.

Before the end of my shift I'd spilled two drinks, one nearly on a customer, and dropped one plate, which scattered plate fragments, steak, and French fries over a large part of the kitchen. The accident happened later in the evening when most of my tables were full. I was already behind, and the time I had to take to clean up the mess made it worse. The customer who had to wait for another steak wasn't impressed either. By the end of the evening, my feet ached horribly from the boots, but I'd survived, and I had twenty-five dollars in tips to go toward a pair of more appropriate shoes.

When the dining room cleared out, I slumped exhausted into a booth with a hamburger and French fries, thankful I didn't have to eat macaroni. After I'd finished, I thanked Susan for all the help she'd given me, then walked through the kitchen to the back door. Trent rested with a cup of coffee at a small deal table near the screen door that led out to the parking lot.

"So, how did you make out tonight?"

"Okay, I hope. I had a couple of accidents."

"Yeah, I noticed. Don't worry about it. Even Susan dropped a plate once." He grinned at me. "You'll do alright."

"Thanks. I promise I won't drop any more. I was so nervous, because I've never done anything like this before."

"It'll come, but it takes a while."

I stood with the screen door half open as I said goodnight.

Trent set his coffee down and turned in his chair. "Where are you living?"

"I rented a basement suite from an elderly woman on the edge of town."

Trent craned to look at the empty parking lot. "You're driving, aren't you?"

"No. I guess I never thought about walking home after dark."

"This is a pretty safe little town, but you still shouldn't be doing that at this time of night. Not a good idea."

"Okay. Tomorrow, I'll drive."

"Why don't you wait until we close? Then somebody can take you home."

"No, I'll be okay."

I was exhausted. If I stayed here, I'd just fall asleep.

"Alright. Tomorrow, come in at eleven. And make sure you drive. I don't want any of my help walking home after dark."

"I will. Goodnight—and thanks for taking a chance on me." I let the screen door close behind me and walked into the softness of the late spring evening.

Dimly lit storefronts illuminated the cracks in the pitted sidewalk between the towering streetlights. Moths flitted through the yellow orbs overhead. The distant sound of truck traffic on the interstate competed with the chirping crickets as I trudged away from the lights on Main Street, then past the municipal park on my weary way to my new home. Everything looked sinister in the darkness. Between streetlights, I quickened my pace. Once, I glanced over my shoulder at the sound of footsteps, but nothing appeared out of the shadows. At the far edge of the park, a car hugged the curb. An unreasonable fear moved my feet to the far side of the sidewalk. The tinted windows revealed nothing, but as I came abreast of the taillights, the front passenger door opened, and a man stepped in front of me. Panicked, I whirled and started to run back toward the downtown lights. Within a few yards, a man stepped from behind a bush and blocked my way. I tried to duck into the street, but his jacketed arm encircled my throat and choked off the rising scream. Another arm closed around my chest while he dragged me to the waiting car. I fought to get away, but he was too strong. The first man held the back door open. They shoved me inside then one jumped in beside me. Again, I started to scream.

The man slapped me. *"Cállate!"* His raspy command to be silent, carried the accent I'd never wanted to hear again. These men were my father's associates, and that guttural Spanish word changed everything. I was in the greatest danger of my life.

# Chapter 6

Hunched over the steering wheel, Frederick shook his head as he fought the weariness from the last seven-hundred miles of driving. He should have taken a room back in Sturgis, but Gram would be waiting for him. Eighty miles ago, and the last time there had been any cell service, he'd called her as he'd passed through the remote ranch town of Broadus. He had to make it. She'd be dozing in her chair, listening for the sound of his car in the driveway.

Once, his eyes closed. The instant his wheels slid onto the rumble strip, panic jarred him awake. Adrenalin kept his eyes glued to the road until the flashing neon from the strip of hotels and the cut-out sign advertising the famous Miles City Bucking Horse Sale came into view.

A tired grin softened his face at the memory of his fling with cowboy culture. In Miles City, the ticket to being somebody mostly revolved around rodeos and ranching. Here, if you couldn't ride . . .well, you were in the wrong town. Cowboy skills were a rite of passage. As the new kid in school, and with a precarious command of English, he'd had to be tough to carve a place. He'd fought his way to the top of more than one school in his native Bulgaria, but here he wanted more than to be feared. He craved respect. In this cow town, riding bucking horses was the best way to make that happen, so that's what he attempted.

The best riders were small, lithe men. Before he was ten, it was clear Frederick would never be that. His heritage trended to chunky, with arms twice the size of his peers. By the time he'd reached his fourteenth birthday, his size had disqualified him at soccer, but his buffalo strength, and cat-quick reflexes made him a rising star in high school wrestling. Then, his parents were obliterated in that tragic plane crash in the Azores, and Frederick had nowhere to go except to a maternal grandmother in America.

Frederick arrived in Miles City, Montana with broken English, a picture of his deceased parents, and a small valise of clothes that he soon jettisoned. Most of the clothes he owned were decidedly uncool at the County High School. Refusing to be a pariah for anything as mundane as attire, the Bulgarian clothes went to the local charity store.

Frederick's chosen sport of wrestling would have won him a scholarship in most big cities, but in this small cowboy town, being on the wrestling team carried little clout in gaining upward social mobility. He chuckled at the memories as he turned onto North 7th, Gram's street. A car idling beside the park showed a glimpse of passion in the back seat, as two heads melded into one. He scanned the rear-view mirror, vaguely disturbed. High school kids had nicer wheels now. That was an Audi. Well, things had changed. Some ranch kid had his daddy's car, out for a night on the town with his girl.

Two blocks later, he pulled into the familiar driveway. The porch light illuminated the shabby clapboard siding. The porch railing still had an unhealthy lean toward the yard.

This would be a good time to stabilize it. On the far side of the driveway, an older pickup slouched in front of an old, single horse trailer. The person who owned it must have rented the basement suite. He sighed. Whoever had made that mistake would soon tire of Gram's constant nosy surveillance. She couldn't stand to leave tenants alone, however saintly they might be.

Frederick retrieved his small suitcase from the back seat and quietly closed the car door. Over the line of cottonwoods along the river, a panorama of stars lit the sky. He sighed, glad to be back, then turned and trudged toward the house. The soft, westward breeze, pungent with the familiar tang of sage and ponderosa kissed his right cheek, welcoming him back to the place that would always be home.

By the time he'd reached the steps, Gram had made it to the door. He set his suitcase on the bench in the entry and gently hugged her frail body.

"Good to be home, Gram. How are you?" His voice still carried a faint European accent; the words pronounced with practiced care.

She smiled up at him. "I'm fine—for an old thing. Do you want something to eat?" He followed her as she hobbled out to the kitchen.

"No, I ate down the road. Just a glass of water, then we better both go to bed."

"Yes, we should, though I haven't heard the new tenant come in. I just rented the basement suite to her. Probably, she's out carousing. She swore she wasn't a party girl, just like they all do. I'll have to watch that one. She'll be looking for a new place—"

"Gram, whoever this girl is, I'm sure she's fine. Where does she work?"

"At the Spur . . . or so she said. I think she lied. Probably doesn't have a job at all, and—"

"Perhaps she had to work late. It's only midnight. Anyhow Gram, leave her alone. Just because she rents the suite from you, doesn't mean you get to run her life."

"I won't have that kind of person in my house." Gram's blue-veined hands trembled on the cushioned grips of her walker.

Frederick patted her shoulder. "Settle down, Gram. I'm sure you made the right decision. She'll be a great renter, and within three months you'll be able to kick her out—or she'll leave. Now . . . let's go to bed. We'll talk in the morning." He hugged her again and walked out to the entry to retrieve his suitcase.

"Lock the front door while you're there."

"Why? We've never locked any doors."

"Well, I do now what with all the crime, and these youngsters terrorizing decent people."

Frederick winced. It was the same the last time he'd come home. Dear old Gram was becoming a prisoner in her own house, more and more afraid to venture out. He'd better see what choices there were for seniors housing. Soon, she would need more care.

"Goodnight. I've missed you, Gram."

"Yes, go to bed. You're working too hard and not getting enough sleep." Her voice rose, querulous and thin. "And you've lost weight. At least that part we can try to fix."

He groaned. "Yes, I'll leave here ten pounds overweight—again." His hand rested on her shoulder a moment as he walked by her and toward his bedroom at the end of the hall.

Within minutes, Frederick was asleep, and it was long past his usual dawn hour of waking before the weariness left his body. He laid still, listening to the morning sounds, the meadowlarks outside the window mixed with the faint sound of a garbage truck starting and stopping on the street.

His last semester had been difficult. The course work wasn't hard, but the intense study regimen took precious hours he didn't have. Now that the agency required more, there was less time for college. However, one day those courses would be valuable, so he persevered.

He swung his legs to the floor when he heard Gram toddling up the hallway.

"Freddy, are you awake yet?"

"Yeah, Gram. I'll be out in a minute."

"Good, because I don't think that little liar came home last night."

"What liar?"

"That Mexican girl who rented the basement suite."

Oh great! She had met a guy and, well . . . probably he didn't have to explain that one to Gram. By tomorrow, the girl would be hunting for a new place to rent.

"How many poached eggs do you want?"

"Two, but I can make 'em."

"No, let me do it. I don't get to cook for you much, now that you're gone."

He pulled a pair of faded jeans over his muscular legs, grabbed his shaving kit and ducked into the bathroom. Ten minutes later, he padded into the kitchen. Gram, hunched over her walker peered through a slit in the closed curtains. "Still no sign of her."

"The girl?"

"Yes. I would've heard her. These old ears are still plenty sharp, and the door down there didn't open. She can get her stuff today and move right out. I'll not have that kind of hanky-panky going on here."

"Gram, whatever happened wasn't here. Besides, you're not running a motel. You rented it to her. As long as she doesn't tear the place apart, that suite is hers. She can do what she wants."

Gram's face mottled with anger. "No, she can't. I'll not have it. She sure fooled me. I didn't think she was the type; so young and innocent looking. Who'd have thought?"

"She might have slipped in without you knowing. Should I go check?"

The old woman broke the eggs into the pan of water before answering. "Maybe you should. It does seem strange, being the first day and all. Usually, they're good for at least a week."

Frederick tiptoed down the stairs and knocked. Twice, he banged on the sun-scoured veneer, with no answer. He tried the key, opened the door an inch and hollered.

"Anybody home?" Silence. He poked his head inside, far enough to see the kitchen-living room combination. Once more, he announced his presence. He hated invading her privacy, but she obviously wasn't here. To make sure, he stepped in and peered around the corner and into the little bedroom. A single blanket covered the mattress. No sheets. A neatly folded sweater lay at the head in place of a pillow. The girl had no furniture, and none of the knickknacks that should grace a young lady's home. His practiced eyes flitted through the rooms, taking in every detail. She was young, conservative—and Catholic. He walked back to the kitchen. Several small packages of macaroni and noodles were mute evidence of her financial standing. A wallet-sized snapshot leaned carelessly against the glass of the small kitchen window. He leaned over the sink to peer at the photograph. A running horse turned hard into a barrel, the rider's left foot only inches from the ground. The girl's heart-shaped face silhouetted against the desert background was calm, concentrated—and capable. He stared at the picture longer than necessary before turning away. He'd gathered any information relevant to the situation. Whoever she was, she had not been here since yesterday.

The door screeched shut behind him, and he understood why Gram would hear her coming and going. After he apologized to the girl for violating her privacy, he would fix the door. As he walked into the kitchen, Gram slid the poached eggs and toast onto a plate.

"She's not there."

Gram eyed him from the other side of the counter. Her scornful laugh needed no explanation. "I should have known better than to rent to that impudent little chit—and a Mexican to boot."

Frederick scowled at her, though his disapproval would do little to change the old lady's lifetime of prejudice. "Gram, you know that's not fair."

She huffed her disapproval of his point of view, then tottered to the coffeepot. "The girl said she had a job at the Spur. Do you suppose I should check with Trent—just in case? Mind you, I know what the story will be. She can pack her stuff and—"

Frederick grabbed a napkin and patted at whatever breakfast remains might remain at the corners of his mouth. "I have to go down to the drugstore anyhow. I'll stop by the Spur and ask Trent—see if she left with somebody."

Gram nodded as her trembling hands attempted to move the cup to her mouth.

Frederick averted his eyes and sighed. It wouldn't be long before Gram would have to leave her home and move to the Manor. That would be a rough day. He finished his coffee, made the few phone calls necessary to his business and drove downtown.

After a stop at the drugstore, he walked the three blocks to the Spur Bar. Trent was wiping at an already clean table in the middle of the room. He looked up at the sound of the door. A slow grin spread over his face.

"Heya' Fred." He wiped his hands on the white apron covering his jeans and stepped forward to shake hands.

"Good to see you, Trent." Frederick surveyed the room. "You'll die here, won't you?"

"I hope not."

"Don't leave. You still serve the best steak in Montana. It would be a shame for anybody else to attempt what you do so well."

"Well, thanks for the compliment, but no, someday I'm going to sell out, move to Canada and just hunt and fish, even if they are all Socialists up there. You want to eat?"

"No, give me a cup of coffee—if you've got any that's drinkable?"

Trent grinned again. "Just made a pot. Sit here at the bar so we can talk while I get some stuff ready for the rush tonight. I'm behind this morning because we're short of help. I hired a new girl yesterday. She was supposed to be here this morning, and—"

"And her name's Dina?"

"Yeah, how'd you know?" Trent set a cup of coffee in front of Frederick, then continued to stack clean glasses under the counter.

"She's renting my grandmother's basement suite. She never came home last night."

Trent's jaw dropped. "No, don't tell me that. Are you sure?"

"Of course. I just checked her room."

Trent dropped his towel and ran a hand through his thinning hair. "I should have made her wait. One of us should have given her a ride."

"You're sure she didn't leave with somebody? Nobody was waiting for her in the parking lot?"

Trent shook his head. "No, Fred, I'd near swear to that. She's new in town, just a kid wanting a job to make a few bucks so she can go to school. And Susan would have said something if she'd been flirting with a customer. No, she walked out of here alone, and she was frazzled. Our servers work hard. She wouldn't have been looking for a party."

"I was afraid of that. We better call the sheriff."

"I'll do it." Trent reached for the phone at his elbow.

"No, let me take care of it—if you don't mind? I feel somewhat responsible, being as how she's staying at Gram's."

"Yeah, well she's working for me, and I let her walk out of here, so I'm responsible."

Frederick nodded. "Whatever." His lips pursed as Trent tapped out the sheriff's office number, punched the speaker-phone button and leaned over the counter.

"Hi, Gail. Is Doug in?"

"Nope. But Bob is. Doug had to go to Billings. Don't tell me you have a drunk this early."

"I wish. No, this is worse."

"Hang on, I'll switch you to Bob."

"Bob's the number two guy," Trent whispered. "A new one."

Frederick nodded, then listened as Trent related the sketchy details of the girl's disappearance to the new man on the force. He turned toward the window and watched the noon-hour traffic. Last night he'd driven down this street, then turned onto North 7th. The expensive Audi at the curb across from the park had drawn his attention, the heads bobbing together for what he presumed was a ranch kid's awkward attempt at passion with his girl. What if it hadn't been that? What if . . . the time had been about right. Had it been Gram's new renter in that car? It was two blocks away from the house, and that's the route she would have taken from the Spur Bar on her way home. Had somebody kidnapped her off the street, taken her to a lonely coulee and raped, or even killed her? He shook his head, casting the thought away. Surely not. Those big city crimes didn't happen in Miles City.

# Chapter 7

I lashed out at my attacker, but his fingers circled my throat, pinning me against the seat. Fear, and his crushing grip choked off my scream of terror. His dark features moved close to mine. Garlic breath again washed over me as he spoke.

"Quiet, *Chiquita.*" He'd used the same endearing term I'd given my beloved barrel mare. "If you even wiggle, I will kill you."

They would kill me no matter what I did, but as the car sped away from the curb, I ceased to fight my attacker, if only to give myself time to think.

The man jerked my head around, threw a scarf over my eyes, and tied it. "Make sure it stays in place. It would be unfortunate for you if it slipped."

The car accelerated to highway speed. I huddled against the door, seeking invisibleness, anonymity. After what must have been a couple hours, the car slowed. The traffic noise indicated we were on the outskirts of a city. I tried to remember which larger towns were within two hours of Miles City. Billings seemed the only option. When we stopped, the man opened the door and pulled me outside. I felt concrete under my feet. He dragged me up three steps, his hand a vise on my arm. I didn't cry out. I would not give him the pleasure of knowing he'd caused me pain. We guided me forward, and I felt carpet under my feet. My hand brushed past a door frame before he pushed me into a chair.

"Do not remove the blindfold. If you take it off, you die." Footsteps retreated, and a door closed. A deadbolt snicked home, and though my eyes remained covered with the scarf, the material was porous enough I knew there was no light in the room. I listened for any further sound. Did I dare to take it off? Was someone sitting quietly in the darkness, waiting for me to do just that? The weighty blanket of silence made me want to scream in terror. Nobody needed to tell me this was because of Papa, but how had they found me? A chill slid down my spine, and the debilitating fear returned. Why did they want to kill me? I had nothing to do with Papa's business.

What seemed like hours later, the door opened, and a heavy tread stopped in front of me. A man jerked the blindfold from my eyes. He flicked a switch, and I blinked in the glaring light. We were in a small cubicle, perhaps a storage room in a house. He thrust a piece of paper in front of my face.

"Read it out loud." My eyes focused on the scrawled statement as he stepped aside. Another man held a camcorder. In a monotone voice, I stumbled through the words in front of me.

"Ricardo, this is your only warning. We always pay for services rendered—either good or bad. You made a mistake. Do not make another. Allahu Akbar." I stumbled over the unfamiliar Arabic words at the end, which made the bearded one holding the camera scowl. After I'd finished reading, the man beside me stepped over and covered my eyes again. Fear raced through every vein in my body. I'd done what they wanted. Would they now kill me? Vengeance for whatever Papa had done? I bowed my head, my teeth clenched against the coming pain as I desperately breathed my last prayer.

"Holy Mary, Mother of God, pray for us sinners now and at the hour of our death. Receive Lord, your servant into the place of salvation which I hope to obtain by your mercy, and . . ." I waited. No bullet. Would that come later, out in some deserted coulee? And would God take me into His heaven? More than anything else I wanted to be sure, but it was too late for that.

A rough hand pulled me to my feet. I stumbled, trying to follow the steps beside me. They again shoved me into a car. Yes, that was it. They would take me to a lonely, wild place to kill me. But if I had to die, that would be preferable to the small room. At least I'd smell the sagebrush, and perhaps hear the meadowlarks one last time. I tried to remember other prayers when one faced death, but who prepares for that when you're barely more than a teenager? All I remembered were remnants from when my great aunt had died three years ago.

"Oh God, give me the grace to prepare for my last hour . . ." It was a little late for any preparation.

The miles spun away too fast to wherever my life was going to end? After a long time, the tire hum lowered in pitch. The car slowed. The crunchy sound of gravel indicated we'd left the highway. The door to my left opened. A hand grabbed my arm and jerked me outside and down a steep bank. Fear coursed through every vein in my body. The man pushed me down. My knees skidded into the gravel. I didn't want to die. I cringed, waiting for the bullet. My lips moved unconsciously as I pled for my life.

"Shut up! Do not take the blindfold off for ten minutes. Somebody will be watching. And if you say anything to the police, you and all your family will die."

I nodded, too numb with fear to speak. A long, shuddering sob broke through my clenched teeth as the squeal of tires on the nearby highway announced their departure.

For what seemed hours, I knelt there, too afraid to move. Tears wet my cheeks. The whine of tires from the occasional car or truck were comforting, but none slowed. Moisture trickled down the inside of the now dirty green blouse I'd worn for my first night of work at the Spur Bar. I squeezed my hands together. Was the time up? Were they watching? After another eternity, I dared to slip the bandanna off my face. I scanned the surrounding area. Nothing. No person watched me, at least none I could see. The bright sunlight of an early Montana morning made me squint. I climbed up the bank to what appeared to be a highway rest stop. The usual pair of painted garbage cans leaned crazily against a white post, both chained like escapees from a federal recycling program. There were no restroom facilities, but stray wads of toilet paper on the ground and my own need were mute testimony that this would have been an opportune place to build some.

I jammed my hands in my pockets to stop the trembling and wished I was more the crying type. This seemed an appropriate time to sit and weep, but it wasn't in me to do that.

Besides, I needed to escape. They might return. I pulled myself over the guardrail that ran the length of the pullout as I thought about the video they had shot of me. Why? What had Papa done now to earn their wrath? As far as I knew, he was their willing and loyal servant. This time, they'd released me, but for how long? If Papa didn't give them what they wanted, would they come after me again? I'd hoped to be safe in Miles City, far from the intrigue of my father's house. How wrong I'd been.

I don't remember how old I was when I first suspected my Papa wasn't just a rancher, but it predated the night I tiptoed downstairs for a midnight snack. Before I reached the bottom, angry voices from the room Papa called his library had frozen me in my tracks. The conversation in Spanish seemed to be between Papa and two men. Both had harsh, gravelly accents. Their voices floated to the stairs where I stood frozen, and eavesdropping.

"Ricardo, we need to get these people into the U.S. If you don't do it, we will find another way. It's not necessary that we work through you." The voice was insolent.

Then I heard Papa, and I was ashamed of my mousy little father.

"Señor, there are problems. The current battles between the cartels have made it more difficult. The Sinaloa cartel is being difficult, and we cannot risk using any passage other than their safest corridor." Papa's voice was the usual plaintive whimper he used with my mother. With me, as with the hired help, it was obsequious and spineless. I loved him because he was my father, but I wished he wasn't so weak, and such a fool.

One of the men's voices again carried outside the room. "Do whatever you have to do. If you don't find a way, there will be trouble."

Too scared to move, I remained riveted to where I stood. Eventually, I heard the office door open, which meant I had to move in a hurry. Papa must have heard me. Before I'd reached the third step he grabbed my arm. Fleetingly, I wondered how he'd moved so quickly? He glared at me. "You are supposed to be in bed, asleep." His voice carried a commanding roughness to which I was unaccustomed.

"I only came down for something to eat," I stuttered.

He sighed and patted my arm. "These are dangerous times, my child. It isn't good for you to hear too much."

"I am not a child—"

"This has nothing to do with your level of maturity, my daughter. It is because I love you, and you must be safe." He patted my hand. "Now go to bed, so in the morning you can practice the barrel racing you are so crazy about."

That night, I wished more than ever that Papa wasn't a weakling, and now a traitor. From that moment, I began to plan my escape from the charade that was my home.

FREDERICK TURNED FROM the window to watch the Miles City assistant chief of police tap his pen on the edge of his desk, which meant he wasn't writing anything on the missing persons report in front of him.

Trent sat across from the policeman. "Bob, I think there's more to this than a bad date. This young lady wouldn't have been foolish enough to get in a car with some man she'd never seen before."

The assistant chief leaned back in his chair, folded his arms and raised an eyebrow. "And how long did she work for you?"

Trent leaned toward the policeman and put his elbows on the desk. "One night, but at least put out an APB on her."

Bob made some notes on the pad in front of him. "No. Not yet. Give it a few more hours."

Frederick stepped forward and stood beside Trent. He leaned over the desk. "He's right."

The assistant chief glared at the newcomer. "I've worked for fifteen years to sit behind this desk. If I make a wrong decision on this one, it'll be my head that rolls. So—tell me sir, what evidence do you have? You've perhaps known her for more than a day?"

His sarcasm angered Frederick. He leaned his considerable bulk over the desk, his eyes riveted on the policeman. "Sometimes, we have to play our best hunches. You of all people should understand that."

The cop met Frederick's glare without wavering. He'd come up the hard way and he was doing his job to the best of his ability, but eventually his eyes slid away. "Okay, if you guys are so sure, then help me out. Give me some evidence, and I'll put out an all-points bulletin. But I'm going to look like an idiot if she met some guy and just—"

"She was kidnapped off the street at 11:45 last night. Right beside the park." Frederick's finger stabbed north in the general direction of the park where Dina had been kidnapped. "The car was a late model Audi—light gray."

The policeman's eyes locked on his once more, then wavered. Frederick watched the indecision flit over his face before the man jabbed at a button on the phone.

"Gail, put out an APB on a Dina Rodriguez; early twenties, Hispanic." He sketched out the needed information, then turned back to the two men.

Trent stood and held out his hand. "Thanks, Bob."

Gail's voice cut in. "Officer Higgins just picked up a hitchhiking female by the Powder River rest stop west of town. The name and description match your bulletin."

"Okay then, scratch the APB for now."

Frederick glanced back from the door in time to see the aging policeman's sigh of relief as he fumbled for an antacid pill.

# Chapter 8

Minutes after I'd removed the blindfold, a black sports car pulled into the rest stop, and though I had a healthy fear of hitch-hiking, there didn't seem to be a choice. A guy stepped out, stretched, and traded places with a girl in black leggings. Neither looked a day older than I, so I hoped they might be safe enough.

I approached them. "Which way is Miles City?"

The man pointed the direction the car was facing.

"Could I catch a ride?"

Both surveyed my bedraggled hair and dirty blouse. The man nervously peered past the guard rail, scanning the ditches like he expected three Caribbean pirates to jump onto the road.

My hands instinctively hid deep in the pockets of my jeans as I fought back the accumulated tears of exhaustion. "I would really appreciate a ride."

They eyed me like I'd crawled out of a sewage lagoon. "No. We don't have room." They jumped in their car and sped toward Miles City.

Discouraged, I trudged out to the highway and walked in the same direction. Three cars sailed by without slowing. They didn't seem to want to take a chance on picking up a hitchhiker. A highway patrolman eyed me as he cruised westward on the other side of the meridian. Two minutes later, his car pulled up behind me. He walked toward me, his right hand close to his gun as his eyes surveyed the surrounding area.

"Hi. Where are you going?"

"Miles City. I live there."

"What's your name?"

"Bernardina Rodriguez." I'd better give him the same name that was on my driver's license, because he would surely ask for that next.

"Your current address?"

"I don't remember the number, but it's the last house on North 7th Street."

"How long have you lived there?"

"Only a couple of days. I just moved to town."

"It's illegal to hitchhike here." He pointed to a sign.

"I didn't know that. I need to get to Miles City."

"Do you have any identification?"

I dug in my purse for my laminated birth certificate.

The patrolman walked back to his car and typed my information into his computer. I furtively scanned the surrounding hills. They might be watching, and they would think I'd told this cop about my kidnapping. They would carry out their threat to kill me. And what would happen to Papa or Mama?

However, there would be no getting away. I'd just have to make the best of it. I clutched my purse as I waited for the cop to finish, thankful that though the kidnappers had pawed through my purse, they'd taken nothing.

The patrolman talked on his radio, then stepped out, decidedly more friendly.

"How about I give you a ride into town?" He opened the back-seat door for me. I slid in, thankful to at least be off the highway and out of sight.

"So, what happened? You had a date that went sideways?"

My mind raced. What should I say? Never would I tell this officer about the people who had kidnapped me, but he'd just insinuated that I . . . Anger brought the blood to my face, but I didn't have a choice. "Yes . . . yes, I guess it didn't turn out too well."

"Who was your date?"

"Oh, a guy—I don't remember his name."

"So—you don't want to press charges. Is that what you're saying?"

"No . . . no, I'm fine. Nothing happened."

"Of course not." His lips flattened as he glanced in the rearview mirror at my disheveled, dirty blouse with the missing button.

A half-hour later, the police car dropped me off in Mrs. Riddler's driveway. Not coming home last night would have me labeled as a party girl, which would undoubtedly earn an eviction notice. Showing up in a police car would make it immediate.

I thanked the patrolman, stepped out and faced the old woman hunched over her walker on the step above the sidewalk. Her gritty, wrinkled face held no welcome.

"Get yer' stuff and get out. I'll have no partyers living here."

I wanted to be angry. 'Partyers' probably wasn't even an American word. I yearned to tell this self-righteous old crow what she could do with her run-down basement suite, but I squared my shoulders and looked her in the eye. At least I tried to. Other than the money I'd earned in tips from my one night as a waitress, I had only a few dollars. And now, not only did I not have a place to live, it wasn't likely I had a job. Scared, and more humiliated than I'd ever been in my life, I crossed my arms, trying to think of something to say that would change the old woman's mind. Nothing came to mind, at least nothing I would tell this hateful old woman. Papa could have bought this despicable little house, for that matter, the whole city block, and here I was standing here begging for . . . No! I would not beg. If I had to sleep in my pickup; some way, I would survive.

Tires crunched on the gravel driveway behind me. Wonderful! Now, I'd endure further embarrassment—in front of one of the neighbors. The old woman and I both turned and watched a chunky, blond man step out of a flashy green sports car. His eyes met mine as he walked purposefully toward the front step where I faced my recent landlady.

"So." The old woman looked back at me. "There's no more we need to say to each other. I'll expect you to be out today." She turned and started back into the house. The man's voice stopped her.

"Gram, we need to talk. I don't think this young lady did anything wrong."

"I'll thank you for letting me run my rentals, young man. I'm not too old for that, and what's—"

"Gram, I'm not trying to interfere, but this isn't—can we talk about it before you decide?"

I turned and surveyed the man who argued my case. Who was he? Why was he sticking up for me? Whatever the reason, I was intensely grateful. As he spoke, I watched him carefully. If he'd immediately disappeared, I might not have been able to describe him in detail, but I could have given a passable description of his passionate, cobalt-blue eyes. They were unlike anything I'd ever seen, the azure of a far-off forested mountain, intense and intelligent. One would never be able to look into those eyes and tell a lie.

The old lady huffed, "Well, . . . alright. But it won't change my mind." She turned to me. "You might as well start packing." She bounced her walker over the doorstep and into the house.

The man turned toward me. "I'm Frederick. You're Dina, I guess?"

I nodded. "Yes, and thank you for sticking up for me." I took a deep breath and squared my shoulders. "I'm sure I can find another place to live."

He nodded. A faint smile played about his lips. "What happened last night?"

"Certainly not what your grandmother thinks, but I would rather not say."

"It might be better if you told me. The police wanted to come here, but I convinced them you would talk to them at headquarters." He raised an eyebrow. "Gram's on the warpath. It won't help your cause if they show up in the yard again. So—your call."

Panic constricted my heart, then coursed down my arms toward the tips of my fingers. What would I tell the police? The same as I'd told the highway patrolman. Nothing. To do otherwise would be too dangerous.

The blue-mountain-eyes bored into mine, but I raised my chin and stared right back.

A slow smile returned to his lips. "Give me a little time with Gram. And don't bother to pack anything. You won't have to find new digs—for now. I can take you down to the police station if you'd like?"

"I can walk but thank you for the kind offer." I didn't want to insult this man who had stopped my eviction, but neither did I need him to cart me around town. Besides, I needed to see Trent and apologize, even if he had already fired me. He'd given me a chance at a job, and I had let him down. What hurt the most was that I would have to let him think the worst of me. But there could be no other story.

I navigated the crumbling stairs to the basement suite I'd left so long ago. My stomach still flip-flopped from the tension with Mrs. Riddler. I sat on the bed and tried to calm down enough to eat more of the noodles, but it was no use. After a quick shower, I changed clothes and trudged to the door, determined to finish the police ordeal.

At the top of the basement steps, a shadow blocked the sun. I looked up and directly into "the eyes". He watched me but said nothing until I reached the sidewalk. "You won't be evicted—for a while."

"Thank you. I appreciate it."

"May I take you down to the sheriff's office?"

I started an indignant protest, but he held up a hand. "Hey, let me be your friend. It never hurts to have someone on your side." His hand looked strong, capable, and suddenly I decided that even if he wasn't friend material, he'd at least be a good bodyguard.

"Okay, I could use some help."

His mouth opened as if he was going to speak. Then he seemed to reconsider. He turned and walked to his car. I slid in on the passenger side. As we passed the park, he turned toward me. "They picked you up right there, didn't they?" He pointed to the exact spot where the men had shoved me into the car.

Though my eyes remained focused on the windshield, fear instantly hypnotized me. Who was this man? How had he known about last night?

"Well?"

"I don't know what you're talking about."

"Dina, I think you do, but that's okay." He gestured with his palm. "You don't have to tell me anything. It's clear you're not dumb enough to jump into a car with a guy you'd never seen before, but the cops are suspicious. They want information."

"So, what if I did get in a car with—?"

"The police may buy that. I don't. And what are you going to tell Trent?" He glanced at me, one eyebrow cocked upward.

An unreasonable anger, brought on by weariness and fear exploded through my chest. "And why should you care? I'm quite capable of figuring out what to tell the police—and Trent!"

We pulled to a stop in front of police headquarters. I opened the door and stepped out.

He stared straight ahead, refusing to answer. "I'll wait for you."

"That won't be necessary," I snapped. Instantly I was sorry. This guy had saved me from having to sleep in my pickup. I wanted to turn around and apologize. Instead, I bit my lower lip and marched through the police station door.

# Chapter 9

Frederick slumped over the steering wheel and watched as Dina disappeared through the solid steel doors. Wow, what a piece of work. Knock your eyes out gorgeous, but an Attila the Hun attitude. He locked the car and strode down the street. She would be in there awhile, and he doubted the local sheriff's department would get much out of her. It wasn't that her story was bogus—she had none. After two turns around the block, he slowed his pace, frustrated at the feelings coursing through his body. So what if she was a looker. That didn't explain why those dark, brooding eyes triggered this crazy desire to protect her? His feelings for her didn't make sense, but then not a whole lot had since the moment he'd seen her standing in the yard doing battle with Gram. A wry grin creased Frederick's face. More accurately would be, annihilated by Gram."

Across the street, a new café had placed a few tables out on the sidewalk. He walked over and ordered a cup of coffee. Absently, he toyed with it while he watched the door to police headquarters. What was she hiding? Why was she afraid to say who had picked her up? He pulled his cell out and dialed a number. He might be able to find out. Before it rang, he changed his mind. Not yet. That wasn't playing fair, and for some crazy reason, he wanted to impress her, or at least not alienate her. If Dina had a secret, it would remain hers. Either she would have to tell him, or . . . or what? How perilous was the information? He tried to weigh any possible danger against the violation of her privacy. Before he'd finished the cup of coffee, he realized that what she wanted already carried a significant amount of importance.

Halfway through his third cup, Dina pushed through the police station doors. She glanced over at his empty car, then turned up the street toward the Spur. Frederick left a generous tip on the table and loped after her, but she'd reached the next block before he caught up to her. "Hey."

She whirled, instant terror etched over her features.

"I can give you a ride."

A jaded smile replaced the fear. "I expected you to tell me to get in the car."

Her mild rebuke flustered him. "I'm sorry, Dina. I . . . well, I just wanted to help you." He met her dark eyes. They weren't doing well at hiding the alarm, but when she spoke, her voice was calm.

"Why don't you let me walk to the Spur? Pick me up there in twenty minutes. I'm sure Trent will terminate our business in record time."

"He might surprise you. I'll be waiting." He watched her march down the street toward the Spur, then turned to retrieve the Mustang.

I LEFT THE POLICE STATION, drained by the probing inquiries. The highway patrolman who had picked me up on the highway had placed me on one side of a table while he and a detective grilled me for at least an hour. They'd tried to be nice as they hammered me with questions. I fearfully dodged every attempt at help. That a couple of drunk cowboys had forced me into a car sounded like a far-fetched lie even to me, though it was at least a half-truth. I had been forced into the car. I added the cowboy part because I couldn't think of anything else, and maybe they were cowboys—in Iran. My story lost credibility as I manufactured more fantasy. I'd fought them off; they changed their minds, and eventually they'd turned me loose. No, I hadn't been sexually assaulted. I thanked God that at least that part of my story held truth. Yes, they slapped me a couple of times but other than that they hadn't hurt me, and no, I wouldn't recognize any of the three men, or the car. The two policemen eventually let me go. They wanted to help, but as much as I abhorred what Papa was doing, telling the police what had happened would be to sign a death warrant for our whole family. Of that, I had no doubt.

When I walked outside, I was sure Frederick's car wouldn't be there. Why would it be, after I'd insulted him and rebuffed any of his offered help? I started toward the Spur. This would be even harder, but it was necessary. Trent had given me a job, and I'd failed him. When I heard the pounding feet behind me, fear clutched at my chest. It was them. They'd watched me go into the police station. I whirled and nearly cried with relief when I saw it was Frederick. He had stayed, the big fool. What a guy for punishment. But an unbidden thrill turned my stomach all mushy, enough that I made an attempt at reconciliation.

I walked into the Spur not knowing what to tell Trent. He was in the kitchen, cooking as usual. Susan walked by me balancing three plates of food. She scowled. "Well dearie, you lasted a long time, didn't you?"

I raised an eyebrow and shrugged my shoulders. This was a time to turn the other cheek. She had every right to be disgusted. From her point of view, she was working tables alone tonight because the girl who was supposed to help her had decided not to show up for work.

Trent looked up when I stepped through the swinging doors separating the kitchen from the dining area. "Hi, Dina."

"Trent, I'm so sorry. I—"

He held up a hand and waved a big steak flipper at me. "Give me three minutes. I'll get these plates out, and then we can talk." He peered at the order board. "Grab a cup of coffee and sit over there." He pointed to a little card table in the back of the kitchen.

I sat with my hands in my lap, too nervous to drink anything. Not that I'd have time. What he would have to say wouldn't take long.

Minutes later, he strode back with a half cup of coffee in his hand and grinned, which was not the way to start the conversation we had to have. "Good to see you, although you're late for work." He held up a hand at my stuttered apology. "No need. I know what happened. It was my fault. I shouldn't have allowed you to walk. From now on, nobody walks home at night. If you don't have a vehicle, then you stay until closing, so somebody else can give you a ride. And that's final—if you want to keep working here."

I nodded, too stunned to speak.

Under his bushy brows, he glared at me. "First, are you all right?"

"Yes, I'm okay."

"Good. Can you come in tomorrow?"

A few tears escaped. I could have managed if Trent had told me what a useless employee I was, but his kindness beat through my fearful defense. "Thank you so much—for understanding. I'll be here tomorrow."

With that, I turned and stumbled out the back door before I completely fell to pieces. As I wiped at the tears, the thought occurred to me that if that Frederick guy saw me crying, he would try to manage my life even more than he was now.

# Chapter 10

I'd hardly finished wiping at my blotchy face before I spotted Frederick's car. He studiously peered at the vacant lot beside the Spur as if it held a diamond mine instead of plastic bags and tumbleweed, and for that I was grateful. I had no wish for him to make a scene over my troubles. After I'd made myself presentable, I trudged over to his car, opened the door and slid onto the leather seat. He glanced sideways but made no comment as he reached down and stuck the console shifter in drive. We took the back streets to his grandma's. The whole way, all he did was whistle along with the country tune that played softly from the stereo. That suited me. Hopefully, he'd not grill me on the details of the most horrible day of my life.

As we turned into the driveway, he asked, "How'd you make out with Trent?"

I bit my lower lip and tried to answer with a steady, nonchalant voice. "Oh, he was great. I go to work tomorrow."

Frederick laughed, a happy, though awkward sound, as if laughing was something he seldom did. I glanced at him to see if he was making fun of me. He wasn't, and I wondered why he would find the news about my job that uplifting.

"Let's celebrate. Would you let me buy dinner?" he asked.

I was exhausted. The thought of eating the unappetizing noodles on the counter clinched it. Besides, I felt safer with him around. "Yes, if I can have a nap first. I'm beat."

"Okay, how about we leave around five?"

I nodded. "Works for me. See you then." I stumbled down the stairs and into my little cave of a basement suite, even more thankful for a safe place to lay my head. Before I fell onto the bed I reached over, fingered the beads of my Rosary and murmured an incoherent, tired prayer of thankfulness. Several times in the last twenty-four hours I had not expected to return. My eyes wouldn't stay open any longer, and I crawled under my one blanket and slept.

Consciousness returned when I realized someone was knocking on the door. Swiftly, I looked over at the clock. It was well past five. "Just a minute. I'll be right there."

Frederick stood on the step, a sheepish look covering his face. "Dina, I'm sorry. I should have let you sleep. We can celebrate another night."

"No. That's alright. I fell asleep and forgot to set the alarm. Give me fifteen minutes, and I'll be ready."

I had a quick shower, slipped into jeans and one of my least wrinkled blouses, and met Frederick at the car.

"Would you like to go to the Ranchman's?" he asked.

I wasn't sure I wanted to spend *that* much time with this man. Besides, I was still tired from last night's ordeal. "How about pizza or a hamburger?"

"Sure. There's a great little pizza place the other side of Main Street."

While Frederick drove into the evening sun, I furtively studied his profile. He was average height, solidly built. His blond hair was so light it was almost white, brushed low over his forehead, or maybe it only looked that way because of the bushy blond eyebrows. I guess I hadn't noticed them before because of the striking eye color. His jaw jutted forward to a broad chin. His thin lips barely covered a set of strong, even teeth. I decided his features were more awkward than handsome, but so what. I wasn't going to dinner with him because he was the love of my life. Besides, so what if he wasn't Mr. Hollywood? I wasn't Miss Dream Girl. I could use a friend, and he'd filled the role admirably. It wouldn't hurt to find out something about him, so I waded right in. "So, you don't live in Miles City?"

"No, I don't."

"But you grew up here?"

"No, most of my childhood was spent in Europe. And you?"

"Mexico—Sonora. My parents live a few miles south of Douglas, Arizona. I went to high school there."

At the pizza place, I continued to try to jump-start a conversation, but every time I tried to find out more about him, he either gave one-word answers or switched the conversation to my past life.

I soldiered on with questions to his reticent answers. "What kind of work do you do?"

"I just finished a master's degree last semester, and I work for a small company that does contract work for the government."

I grimaced at his evasive answer. "What kind of contract work?" A conversation with this guy was like trying to row a boat with the anchor down. He seemed preoccupied, and I wondered if he'd invited me simply because he suspected I didn't have money for anything but Chinese noodles and macaroni. I waited for an answer while he worked his way through another wedge of pepperoni pizza.

"Oh, we get a lot of contracts nobody else wants, stuff that's let out for whatever reason to the private sector."

I swallowed the last bite of pizza. "That's the most evasive answer I've ever heard."

He leaned forward while his hands twisted nervously together on the table. "I'm sorry. I didn't mean it that way. Sometimes we do offshore work."

"What's that?"

He smiled and shrugged. "I'd rather talk about you. My job is so boring, I try not to discuss it." He abruptly moved his hands to the arms of his chair. "So—are we done here?"

I nodded, piqued at his cloddish conversational manners. Nice guy—if you didn't have to talk to him.

The waitress brought the bill. Frederick reached for it, but I'd changed my mind. Better if I paid my own way. I dug in my purse, but his hand on my arm stopped me. "Please, may I catch this? It would be a rare pleasure."

I shook my head. "We should stay on even terms." I glanced at the bill and laid out my share.

His face reddened. "Dina, I'm sorry. I wouldn't have insisted we go out to celebrate if I'd known you wouldn't let me pay. I'm sure you don't have the money to be eating out—I mean . . ." he stuttered, "I—I meant after you only just got a job and all."

Unreasonable anger drove me to my feet. "I don't need anyone to tell me whether I have enough money to go out and eat." I turned and swept toward the door and out to the car while I calculated how many meals I would have to miss to pay for my extravagance and pride. Had he really meant to be so overbearing?

Both of us remained silent on the way home. I needed to apologize but decided doing that once in a day was more than enough. Frederick idled to a stop at the red light on Main and punched the volume up a couple notches before he turned toward me. An old Vince Gill song masked the tension between us.

"Would you like to walk for a few minutes in the park before we go to the house?"

"Sure." It wouldn't hurt to indicate a little regret for rebuffing his generous offer of dinner.

As we walked, the sun slid behind a far-off butte. Warm spring air carried all the small-town sounds of early May. Birds sang their last sonatas of the day, and I realized how fortunate I was to be here.

On the far side of the park, we had a view of the rodeo grounds. Horse trailers and pickups clogged the parking area. I craned to see into the arena.

Frederick answered my unspoken question. "They always rope steers on Thursday nights. At least they have as long as I've lived here."

"Really? Let's go watch. I love to rope."

Frederick's head swiveled around, his eyebrows raised. "You can do that?"

I nodded, not willing to share more with somebody who no doubt thought that was beyond a girl's capabilities.

"We'll cut through here." Frederick led the way through a small ravine that led to the grounds. "In Miles City, this is where you'll find the action." He chuckled. "I spent a fair share of my time here during high school. You do know that the bucking horse sale is next week, don't you?"

"No, what's that?"

"Oh girl, tonight you're going to get an education. Miles City is all about the bucking horse sale. That's nearly why it exists."

My mind flipped back to the brochure at the truck stop in Phoenix that had given me the desire to drive this far north. Frederick and I stood by the arena fence while I told him about my good friend Raul. "I turned many steers for him—though only at the ranch, but I do enjoy roping." He kept a couple horses at Douglas, so he could rope in Arizona and New Mexico without having to go through the hassle of getting horses across the border. My throat tightened as I thought of my sensational Chiquita.

Two ropers walked their horses up the arena from the catch pen at the far end. One of them glanced at us and stopped his horse. "Hey, Fred. How you doin'?"

"I'm doing well, Hardy. Good to see you again."

Hardy glanced at the next team of ropers barreling down the arena toward him. "Don't go away. I'm right in the way here. Stay put, and I'll come outside." With that, he trotted his horse up to the gate, and back toward where we stood watching the ropers. His big, well-muscled bay gelding wasn't fancy, but he was well-broke. Hardy rode up to us and stepped off to shake hands with Frederick. "Man, I haven't seen you since summer before last. You still doin' that spy stuff?"

Frederick chuckled. "Yes, nothing's changed there. I still work out of Omaha, but we're opening a new office in Albuquerque and it sounds like they'll shuffle me down there before too much longer."

Spy stuff? It was my turn to stare at the man who had shown an interest in me. He'd talked more to this Hardy guy in two minutes than he'd said to me through the whole meal.

"Hey, who's your girl?" Hardy asked.

Frederick's face reddened enough I almost laughed. "I'm sorry. This is Dina Rodriquez. She's renting Gram's basement suite. She wanted to come watch the roping. Apparently, she did a lot of that back home." Frederick glanced sideways at me. A skeptical smirk played at the corners of his mouth.

Hardy stepped forward, and I held out a hand. He captured mine in his rope-calloused fingers, while his eyes roamed over my face. "Fred, if you don't capture this one, then I'm going to. Dina, are you a header or do you rope feet?"

"I don't heel steers very well. Mostly, I'm a header."

"Well, don't let it be said that a Miles City cowboy didn't give a good-lookin' girl like you every chance. Here, get on Badger and go rope some steers. Fred and I have some catching up to do anyhow."

"Phil," he yelled to a man inside the arena. "You got a new partner. This is Dina. She's going to turn some steers for you." My face colored as twenty male heads swiveled my way.

Phil gave a desultory wave, clearly not excited to run his heel horse down the arena while some girl missed steer after steer.

"Hardy, are you sure this is okay?" I asked. "I don't want to mess up your horse—plus ruin your evening."

"You're not ruining anything, and Badger knows more about roping steers than you and I put together. There ain't nothing you can do to mess him up. Back him in the box and nod your head. He'll do the rest. Hold him in until you get to the horn, 'cause he will duck out if you let him."

"All right. If you're sure."

"Go. Leave us here to reminisce, and if Fred gets too cocky, come and see old Hardy. I'll tell you all about when a dumb kid from Bulgaria showed up after school to try to ride bucking horses—and a few other stories."

Frederick smiled. "Don't believe a word he says."

I slipped my long black hair into a ponytail, shortened the stirrups, and rode into the arena. After loping a circle to get acquainted with this solid old campaigner and swinging Hardy's rope to get the feel of it, I rode up beside Phil to introduce myself.

He nodded a greeting, still not keen on roping with some unknown girl.

"We're next." Phil spat a brown stream of Copenhagen into the sand and spun out a loop.

I took a deep breath and talked to Badger while I backed him into the box. So far, he hadn't told me he didn't like women. Phil was already waiting and ready. I didn't know how hard Badger broke out of the box, so I held the horn with my loop hand before I nodded. Badger broke smooth and positioned me right at the steer's hip. It was too easy, and I almost missed. I dallied quickly, and it was good that I had. Badger ducked away from the steer and headed for the far wall, the brindle steer bouncing behind him. Phil nearly swallowed his Copenhagen before he snared both hind feet. We made three more runs before I rode outside the arena and handed Hardy his wonderful old horse.

"Hardy, thank you so much. I never expected I would get to rope. You made my day."

"You're most welcome. Come anytime. You rope well, and what's more important, you ride him right. You're not in his mouth all the time, which means you can ride my horses whenever you want."

"It's been great seeing you again." Frederick stuck out his hand, and Hardy shook both Frederick's and mine.

Frederick and I strolled through the coulee and back to his car. I glanced sideways at his face, wondering how he'd taken the evening. His face remained calm and unruffled.

Eventually, I summoned up enough nerve to speak. "I've no doubt you had other things to do tonight, and now I've taken up your whole evening."

"No, I had nothing important. This has been fun. You didn't tell me you could rope like that."

"And I never would have guessed you were a spy."

"I'm not a spy."

"Well, what are you? That's what Hardy said."

"Hardy wouldn't know a spy from a prairie gopher. That's not what I do."

There was little sense in pursuing this further. I leaned back against the seat, all the anger and fear of the last few days forgotten while I basked in the joy of the warm evening. I had a job and a place to live, and now I'd spent the evening roping steers. Life didn't get better than that.

# Chapter 11

Frederick idled down Main before turning onto North 7th. The evening sun carried unusual heat for early June. Across from the park, he pulled to the side of the street and parked in the exact spot where the other car had been last night.

I looked straight ahead, suddenly wary. "Why are you stopping here?"

"Perhaps you would humor me for a few moments. I promise, it won't be long."

"It better not be. I'm tired, and I would just like to go home."

Why did the guy affect me this way? He'd just given me the most wonderful evening. I had no reason to snap at him.

"Walk with me for a few minutes?"

I sighed and stepped out onto the sidewalk. Frederick strolled toward the town center. I trailed behind him, but after a few yards he stopped and turned around, facing the car.

"There were two of them, weren't there?"

My eyes darted to his face.

He walked to where the man had stepped from the car onto the sidewalk. "Right here is where they grabbed you?"

I folded my arms and watched him, not daring to answer.

"May I see your purse?"

"Well, why not, Mr. Detective." I pulled it off my shoulder and held it in front of me. "Perhaps if you paw through it you may find a magnifying glass and a funny little British hat, but I must warn you, I gave my last pipe away."

Frederick said nothing, which made my Sherlock Holmes sarcasm fall flat. He reached over, turned my dangling purse around and stared at it for a moment.

"Well? My arm's getting tired."

"Sorry. That buckle's been damaged for a while, has it?"

I snatched my purse back and looked at the two small decorative, sterling silver buckles. One was broken, part of it missing. I shrugged. "Probably."

He bent and picked a piece of metal out of the grass by the edge of the sidewalk.

"It broke last night when you were struggling to get away."

He offered the piece to me. With a sense of dread, I held out my hand. How had he known? I didn't have to look at the buckle to know it was a perfect match. My eyes dropped. The gathering blanket of darkness helped obscure the confusion and fear. Maybe he *was* a spy?

"I wish you would let me help you." A distant street light shimmered in the distance, enough to see the softness in his eyes. I wanted to trust him, to have all my fears swept away, but somewhere out there, those men watched. They would find out if I told somebody. Confiding in anyone was too risky. I shook my head. "This is my problem, and no—I cannot tell you."

"As you wish, Dina. But I think there is great danger in whatever you're doing. When you need help, I will be there."

I raised an eyebrow. "I do not need any help—but thank you."

His eyes roved over my features. I tried to read his thoughts. Was there more in that gaze than concern for my well-being? The thought brought a rush of blood to my cheeks. Whoever he was and whatever his feelings, he was not a man I needed to fear.

Frederick jammed his hands in his pockets and gazed across the street to the park. "Dina, perhaps neither of us can be as candid as we would wish." He hesitated, his gaze centered on something unseen in the now dark distance. "I cannot tell you exactly what I do, but I did not lie to you. I do work for a company that supplies a service to the government. But it is also a job that allows me to ask for any type of available intelligence." He gestured at the ground where he'd picked up the broken piece from my purse. "This was not the work of two cowboys who had a few too many at the Bison Bar."

I clutched my broken purse between my breasts. "If you want to help me, then leave this alone. I cannot tell you, or anybody. Trust me . . . please." My voice ended on a high note, the fear once again driving me near to tears.

He stood, eyeing me in the darkness, then nodded. "Okay—at least for now. Let's go home. You must be exhausted. And . . ." He grinned. "I guess you have to be at work tomorrow."

"Yes, thanks be to God; I still have a job."

His head swiveled around like I'd said something insulting.

"What's wrong? You don't believe in God?"

"Actually, I do. More than that, I believe in Jesus Christ as the only hope for mankind."

"Interesting. Well, I do too."

"But you're Catholic?"

"Aren't you?"

"Definitely not."

That gave me more reason to avoid him. "I think we better go home. I'm exhausted, and we don't want to even go near that discussion."

Frederick nodded, and we walked back to the car. The few blocks to his grandmother's house passed in silence. He'd wanted to help me, and it had been wonderful to go to the arena and rope. But there hadn't been one issue we'd discussed tonight on which we agreed. Actually, I couldn't think of a positive attribute the man had. He was a nosy Protestant; he wasn't good-looking, and besides, with his build, in later years he would probably run to fat. What was there to like about him?

# Chapter 12

After my third shift at the Spur, Susan's rapid-fire instructions started to make sense. But serving people in a steakhouse, even in a town as pleasant as Miles City, was much harder than I'd thought it would be. Nevertheless, I was determined to succeed.

Trent gave me advice on how to make the most of every trip from the kitchen. Even Susan, who expected perfection of herself and everybody who worked with her backed off with her criticism. If I waitressed for the rest of my life I'd never be as capable as she was, but at least I quit dropping plates.

Frederick might as well have been invisible, for all I saw of him. Once, when I backed out of the driveway on my way to work, he was standing at the living room window. He gave a friendly wave, then disappeared.

I never walked to work again, and every night I scoured the parking lot before skittering from the safety of the restaurant to my truck. The evening after the kidnapping I tried to call home, but my parents' answering machine kicked in. Disappointment mixed with relief washed over me. I wanted to hear their voices, but I wasn't sure I'd be able to respond with anything but anger. I left a message that

I was fine, had a job, and was planning to enroll in Miles City Community College in the fall. Mama would appreciate knowing I was okay. The kidnappers would have given Papa the video as a warning, and I wanted him to know they'd turned me loose.

For the hundredth time, I wondered what orders Papa had refused. What had he done to fall so far out of favor that they would kidnap me?

The following Thursday night, I stood at the screen door at the end of my shift. The parking lot, swaddled in the warmth of a Miles City night in May, still held a dozen cars, and it took me a few seconds to locate my pickup. I'd always parked as close to the door as possible, but this afternoon when I'd arrived for my shift, a freight truck had been unloading meat, so I'd had to leave my pickup further away from the building. I dug in my purse for the truck keys. After I had them firmly in hand, I scurried into the parking lot. A late model car left little room beside my pickup. The dim light from the street outlined a heavyset man slouched in the driver's seat. As I reached for the driver's side door, the passenger side window of the car slid downward, a perfect match for what my heart was doing.

"Dina? Can I talk to you for a few minutes?"

Instantly, I dived into my pickup. The man stepped out and rested his hands on the roof by the driver's door.

When I realized it was the balding detective who had grilled me at the police station, I lowered the window. I had no reason to talk to him. In fact, I had several reasons not to even be seen near him. "No. I'm tired, and I want to go home. Perhaps some other time."

His flat brown eyes bored into mine. "Okay, I'll drop by where you live in the morning. Either way, you need to talk to me."

That would never do. If any more police cars pulled into Mrs. Riddler's driveway, my precarious tenancy would certainly be over.

"So, what do you want? I already told you everything."

"Sure you did. Would you get in the car for a minute?"

"No, I won't. I have nothing more to say." My eyes skittered around the parking lot. Were they watching? A vehicle hugged the back fence, the color indistinguishable. Fear clutched at my throat. The red taillights seemed familiar and brought instant panic. I jumped in my pickup, slammed the door and drove away. The car at the back of the lot followed me. Through the downtown area it stayed well back, but as soon as I turned onto North 7th it edged closer until he was right on my bumper. I drove faster, then slid into the driveway, the tires screeching loud enough to announce to Mrs. Riddler she could add reckless driving to my growing list of faults. Would they follow me into the yard? I shut the engine off and watched the car slow, then cruise on down the street. I sobbed with relief, wondering whether I could run away from here? But where? The inky shadows enveloped the yard as my headlights dimmed and went out. Still I sat with my hands gripping the wheel, wondering how to escape from this nightmare. Running farther would take money, and I had little enough of that commodity. I stepped out of the pickup and eased the door closed, trying to make as little noise as possible as I hurried up the dark sidewalk.

"Good evening."

My breath caught in my throat, as I stifled a scream. Frederick sat on the top step.

"I'm sorry. I didn't mean to startle you."

"Well, you did."

"That was the car, wasn't it? They followed you home."

Suddenly, my need for a friend and ally became at least as large as my fear of the kidnappers.

"Yes." That one simple word unleashed a torrent inside me that was bigger than the few silent tears that threatened to fall in the darkness.

Frederick stood, took my hand and made room on the step for me to sit beside him. I offered no resistance.

A quarter moon nearly eclipsed by the luminescent stars seemed only a high ceiling above us. Crickets chattered to each other in the night, and a faraway dog voiced his uncertainty and fear to the sliver of light in the sky.

"How did you know?"

"About the car?"

"Well, that for starters."

"Coming to Grams, I drove right by the park and saw it. What I mistook for a couple of kids making out in the backseat was you struggling to get away. Then when Gram told me you hadn't shown up, I went over to the Spur and talked to Trent. I suspected from the way he described you that something had gone horribly wrong."

"I can imagine what your grandmother thought."

"Actually," Frederick chuckled. "I think she likes you." He spread his hands in a helpless gesture. "At this stage, there's so little in life she can control. But I do pity anyone who has to rent from her. She harassed the last girl until she'd had enough and moved out. If you can find it in your heart, try to understand."

I mumbled a response through my gritted teeth. In my heart or any other way, I had no desire to put up with Mrs. Riddler's prejudice, but it didn't seem productive to say so.

"Dina, I'm so sorry for not stopping that night. I could have helped you, and I drove right on by."

"No. It would have been more dangerous for both of us if you *had* stopped. I've never been so afraid in my life, but it was better you didn't get involved." Our shoulders touched lightly. His arm felt strong and capable. "So why did you suspect there was more than I told you?"

"I made a few calls. We have contacts in the intelligence community. There was no demand for money, so that narrowed it to two international criminal organizations that might have an interest in you or your family. The first is the Sinaloa Drug Cartel."

"And you eliminated them?"

"Yes."

"Why?"

"We wouldn't be having this conversation if it had been them. When they abduct a victim, their loved ones never see them again."

I stiffened. "And the other option—or are you just fishing?" Instantly, his fingers stopped working against each other. Even without seeing his face, I knew I'd hurt him.

When he spoke, his words were clipped. "I would not do that. What I did do is contact a friend in the CIA. He divulged nothing, which may mean they either don't know, or they have a big operation and they don't want anybody messing in it. Typically, they tend not to act until a few innocent people get killed. In the end, they capture the bad guys and a lot of good press. I'm not willing to allow you to be collateral damage in one of their drug busts."

While he spoke, I sensed his eyes roving over my face and hair.

"So, if you can do any security check you choose, then I guess you are aware of my family's background?"

His hesitant denial only left me with more questions.

"Why not? If you have that kind of connection, you should have discovered all the information you need."

He hunched forward as he stared into the darkness of the stairwell. "Yes, that is true, but . . ." He leaned forward, his elbows on his knees, fingers laced together in front of him. "I decided I would not ask for anything regarding your family. I want to hear from you if there's something I should know. Whatever you choose to tell me about your family will always remain private."

His face turned toward mine, and now the night did little to hide what was in his eyes.

I stared out at the dark street. If this man cared enough about me that he wouldn't infringe on the privacy of my family . . . suddenly I understood, and the realization left me uneasy. His comforting, strong presence had a price. Frederick wanted to be more than a protector. Was I willing to go there? He *was* nice—that is, when he wasn't making me angry.

# Chapter 13

My dream of being a barrel racing sensation still lay shattered in that dusty Mexican border corral. Since I'd crossed the border without my beloved Chiquita, there had been no time to think about another horse. But the evening when I'd been able to ride Hardy's Badger had brought it all back. It was why I was here, and though I didn't have the hard-running Chiquita to power us to the top, I was still determined to win a college scholarship. Without the right horse, that would never happen. Was another Chiquita even possible? I had to find out.

After my Monday night shift at the Spur, I hunched under one of the four bare light bulbs in my apartment, feet propped against the bed. Barrel racing magazines and newspaper classified ads lay strewn across the floor. I chewed through the last bite of an apple while I surfed for more online barrel horse ads. A few of the horses appeared interesting, but they were all several states away, and cost twenty to thirty thousand dollars. Not even Papa would spring for that—as if I would ask.

An hour later, I closed my laptop in disgust, my confidence scattered with the high desert wind. The odds of buying a good horse on my terms were slim to none—but I had to try. Every ad that had a price tag attached made my jaw nearly hit the floor. I hoped horses were cheaper in Montana than all those crazy-priced ads for barrel prospects in Oklahoma and Texas.

I shoved all the newspapers and magazines into a pile, sponged off my face and fell into bed, full of hope that tomorrow, my day off, would bring a new start. I had arranged to look at two outstanding prospects. Both horses were well started, with excellent breeding.

Incidents during my work day competed with the sleep I badly needed. I had snapped at a customer. He had been drunk and unruly, but still, I shouldn't have . . . I needed a horse, not just any horse . . . but how would I pay for one . . . those men, my father's associates—where were they now?

I left the house before eight. My first stop was eighty miles away, and I wanted to be on time for my ten o'clock appointment.

As I drove east on the interstate, I mulled over the possibility of additional problems with my kidnappers. I'd seen no more of them, but I still kept an eye on the rearview mirror, and though I refused to live in fear of what they might do, neither would I give them opportunity.

A week after my kidnapping, Papa had called to assure me that the issues were all resolved, that my abduction had been a mistake. I listened while the anger built in my chest. I wanted to scream out accusations, bitter recriminations that went back to my childhood. I wouldn't be in this trouble if it wasn't for his illegal border smuggling activities. Before I erupted, Mama had taken over the phone to insist I quit living like a tramp and that I should come home to my rightful place. Strangely, she never mentioned marriage to Eduardo. I informed her I was quite happy and had no intention of returning to any place in Mexico. That ended our conversation. She never addressed my troubles with Papa's crazy clients, which meant she probably didn't know, and I wasn't about to tell her. She'd be on the next plane, and that was the last thing I needed.

Frederick and I had only talked once since the night on the front step. Often, I wondered what I would tell him if he again quizzed me about my abductors. Had Papa told the truth, and the men who had kidnapped me would now just go away? All I could do was hope.

A few miles north of Glendive, I pulled through an ornate steel gate and into a definitely upscale ranch yard. A tall, capable-looking lady walked down the steps and introduced herself. We made small talk about the weather and other unimportant subjects as we made our way to the barn. She led a lanky, gray gelding out of his stall. He stood quietly while she saddled him. After I had warmed him up in the arena, we did an easy run. The next time I pushed him hard. There was no doubt he had a big gas tank. The question was whether all that speed was controllable, and most of all, whether he had the desire to win.

Picking barrel horses is like choosing from top Olympic contenders for the hundred-yard dash. When there's equal ability, it is often the contender who wants it the most that wins. In barrel racing—we call it "heart." A horse can be a great athlete, able to run and dig out of the turn, but he has to want to give everything. Few horses have it. Chiquita did. This horse might.

I jumped off, loosened the cinch and walked the gelding around the arena to cool him down—and give myself time to think. He'd just turned six. Barring injury, he had many good years ahead, lots of time to settle down to overcome his aggressive charge at the first barrel. I walked back to the lady. "How much were you asking for him?"

I had little doubt he would be expensive, but I was unprepared for her answer.

"Twenty-two thousand." She didn't even blink.

I sidled around to again inspect the gelding's feet and legs. My eyes traveled up his hocks, then to his sloped and muscled hindquarters. This horse could work for me. With him, my dream had a chance. I ran my hand down his hip.

"Could I give you part of it in a couple of months, and then make payments on him?" That was asking for a lot. I guess the lady thought the same thing.

"Nope. I want a certified check when he leaves the yard. You ride well, and I'd like to see you take him because I think you could win on him, but business is business. For you, I'll take eighteen-thousand because I need to sell him, but I gotta' have cash."

"I understand, but I wouldn't be able to raise that kind of money in one lump sum. Thank you so much for showing him to me." I drove out of the yard and tried not to look back, because a little bit of the dream had died. That horse might have been the one to win on, and I'd had to walk away.

The other horse belonged to a couple who specialized in training barrel prospects. They always had several of their own, as well as clients' horses listed for sale, so I thought it would be beneficial to meet them and look at the mare they had advertised. Even if she wasn't suitable, they would know I was looking, and . . . well, something might work out.

Both the man and woman were riding in the outdoor arena when I pulled up to the barn. After introductions, they took me inside their barn to the mare's stall. She was a small palomino, less than fifteen hands, but with large intelligent eyes that reminded me of Chiquita. I loped around the arena to warm her up, the excitement building in me. She was so responsive, instantly moving off my leg. When I broke her around the first barrel, she had the same fluid bend as Chiquita. She was light and supple, and by the second barrel, little doubt remained. This mare could run with any horse, at any rodeo in the country.

After I'd finished, I walked her around to cool her off, the same as I had with the gray gelding. But that horse couldn't even pack this little lady's lunch. I stepped off and led her over to where the couple watched.

"Nice isn't she," the lady said.

"They don't come any better." I shrugged. "But you already know that. How much hauling has she had?"

"Connie Duke won seven or eight pro rodeos on her after her horse pulled a tendon at Fort Worth. She's been over the road enough to be solid."

"Yes, if Connie rode her, that gives her all the credibility she needs."

"So, think about her. She won't last long, but you ride her well. If you want her, we'll help you all we can."

"I would like to have her. Perhaps—"

"Tell you what." The man walked up to the mare and rubbed her neck. "Give us half down, and you can make payments on the rest. We'd love to have somebody buy her that would really campaign her."

"Oka-ay." I hesitated. So-o, how much would I have to have down?"

"Twenty thousand."

"Twenty thousand dollars?" I wanted to be the cool in-control horse buyer. That was hard to carry off with my tonsils showing. "I'll have to see if I can raise that much money."

"It's a lot of cash, but there aren't any shortcuts with barrel horses," the woman said. "You get what you pay for. There are cheaper ones, but you won't win anything with them." Her friendly eyes crinkled. "I suspect you are aware of that, or you wouldn't be here."

I nodded. There was nothing more to say, so I thanked the people and told them I would be in touch. Somehow, I steered my truck between the gateposts and hammered down the potholed gravel toward the highway. I had to have that mare. Never in my life had I been faced with the possibility that something might be unaffordable. If I wanted it, Papa bought it. But my refusal to live with my father's smuggling activities had changed everything. I could never go back, and as the dust behind me obscured their ranch gate, I realized the sorrel mare would never be mine. When I turned onto the highway, the ice-cube-sized hope that was left of my dream melted away. My affluent life lay behind me, and so did any possibility of ever having another horse like the blazing fast Chiquita.

# Chapter 14

Frederick lost count how many times he'd started to punch in the number. Now he had no choice. He let it ring until the familiar growl sounded in his ear.

"Yeah."

"Can you meet me tomorrow night in Madagascar, at the number two location?"

Stirling Associates always used code names over the phone, even inside the country. Every agent memorized them as well as the code names for several dozen other major cities in the world.

A second of silence passed before the man answered. "I'll be there at the usual time."

"Good." Frederick disconnected. Though every conversation was encrypted, he never wasted time on the line, and he always changed physical locations after calling. He left the rest stop east of the city and drove downtown. After parking on a side street, he hurried toward the Spur Bar, then wedged into a small space at the back where Trent kept the garbage cans. A faint odor of wilted lettuce and rotten tomatoes made him take shallow breaths as he melded into the shadows of the back wall. For a week, he'd kept an uncomfortable vigil here. Would this be the night they made their move? The evening air had cooled, and he shivered as he peered into the parking lot. The gray Audi had moved from its usual spot on the far side of the lot. This time, they had parked behind Dina's pickup. His eyes narrowed. Adrenalin cascaded through every cell of his body. The waiting was over.

Twenty minutes later, he watched Dina open the back door and scan the parking lot before she hurried toward her pickup. She was starting to get careless. For days, she had parked right outside the door, her vehicle hugging the building so it was only a few steps until she could drive away. Tonight, her pickup was halfway across the lot. He wanted to follow her with his eyes. Instead, he watched the car. She'd nearly reached her pickup when two men stepped forward to intercept her. Frederick trotted away from his hiding place and yelled at her. His hand brushed at the gun inside his vest—just in case. "Dina. Hey, wait a minute."

The men hesitated at the sound of his voice.

Dina whirled, still unaware of the danger. "What are you doing here?"

He stepped close to her and squeezed her arm. "Keep looking at me. Do not turn around. Get in your pickup. I'm coming with you, so unlock the passenger door." Fear instantly froze every muscle in her face. Her eyes widened as she followed his instructions. Frederick moved nonchalantly to the passenger side, though his attention never left the two figures in the corner of his vision. The two men immediately walked back to their car. Whatever they'd planned for tonight would be postponed. But to protect Dina, he had to know who they were. He could no longer wait for her to take him into her confidence—if she ever would.

"Let's go." Frederick's eyes were glued to the right side rearview mirror. "Turn left. Go down Main and turn right onto the Broadus highway." He watched the car pull onto the street behind them. It followed at a reasonable distance until the intersection loomed ahead. Their tail then turned into a side street and disappeared. "Okay, pull into that hotel parking lot and turn around, so we're facing the highway."

"It was them, wasn't it?" Dina's voice was weary.

Frederick nodded. "Until now, they were just giving you a reminder. Tonight was different."

"Why? What do they want?"

"I'm not sure. You tell me."

She looked straight ahead at the pulsating red and purple neon advertising Miles City's best hotel deal. "I guess I should have told you everything before."

"It would have made it easier." Though he hadn't intended it, his voice held an edge of sarcasm.

"I don't know who they are for sure, other than they are people who have an atrocious English accent and an even worse Spanish one. I think they are from the eastern countries."

"What do you mean? Like China?"

"No, like Iran or Syria. Somewhere over there."

"How is your family connected to them?"

"My father has been involved with these men for years." She turned to face him. "Frederick, tell me I can trust you, because if you betray me, then my father will die, and probably all my family. They made that clear."

"The night they kidnapped you?"

She nodded.

"Why didn't you tell me? How can I help you if—"

"Frederick . . . stop! I need to hear something about you. Who are you? You've stood up for me, but how can I trust you when my family's lives are at stake?"

"Wow. Talk about two people with secrets." Frederick swiped at his forehead, then leaned back against the seat. "To disclose anything about my work is just as dangerous for me. Other people's lives depend on my silence, and to a large degree my anonymity as well. So how much can I trust you, Dina?"

Her eyes searched his face. Finally, she reached across the console and slid her hand into his. His other hand enveloped her slim fingers. Their eyes met.

"So, I'm going to trust you, Dina Rodriguez. I hope that means you will also trust me, because I'd like to help."

"Do I have a choice?"

"No."

A sad smile touched her lips. "I didn't think so." She swallowed the tears that threatened to spill down her cheeks. "I only want to live my life like a normal person, to follow my dreams, away from whatever my father does. I don't want to die, and I don't want Papa to die, no matter what he's done. Why can't these people just go away?" Angry tears wet her green uniform blouse. She reached into the middle console for a small package of tissues.

"Dina, I don't understand why you're faced with what you're going through, but I am convinced that God is in control of every facet of our lives. I've had to learn that the hard way. My parents were killed in a plane crash when I was twelve. I had no other relatives except a grandmother I'd never met in some faraway cowboy town in America on the other side of the world. I won't bore you with the details—"

"I'd like to hear them."

Frederick chuckled. "Okay, I will tell you, but not tonight. Let's save that chapter for another time." He leaned toward her, still holding her hand. "Tonight, I need to hear about you."

"No." She pulled her hand away. "First, tell me who you are. Not where you went to school, or where you live. Who is the real Frederick—the one Hardy said was a spy? How does he spend his waking hours?"

Frederick sighed heavily and leaned against the passenger door. His eyes never left her face. What if this was a mistake? What if this girl wasn't who she seemed to be? Revealing anything about his role with Stirling Associates could prove disastrous.

"Okay, I understand." Her voice hardened. "Sorry, Frederick. Trust has to work both ways." She leaned forward to turn the ignition key.

"No." He reached across and touched her shoulder. "Give me a minute. It's just— there are others to consider."

"And what about me? Those men told me what would happen if anything was leaked to the police. If you betray me, my family will die. They will kill them."

"Okay, I got it, and I believe you. So . . ." Frederick stared through the windshield at the deserted street, then turned toward Dina as he spoke the words that could end his career. "I am part of a small company that does undercover work, mostly for the U.S. government. Sometimes we work in countries where Americans aren't welcome. We spend a lot of time and resources in Mexico and Central America because of the drug cartels, most of the time with the host country's approval. In rare circumstances our people just quietly slip in and do what needs to be done."

"And what's your job?"

"I don't have a title. Perhaps Special Operations Coordinator would best describe how I spend my time. I deal with planning and forward reconnaissance, so our undercover agents are as safe as possible. We maintain constant contact with relevant government agencies."

"And you manage that as well?"

"Sometimes. Presently, things are quiet, so I've been able to stay here longer than I'd planned." He squeezed her hand. "Now . . . your turn."

"Okay. I'm not sure if what you told me explains everything about you, but I guess it's a start." She took a deep breath. "My parents own a large ranch in Sonora. My father married my mother for her money. Mama married Papa for his American citizenship, or at least that's my perspective on my family." Dina paused before continuing, trying to marshal her thoughts. "Their relationship is strange, and yet at times I've suspected they love each other dearly."

Frederick tapped an index finger. "Tell me about your father?"

Dina glanced at him, wondering why he'd asked, though she was sure she'd not have to wait long to find out. "There's not much to tell, at least not much that's good. He started as a coyote, smuggling illegals and sometimes other contraband.

"A coyote?"

"A people smuggler. Along the border, that is a respected profession."

Frederick waved her explanation away. "I'm familiar with the term, but it seems out of character . . ." His voice trailed off.

"Mama says a lot of businessmen got their start that way. Unfortunately, my father went from smuggling Mexicans across the border to this."

Frederick hunched over the console. "What do you mean?"

Dina stared out into the night, her whole body suddenly full of tension. How much more information should she give this man whom she'd decided to trust?

"Honestly, I can't say. All I know is that the people who come to the ranch are evil men, and they are not Mexicans or Guatemalans."

Frederick's finger now tapped on a piece of plastic door trim. What Dina had told him vindicated his decision to call for the meeting tomorrow night.

"I despise what my father has done, and what it will do to our family when he is exposed, but I will not be the one who causes his downfall."

"Who do you think kidnapped you?"

Dina shrugged. "Whoever they were, they had the same bad accent as those who my father often met on our ranch."

"This may be a weird question, but is your father of the Muslim faith?"

"Papa? No, of course not. He and Mama are devout members of the church."

"The church?" Frederick's eyebrows rose.

"The Catholic church. Right—I forgot. You're a Protestant."

"A Christian."

"Meaning, I'm not?"

Frederick cringed at the anger and hurt in her voice. "No-o, that's not exactly what I meant."

"Well, that's what it sounded like."

"Dina, I didn't say that." Frederick held up both hands in a mock surrender. "Probably we need to have a religion discussion. Hey, how about we go on a picnic on your next day off? We can both take sharp knives and fight to a bloody finish for our faith. At the end of the day, the vanquished shall promise to renounce all ties to their church and join the victor's."

She gave him a withering glance. "A picnic with you would be boring, and I don't think you're at all funny. Unlike you, I cannot be flippant about God—or my church." This time Dina did start the pickup. The tires spun on the gravel parking lot as she pulled across the highway and onto Main Street. At the house, she slammed the shifter into park and opened the door.

Frederick held up a hand. "Hey, I need your permission for something."

"What?" He didn't have to see her face to hear her anger.

"I have a meeting tomorrow with my superior. I would like to ask a few questions about you—your family. If I had a better idea of who we're dealing with, we might find a way to protect you, and your father."

"Do whatever. Lock the truck whenever you decide to get out." She slammed the driver's side door, flounced over the sidewalk, and disappeared down the steps.

Frederick bit his lower lip, wishing it had been his tongue. He seemed to have a talent for making her mad—another calamity in their faltering relationship. And more and more he was aware that . . . the most disastrous thing that could ever happen was if this girl walked out of his life.

# Chapter 15

After crawling out of bed the next morning, I glanced out the tiny kitchen window. Two hours before noon was long past my customary waking hour. I'd always been an early riser. Now, I seldom returned home from the Spur before 1:00, and last night had been much later.

I sat on the edge of the bed, yawned, and then peeked out the kitchen window. Frederick's green Mustang was not in the driveway. Where had he gone for this meeting? What would he discover? Instant fear skittered through every vein, followed by dismay. I'd come to depend on his protective presence. Had last night been the final straw? Had he left; gone back to Omaha? I pushed off the bed and padded toward the shower. If he was gone, so be it. I would survive. In fact, my life would be easier without him. At least then I wouldn't have to hear the constant innuendo against my faith. What had he said? He wasn't a Protestant? I gritted my teeth. He'd said he was a Christian, as if I were somehow disqualified from that saintly state because I was Catholic. Maybe his picnic wasn't such a bad idea. It would be a good time to straighten him out once and for all, and besides, he needed to understand that anything more than an arms-length friendship between us was *so* not going to happen.

Later, I marched up the basement steps, intent on checking out the second-hand store across town for a table and chairs. Thanks to my squeaky door, when I reached the top of the stairs, my landlady toddled outside.

"Good morning, Mrs. Riddler. It's another beautiful day." I gave her my sweetest smile.

"Humph. In another hour, you'll be able to fry an egg on the sidewalk, and by this time next month, you won't even be able to poke your head outside. Mind you, I suppose you're more used to the heat. There probably isn't much for air conditioning where you come from. I can't imagine any of those little adobe huts having that."

I smiled sweetly. "Yes, I suppose we are better acclimatized to heat. Sonora gets very hot in the summer." Inside, I steamed. It would do no good to inform this old woman that every room in my parents' house had the best air conditioning money could buy, and that her little house would have nearly fit inside our *sala*.

Mrs. Riddler then fixed me with her flinty eyes. "Come up here, young lady. I want to talk to you."

She turned and bounced her walker across the sill and into the living room where she dropped into her chair. I followed her inside. Surreptitiously, I scanned the area to detect any sign of Frederick's presence. No male items graced the room, which meant he'd probably left for good. A great weight squeezed my chest, as if I'd lost something or someone near to me. Though obnoxious, the man had at least offered protection from those who followed me.

"Sit." The old woman pointed to the couch.

Gingerly, I perched on the edge, my hands folded in my lap. This sounded like an eviction. She'd only been waiting until Frederick left.

"I am not happy with the time my grandson seems to be spending with your affairs. If I had my way, you'd have been gone long ago." She now stood directly in front of me, both hands trembling on the grips of her walker. "I am aware of what your intentions are, and let me tell you young lady, he is not for you. Frederick has a brilliant career ahead of him. He needs a wife of his own kind and station in life, one who can help him to succeed. You would drag him down in every way." The old woman's eyes flashed with anger. "Now, I demand that you leave him alone. You certainly have enough assets to turn a man's eye, but I insist you use them elsewhere. If you defy my wishes, I will take other action."

My cheeks burned as the accusations escalated. When she was finished I stood in front of her walker, my hands at my sides, clenched with anger. "Mrs. Riddler, I have no intention of trapping your grandson with whatever charms you accuse me of possessing. We have been thrown together in some distressing circumstances. I have appreciated his help. However, let me assure you; Frederick is the last person I would ever consider marrying, and if by chance I change my mind, you will be the first to know." I whirled and strode out of her living room and down the steps to my suite. The table and chairs could wait. I wouldn't need furniture here anyway. Though it was still two hours before I had to be at the Spur, I quickly changed into the green blouse and jeans I wore to work and left the premises. I could no longer bear to be on the same property as that frightful old woman.

# Chapter 16

Even at six-thirty in the evening, the air carried the clammy moisture common to the corn belt of America. Frederick threw his bag into a taxi and gave the driver directions. Twenty minutes later, he walked into what might have been the seediest dive in Omaha, Nebraska. The pimp standing at the end of the bar turned to view the newcomer. A black dude with bulging biceps in a leather jacket with ripped-out sleeves watched his approach in the mirror behind the bar. The several other customers spread throughout the room ignored him. Those seemed sky-high, stoned on some lethal substance. The pungent aroma of marijuana saturated every corner of the room. Frederick avoided eye contact, strolled to a table in the back corner, and slouched into a red Naugahyde chair. The bartender made no move to offer refreshment, but the leather jacketed gym rag picked up his drink and moved to a table where he effectively blocked the door. Another black occupant, dreadlocked and skinny, wandered toward Frederick's chosen seat. He placed both hands on the table and spoke. "Hey whitey, ya wanna' buy some weed?"

Frederick shook his head, his eyes fixed on the entrance. A tall, gray-haired man pushed through the metal door and moved to the bar, a noticeable limp slowing his progress. He leaned an elbow on the shiny surface while he surveyed the room. An electric tension saturated the air as the man's eyes took in the occupants. He sauntered over to Frederick's table, his quiet face giving no hint of his intentions. Frederick stood while the man turned and waved at the assorted characters. "At ease, people." Instantaneous obedience filtered through the room, no less dramatic than if he'd given the same order to a platoon of Marines. Those who were stoned and inebriated were sobered. The pimp turned into a family man wanting his shift to end so he could go home to his wife and three kids, and the hooker at the end of the counter left to change out of her skimpy uniform. After the veteran agents were dismissed, the bartender taped a makeshift sign to the exterior of the door and locked it. Due to a burst pipe in the men's washroom, the Vermillion Club would be closed for the evening.

Frederick reached across the table for the proffered hand. "Adrian, I appreciate you coming. It was short notice."

"What isn't in this business?" The raspy volume of the words was blunted as if the larynx had already lost to the devastation of nicotine. "Sit." The man motioned to the chairs. "How is your grandmother?"

"For her age, quite well. Thank you for asking."

"Are you ready for an assignment? We have a problem in Guatemala that will require your attention. It may not be as difficult as the last one, but infinitely more dangerous. The Guatemalans need help with cartel goons filtering across the border."

"How soon?"

"Thirty days, no more."

"Los Zetas?"

Adrian's square chin inclined in a barely perceptible nod. "Yes, they're using remote ranches in Guatemala as storage depots for Columbian cocaine, before running it north into Alabama and Mississippi." He picked up his cup and drank, never taking his eyes off Frederick.

"So why have you called an old man away from his hearth?"

Frederick leaned over the table, his voice quiet in spite of the obvious security. "Are you aware of any smuggling operations on the Arizona border? Douglas area. Possibly ferrying Muslim militants into the country."

"Which militants? There are at least a dozen groups, though the most likely are Hezbollah, ISIS, the Muslim Brotherhood or al-Qaida."

Frederick shrugged. "I don't know yet. Does the name Rodriguez mean anything?"

"A common name in Sonora. Not Ricardo, by chance?"

"Might be." Frederick hesitated. He wished he'd at least gotten that much information from Dina. "He's an American, married to a Mexican woman."

The silver-haired man moved sideways in his chair and placed both hands on the table. "That sounds like Ricardo. If it is, then yes, I'm familiar with him. A number of years ago, we tried to recruit him as an informant."

"Is he connected enough to run a high-level operation?"

Adrian's big-knuckled hands writhed against each other, his fingers massaging at chronic pain. "Interesting question." He glanced suspiciously at Frederick. "At one time, we decided he was no threat. But I've often thought there was more to Ricardo Rodriguez than anyone suspected. He worked as a low-level coyote, ran illegals across the border, and dealt in the odd lot of contraband or livestock. The Border Patrol nabbed him at least a half-dozen times, but curiously, he avoided any prison time." Adrian shrugged. "Friends in high places? Perhaps, but it all seems odd, and so far, the cartels haven't killed him, which means he's not stepped on their toes. Ricardo has always led a charmed life. If you meet him, you'll swear he's an incompetent idiot. He may be, but he married into a wealthy Sonora family, and he raises some of the best horses in Mexico. Most believe it's his wife's intelligence that keeps the ranching business together. I'm not so sure."

Frederick cataloged every word. From Adrian's response, it was clear that no one knew Ricardo, this parent Dina had grown to despise. Who really was this man who engendered such conflicting emotions? An hour later, Frederick felt no closer to understanding Dina's father.

"Enough, though I wish I could tell you more." Adrian crossed his arms and leaned back in his chair. "The arthritis gets worse every year. Soon, I will want to be a full-time grandpa, a role I quite look forward to filling." He maneuvered his chair sideways and stretched out his legs. "I suspect the Feds are running an operation in that border sector. Whatever they are doing is top secret with only a few agents involved. They haven't made us privy to any information, and they won't until they need someone to risk their neck across the border. That's when we'll become significant enough to be a part of the loop," he growled. "But that's the way it has to be."

Frederick stared into the mirror behind the bar and tapped an index finger on the polished table top. Dina had indicated her father might be a conduit for a radical Muslim group, perhaps al-Qaida. Whoever it was, they were desperate enough to kidnap her to put pressure on her father. The question was, why? What he had just heard from Adrian didn't line up with Dina's description. If this Ricardo was her father, and he had the infrastructure and connections to spirit hostile operatives into the country, then he was neither a small player, nor a fool. A huge piece of this puzzle was missing.

Adrian sat with his chin resting on his gnarled, thin fingers. Finally, he raised his head and signaled to the man behind the bar. "Alex, run this name through the system. Ricardo Rodriguez Ortega. Probable address is Agua Prieta, Sonora. Just the usual, nothing classified for now."

Ten minutes later, the supposed bartender laid several pages in front of Adrian. He pushed them across to Frederick. "You need the info—you read it."

Frederick took a deep breath and picked up the five pages of data. They contained the usual data found in a credit rating and criminal activity report, most of it either old or useless. He flipped through the first four pages. The family had money, connections, and credit. The Border Patrol had picked up Ricardo nine different times for smuggling illegals. The odd thing was that not once had he been charged. The last page held the answer he needed. Ricardo's name, listed in the traditional Mexican way, stood out as if underlined in black. The names of his wife and two children were printed below. Frederick's eyes riveted on the last one: "Bernardina Rodriguez Loera." Ricardo, the man who had started as a "coyote" on the border had graduated to the big-time, and he was Dina's father.

Adrian winced as he sought to find a more comfortable position. "If you want, I can call in some favors. A couple guys in the agency owe me. One of them will have enough information to piece it together."

"Much appreciated. Frederick's left jaw muscle twitched with the tension coursing outward to each limb. If he got this wrong, somebody would die, and it might be the girl. His life was about instant decisions. This time . . . well, nothing had changed. He leaned across the table. "Which terrorist group is Ricardo is dealing with? Something went wrong, and they're putting a lot of pressure on him."

Adrian raised a questioning eyebrow. "Hmm, I'm not sure I can pull *that* much information."

"Whoever he's involved with kidnapped his daughter. They put her through the usual terror, complete with a video to send to Daddy."

"They didn't kill her?"

"No. They just roughed her up, then turned her loose." Frederick pushed his chair back. "I'm going after these guys."

Adrian's eyes narrowed. "This sounds personal."

Frederick ran his fingers through his hair. "Adrian, you may be right. I'm not sure of anything on this one, so if you're upset, I understand."

Adrian nodded, but made no comment as he stood and held out his hand. "I'll find out what I can and get back to you in a day or two. But be very careful, Frederick. Don't let this . . . this relationship cloud your focus. I need you to take over—and soon."

# Chapter 17

Since I'd started work at the Spur Bar, Friday nights had always been busy. Tonight, a herd of horses in the restaurant wouldn't have disturbed a soul. Two hours from now, that apparently would all change.

The third weekend in May is the most important celebration in Miles City—arguably the most prestigious event in Montana. The bucking horse sale almost doubles the population of this small town with buyers, sellers, and bucking horse riders from all over North America. For now, the crowds had deserted the downtown in favor of the evening performance at the fairgrounds. Susan had warned me. "Tonight, between nine o'clock and closing time will be the busiest shift of the year."

Tomorrow and Sunday featured afternoon performances at the fairgrounds, and even though Trent hired extra help, he'd warned us, we'd work harder than we ever had before. I'd gained enough proficiency to nearly hold my own with Susan.

Two couples walked through the side door by the bar and waited to be seated. I gathered up menus and greeted Hardy with a big smile.

"Dina, I didn't realize you worked here."

"'Fraid so. Trent had a soft moment, and now he's stuck with me. Are you going to eat, or would you like to sit at the bar?"

The blonde girl beside Hardy elevated her nose about a hundred degrees before she responded to my question. She was the same one who had worked at the hotel where I'd stayed on my first night in the town.

"We'd like a table in the dining room." Hardy's friendliness hadn't pleased her.

"Please, follow me." I took them to a table by the far wall.

"I suppose you don't get to go to the bucking horse sale," Hardy said.

"No, Trent has me dialed in to work every day. Nobody here gets time off this weekend."

Hardy chuckled. "Yeah, but you girls are going to load up. You'll make more in tips in the next two days than the whole rest of the year."

"Ha, I hope you're right. My horse fund isn't growing nearly fast enough." I didn't add that at least now I had sheets on the bed, and real food to eat, for which I was very thankful.

By Sunday night, my feet were so sore I could barely hobble, but a small sense of pride took away the ache. The bucking horse sale weekend was over. I'd made it through—and pulled my weight. Susan had only come to my side of the dining room once to help, and an hour later I'd been able to return the favor.

After my shift, I wearily scanned the parking lot before opening the screen door to brave the run to my pickup. Even though there were still a couple groups having impromptu tailgate parties, I was cautious. There seemed no opportunity for my stalkers to approach me in this crowd, but I'd take no chances.

When I pulled into the driveway, Frederick's Mustang sat in its usual spot. A thrill shot through me, or maybe it was more that I was weak with relief. I didn't even want to think about how to reconcile those two emotions.

I tiptoed toward the stairs that led down to my basement suite. I shouldn't have bothered. When I attempted to wrench the ill-fitting door open, it would squawk louder than a whole flock of crows. Frederick had said he would fix it, but probably that mean old woman had told him not to bother. It didn't matter to me. As soon as I found another place, I would leave. My face burned as Mrs. Riddler's cutting words came back to me.

"I am quite aware of your intentions."

I certainly had no designs toward her sainted grandson. In fact, I recognized the same obtuseness in him as his grandmother.

"And let me tell you young lady, he is not for you."

If she only knew how much I disliked her grandson.

"You would drag him down, in every way."

My fists knotted in anger.

"If you insist on defying my wishes, I will take other action."

Huh! She wouldn't have to. Tomorrow was my day off. I would use it to find another place to live.

Suddenly a figure stepped in front of me. "Good evening."

My heart jumped into my throat. “At least you could say something, so I know you’re there,” I snapped.

“I’m sorry. I didn’t mean to scare you.” Frederick chuckled which made me angry. Suddenly, he sobered. “Let’s start over. How are you?”

“Fine—and exhausted,” I sighed, pushing the unreasonable anger away. “How’d your trip go?” I wanted to find out what he’d discovered about my family’s adventures on the border, but with the wild weekend at work, I hadn’t had time to even ask.

“Good. We should talk. How about that picnic?” He held up his hands at my hesitation. “We can steer clear of church stuff. I’ll bring something to drink and . . . no, on second thought, how about we stop at Subway and grab a sandwich and drinks. That should fill the bill quite well.”

I crossed my arms. “I haven’t said I’d go, yet.”

“Oh—I guess you didn’t.” He hesitated, his fingers shoved deep into his pockets while he shifted from one foot to the other. He reminded me of a boy in eighth grade who had asked me to go to a dance. Thinking of that made me feel sorry enough for him, I capitulated.

His teeth flashed in the dark, and the thought occurred to me that when Frederick smiled, he was actually good looking, but there was no need to tell him that.

“Okay, we’ll leave whenever you get up. I have a friend who has a ranch down on the Tongue River. It’s a beautiful spot. We could go on a little hike—if you want to.”

“I don’t. I’ve hiked about a hundred miles this weekend at the Spur. In fact, if you make me walk more than fifty feet, I’m out.”

"Got it. No hiking."

Despite being exhausted, I smiled at his enthusiasm. "Goodnight. I'll be ready around ten thirty."

"Goodnight, Dina." His voice was soft and musical, and as I felt for each dark stair with my foot, a disconcerting thought destroyed my concentration and I nearly fell to the bottom. My heart was doing crazy little flip-flops over a simple picnic.

FREDERICK WAITED FOR Dina at the top of the stairs, well before the specified time to leave. When she appeared at the porthole-sized kitchen window, he waved.

"Give me ten minutes. I slept late," she shouted.

"No rush. Whenever you're ready."

Finally, she skipped up the stairs in a red blouse, jeans, and tennis shoes.

Mesmerized, he stared as she reached the top.

She stopped and looked down at her front. "What's wrong? Did I spill jam on it?"

"No—no you look marvelous."

Her face flushed. "Oh, . . . thank you. It's just an old blouse. I had nothing else clean to wear."

"So, you're ready?"

"Yes. But if we have to go over some rough roads to find this mystery ranch, we should take my pickup."

"No, my car will be okay. I'll take it easy."

"Frederick, that's dumb. It doesn't make sense to tear the muffler off that expensive sports car just for a picnic."

"No. We'll be okay. We're taking my car." His voice had an edge to it.

"Why do you always have to be so stubbornly chauvinistic? You can drive my pickup if it makes you feel better." She tossed a stray lock over her shoulder and stamped toward the expensive Mustang.

"And why do you argue over every little item?" He followed her and opened the driver's door. "Fortunately, I already bought the sandwiches, or we'd never get out of town because you would argue over that too."

"No, I wouldn't. I always order roast beef."

"Then this is my lucky day. Come on. Let's go."

"I—I . . ." She shook her head in defeat. "Arguing with you is like hitting a brick wall. All you do is hurt your hand."

He turned and grinned at her. "Then quit hurting your hand."

She scowled but remained silent as they drove west. Just before the Hysham exit, Frederick turned onto a gravel road, then bounced over a cattle guard and through a fenced pasture. The low-slung Mustang did not do well. Dina glanced sideways at him and smirked when the undercarriage scraped bottom for the third time. The muffler now had a distinctive and new vibrato. Frederick squirmed in the expensive leather seat.

The dirt track they followed stopped at the river. Scattered willows grew among the gnarled cottonwoods. The grassy bank, chewed to a smooth green carpet by the nearby range cattle had invitation written all over it. Frederick scooped up the lunchbox and led the way down to a shaded area by the riverbank.

"Hey, did you ever fly-fish?" he asked.

"I have never caught a fish in my life. That is one opportunity most Sonora-raised kids don't have."

"Would you like to try it? I brought some gear."

"Maybe later. It's time you told me about the men who are following me, or is there a reason you've avoided the subject?"

His jaw clenched. "You're right. I have, because I needed more information. It came last night."

"Who are they?"

Frederick mauled a green willow stick while he stared out at the water. "Do you know anything about al-Qaida?"

"No, other than they're terrorists, but everybody knows that. What are you saying?"

Frederick tore a piece off the twig and tossed it in the river. "Tell me about your father."

Dina shrugged. "I already have. What more do you want?"

"Who is he—really?"

"Sometimes, I don't think I know. When we were growing up, Papa was always very good to my brother and I, but what he does is despicable. If he's the one helping these crazy assassins, how can I do anything but despise him and everything he stands for?"

Behind the sunglasses, Frederick's eyes narrowed, wondering what of the information he'd gained from Adrian he should share? He flipped another piece of the twig into the water, then watched as it swirled into the current and floated downstream.

Dina moved onto her knees and faced him. "So, it was al-Qaida terrorists who stayed at our ranch?"

"That's my guess."

"They kidnapped me, then turned me loose to force my father into something?"

Frederick shrugged. "That's the way I see it. He didn't co-operate at the level they felt he should, so they grabbed you to show him they're deadly serious, and capable of hurting anyone in his family."

Though it was a hot day, Dina shivered. "It's difficult to believe that my father cared so little that he would expose us—his family—to that kind of danger."

Frederick nervously twisted his hands together, trying to concentrate. Why did he always feel so inadequate when he was with this girl? It was like a perpetual first date. "Dina, don't be too hard on your father. Sometimes things aren't what they seem. He may have reasons for what he's doing."

"What are you talking about? He sold his family out to the evilest people on the face of the earth, and then you say it's okay, like it's not his fault?" She threw up her hands. "Sorry, Frederick. Go peddle that psychobabble to somebody else."

His face fell as she got to her feet, then marched down to the riverbank. He hadn't meant to sound like he was making excuses for her father.

She turned and yelled up at him. "You don't understand what it was like to watch a father who never stood for anything in his life. You've never lived with that kind of disgusting, cowardly behavior."

"What are you talking about? At least you had a father."

"It would have been better not to have had one than to have a parent so devoid of principle he would sell out his own family. And it doesn't matter what happened in his life. What he has done goes against every principle I've ever held to be true." She marched up the bank and stood in front of him. "Most people stand for something. Growing up, I was convinced my father stood for nothing. I was wrong. He stands for evil." She glared at Frederick.

Frederick's hands twisted at the last remnant of willow stick in his hand, refusing to meet her eyes.

"Perhaps you can tell me how you harmonize your no-fault, see-no-evil view of my father with your supposed faith?"

His face colored. "I thought we weren't going to bring the knives?"

"Okay. I take it back. But what you're saying doesn't make sense. How can you have a God who demands responsibility and righteousness, yet you're willing to make excuses for my father who is involved with a group that has killed hundreds of innocent people?"

Frederick grimaced and flung the last of the stick in the water. "First, I wasn't making excuses for whatever he's done. All I'm saying is that there might be more than we know. My parents were taken from me when I was twelve. Can you, or anyone give me a reason? Nobody can. That plane crash changed and shaped my life, and I will always carry a deep pain from that event. Do I understand why it happened? Hardly. All I can control is my response to the hurt and tragedy in my life."

Frederick watched the anger drain from her dark eyes, only to be replaced with the torment of her father's betrayal. That—he couldn't take away.

# Chapter 18

The morning after the picnic, I washed the dishes and cleaned up the kitchen while I thought about Frederick. Though the day had been marred by arguments, it had still been fun—or was it more than that? We were spending more and more of my off-work hours together. I tossed the last piece of tarnished mismatched cutlery onto the drain board and dried my hands on a dishtowel. How did I feel about this guy? What about our faith differences? And most of all, was there any future with him? Too often, when the religion subject arose, we fought like a pair of banty roosters.

A few minutes later, the man himself knocked to see if it would be okay if he tried to fix the squeak that announced my every movement to Mrs. Riddler. We chatted amiably, until he noticed the little corner shrine. I'd placed it there because I'd grown up with one. It was as much a part of my parents' home as the dining room table.

"So, what's that?" he asked.

I glanced to where he was pointing. "Sort of an attempt at an altar. It's not very good."

Frederick glanced at me and smirked. "Right; I forgot. You pray to idols."

"I don't pray to idols. The focal point of a home should be something more than a television set."

"Fair enough, but why do you have a crucifix and beads and all that other stuff?"

"What's wrong with a crucifix?"

"Lots. Jesus isn't on the cross."

"I know that. He arose from the grave; otherwise there would be no reason to hope for eternal life."

"And isn't that what you Catholics do; hope by working hard enough that you can get to heaven?"

"Yes, for your information we do good works. We are saved through faith and works inspired by the Holy Spirit, unlike you Protestants who say one little prayer and think you can go on your merry way still being jerks. Thanks for fixing the door." I grabbed my purse and marched past him and up the steps. I was an hour early for work, but so what. I'd rather spend the time standing on my head than listening to that self-righteous, insufferable man.

As I drove toward the Spur, I thought about our running argument. Did we believe the same things, or were there fundamental differences in our faith? And if there were, did that mean the end of our relationship? Would he give up any of his cherished Protestant hang-ups? I squelched a decidedly unladylike snort. Him? Not likely!

I edged my pickup into the nearest parking spot behind the Spur and decided to go for a walk, a dumb idea. That's all I did for eight hours on my shift. I didn't need any extra miles.

Perhaps it was the uneasiness over our argument that led me toward the fairgrounds. I needed to feel the familiar sandy dirt of a rodeo arena under my feet. Soft drink cans and hot dog wrappers littered the grandstand area. Discarded coffee cups and cardboard spilled from a nearby trash can. Fresh dust clung to the pipe pens behind the bucking chutes. The bunting and banners fluttered listlessly, like the forlorn finale of a mud-splashed and spurned flamenco dancer.

I strolled past the pens which would mostly remain desolate and silent until next year's bucking horse sale. Next year, I would try to get at least get one day off work so I could watch this extravaganza that drew bucking horses, cowboys, and stock contractors from all over North America.

A lone horse stood in the farthest pen from the chutes. She nuzzled a flake of hay and ignored me as I strolled up to the gate. The chain rattled as I undid the latch to go inside. I missed being around horses. They'd been a part of my life as long as I could remember. The mare stood quietly when I walked up to her. I ran my hand down her well-shaped neck. Was she somebody's rope horse, or perhaps some girl's barrel horse? I stepped back to look at her conformation. She had the same powerful, sloping hip and short back as Chiquita. The mare turned her head toward me, her well-spaced, intelligent eyes aware of every movement I made. Brown pixie ears flickered back and forth.

"Y'all are looking for something?"

I whirled at the unexpected voice. A man in a blue checked shirt stood at the gate. I'd failed to notice him, or the truck and trailer at the far end of the alley.

"Oh, no. I'm sorry. I was just walking around the grounds and saw your horse, so I stopped to pet her. I hope that was alright."

"Well, you'd best get to pettin' because in two minutes the witch is going to Billings to the horse sale."

"Why? What's wrong with her?"

"She's a loser who just had her last chance. Ike Fenton hauled her clear from Kansas to the bucking horse sale. All she did at home was buck everybody off, but she didn't buck here. She thought she was in the Preakness, and if she had been, she might have placed." The man chuckled. "The pick-up men couldn't even catch her. Anyhow, Ike said he'd lost enough money on her, and to send her to a meat horse buyer."

"How old is she?"

"I haven't a clue, but if she'll let me look in her mouth, I can soon tell ya.'" The man eased up to her and ran his hand expertly down her nose. He tucked two fingers inside her lip and opened her mouth. "Five—coming six. And no, lady, you do not want to own this horse."

"What will he get for her in Billings?"

"Oh, I reckon about thirty-five cents a pound. She weighs—let me see . . ." He stepped back and eyed the mare. "Probably a hair over eleven hundred, so I suppose after he pays commission and gives me something to haul her, he'll be lucky to put two hundred and fifty bucks in his jeans." The man opened the gate and popped his whip at the mare. She whirled and loped toward the alley and waiting trailer.

"If I offered three-hundred right here, would he take it?"

The man turned around and looked at me with a hint of disdain—and pity. "What are you going to do with her? Just because she's built like a derby winner doesn't mean she's any good."

"I understand that. I have no problem with sending renegade horses to a meat buyer, but I'd like to spend a little time with her."

The mare stood halfway down the alley. She tossed her head, wanting to get back to the sweet-smelling hay at my feet.

"Listen, young lady, I'll ask Ike if you want because he'll lose less if he takes your three hundred, but for whatever it's worth, don't do this. You're wasting your time, and you'll probably get hurt."

I didn't argue. He was right, and yet . . . I watched the mare as she inched toward the hay. The man waved his whip at her, and she jumped away, again fluid-smooth like Chiquita had been. But there the resemblance ended. Chiquita had not only been athletic, she had a kind, willing disposition, and incredible heart. Who knew what this mare had, other than attitude?

As the man punched numbers into his cell phone, I started to get excited. He propped a booted foot on the bottom rail and leaned against the fence, waiting for an answer. "Ike? Troy here. Would you take three-hundred for that ding-bat mare you left here?"

Silence while whoever was on the other end gave his answer.

"Some girl wants her."

A longer silence. Probably Ike would say no. That would be best, and it would take the decision out of my hands. I needed to be saving money like crazy to buy a ready-made barrel horse, not messing around with some untrainable outlaw. The man was right. Trying to make something out of this mare was a good way to get hurt.

Troy snapped his phone shut. "Ike said she's been through five trainers and bucked them all off. That's how *he* got her." He shrugged. "The mare's had more than enough chances. But, if you'll give three hundred, she's yours."

"Can I meet you in front of the bank? I'll get some cash and pay you there. I'd bring it back here, but I have to be at work in fifteen minutes."

"Where do you work?"

"At the Spur."

"I'll stop by this afternoon and get the cash and an address, so Ike can send you a bill of sale."

I didn't have time to even give a second look at my new purchase, which was just as well. A lead weight rolled around in the pit of my stomach. Why had I done such a foolish thing? Where would I board this crazy horse? Frederick's grandmother had a postage-stamp-sized acreage behind her house, but that was a non-starter. We weren't on speaking terms except when the rent was due. I had made every attempt to avoid her since her insulting comments about "my intentions" with her precious grandson. Mrs. Riddler's fondest desire would be for me to move elsewhere. The feeling was mutual, but now I had made my departure doubly difficult. How would I find an affordable home for me and my three-hundred dollar bucking horse—one that hadn't even done a good job of that?

# Chapter 19

When my Tuesday night shift ended, I pushed the back door at the Spur open to check the parking lot. It had been days since I'd seen the familiar gray car, and again tonight there didn't appear to be anything in the lot to cause alarm. Nevertheless, I'd no intention of being careless. After I'd double-checked the surrounding area, I hurried to my pickup. Only when I was inside with the doors locked and engine running did I breathe a sigh of relief.

At home, I parked in my usual spot. Frederick's car had been missing when I went to work. He hadn't returned. I wished he'd told me he was going to be gone, but of course he hadn't, which meant tomorrow I would have to face Mrs. Riddler alone. It would have been nice to have him smooth the water for me when I asked his grandmother whether I could keep a horse on her property. After all, we *were* friends.

No light peeked under the curtain of her living room window, but I still tiptoed past the living room window and front door. The last thing I wanted tonight was any confrontation. I trudged down the steps, wondering what I would do with my new horse after Mrs. Riddler declined my shaky proposal. The mare had to be moved somewhere. I had no money to keep her at the fairgrounds where I'd have to buy hay for her all summer. It would be expensive enough to do that during the long Montana winter.

Next morning, I awoke in a cold sweat after dreaming about facing Mrs. Riddler. I swung my feet over the edge of the bed and padded to the bathroom. Now I was awake, the prospect didn't seem quite as daunting. She would say no, and then I could get to work finding another place to keep the mare—and me.

After a piece of toast and some orange juice, I prepared myself for war. At the top of the steps, I investigated the little pasture. Too bad I had to move. It would have been so perfect to have the mare right here. I knocked on Mrs. Riddler's door while I tried to quiet the butterflies flitting around my stomach.

"Who is it?"

"It's just me. I wondered if I could talk to you for a minute." I opened the door and stepped inside.

"Well, I'm busy. What do you want now?" The old lady hobbled toward me.

Oh, no. This had been a bad idea. Mrs. Riddler had never spoken with any civility. However, her disdain was usually not as open and overt. Whether it was my heritage, youth, or something completely hidden that caused her enmity, I realized this wouldn't work. I should have found a different place.

"Well, spit it out. What do you want?"

My mouth flew wide, and I stuttered, "Nothing, Mrs. Riddler." She turned to toddle back to her overstuffed, purple chair. I swallowed, my throat suddenly dry. "I bought a horse, and I was wondering . . . well, if you knew of anyplace—"

"A horse?" She turned, her beady eyes shooting virulent jets of fire. "What are you going to do with a horse? I suppose you came to ask me whether you could use my back pasture, didn't you?"

Despite my resolve to be in charge of the conversation, I felt the blood rush to my cheeks. "I'm sorry, no, Mrs.—"

"What do you mean, no? Where else are you going to keep her? I love horses. Haven't had any around since Earl passed away, and that was twenty years ago."

"That . . . Mrs. Riddler, that is so kind. I will pay—"

"Go on with you. I won't charge you any extra for something I never could rent anyway.

You'll have to find a water tub. There may be an old one out there buried in the grass, but it's probably rusted through and no good."

"I don't know how to thank you. That is so generous."

"Oh, I'll think up something extra you can do. Now, go get your horse." She dismissed me with a wave of her hand, and I made a hasty exit before she changed her mind.

Ten minutes later, with the trailer hooked up, I rolled out of the yard. At the fairgrounds, my confidence deserted me. If this horse had been to five trainers she might load easily, but what if she didn't?

The mare's ears pointed toward me as I walked into the pen, but when she saw the halter in my hand, she trotted away. I talked softly to her but let her escape. After a few minutes, she lost interest in running past me and stood in the corner. Nevertheless, when I walked up to her, her neck remained stiff, her nose elevated, not a sign of a well-trained and willing partner.

I tied her to one of the stout corral posts, then backed my trailer into the alley. If she pulled away from me, I didn't want to be trying to catch her in downtown Miles City. Then, I walked her up to the trailer. She led well, her splashy white face and big intelligent eyes right at my shoulder. I looped the lead rope over her neck and she stepped inside without hesitation. Cautiously, I reached for the butt chain while I soothed her and petted her muscled rump. Suddenly, she threw herself over backward, banging her head in the process. I jumped out of the way, as she came boiling out of the trailer. Blood trickled from a cut on the top of her head. I grabbed for the lead rope, but she jerked away and ran to the far end of the alley, tried to jump the fence, and landed flat on her back. She was crazy.

Nobody needed to tell me what would happen next. She had a barrel-full of bad attitude, and now she was hurt and scared. I caught her and led her up and down the alley, but when I tried to load her, she refused to budge. Twice more I tried with no more success. She wasn't going anywhere near that trailer, and even if I did manage to load her, what would I do when I got her to Mrs. Riddler's? I couldn't train in a pen with broken down barbed-wire fences and grass two feet high, so I either had to haul her back to the fairgrounds, or some other place with a round pen and the proper facilities.

Desperate for a solution, I glanced at my watch. In a half hour, I had to be at work. I led her toward the trailer. At this rate, I would need every minute and I didn't know what to do. She stood splay-footed, her eyes wide with distrust and a long-held fear. I felt as if I were a child playing piñata, blindfolded and helpless while I desperately flailed to reach the sweet spot inside this crazy mare. I stepped back, the lead rope loose in my hand and talked softly to her while I tried to keep the mounting frustration from my voice. "Hey, mare. What was your name before? You've been through five trainers? Probably every one of them had a name for you, most of them not repeatable. So, your new name is . . . hmm—Piñata. Whatever possessed me to buy you? You've had such a long history of failure, but now Piñata, we're stuck with each other."

When I gave up and turned her back in the pen, Piñata had an unbroken track record. She was not in the trailer. Our first day together had been a dismal flop.

# Chapter 20

After another hard shift at the Spur, I was exhausted. But before I crawled wearily into bed, I knelt and said a quick prayer before the tiny shrine in the corner, the spot where Frederick had accused me of worshipping idols. Where had he gone? I hadn't seen him for days. Would he come back? The thought that he might not, panicked me more than I wanted to admit, which made me wonder. Did he really believe what he'd said about my little altar, or had he only wanted another argument?

The next morning, I again drove to the fairgrounds. Either the mare had to load in the trailer today, or I would have to buy some hay.

When I got within sight of the pen, I could see Piñata dozing in the shade, her bright sorrel coat glistening in the morning sun. I backed the trailer into the alley and again tried to load her. She had a long memory. Today, she fought like a cornered tiger and refused to get anywhere near where she had hurt herself. Finally, she lunged away, tearing the nylon lead-shank out of my clenched hands. I grimaced with the pain from my rope-burned fingers.

"That's quite the mare."

I turned to see who had witnessed my failure. The voice came from a weather-beaten old man outside the alley. He carried a knobby, wooden walking stick that looked to be nearly as old as his sweat-stained silver-belly hat. Well-worn jeans puffed away from stick-thin legs, and a black neckerchief at his throat topped a blue, long-sleeved shirt, all of which framed a deep-lined, leathery face. He paid no attention to me, his eyes fixed like little homing beacons on the mare. I ignored him, caught the mare and led her back—or tried to. Each step was now a fight, one I had already lost.

"Young lady, I surely don't mean to intrude on your business, but I reckon I could help you—that is, if you want?" The old man's voice was low, the syllables drawn out enough I had to strain to understand him. He leaned on his stick, while his watery blue eyes followed the mare's every move.

What did I have to lose? There was no chance of her loading in the trailer before I had to go to work. "Yes, I could use some help," I replied testily.

"Where did you want to take her?"

I told him I had to take her home, and then haul her back to the arena to start her training.

He nodded, his eyes occasionally meeting mine while we talked. "So, you'd like for her to get into the trailer, preferably when you loop the lead rope over her neck and tell her that's what you want?"

"Of course." I glared at the old man, wondering if he was making fun of me.

"That sounds like a simple procedure, but sometimes we get in a hurry and start with the end result, instead of taking baby steps, so the horse learns not to be afraid." He crawled painfully into the alley and stood beside me. "You take this mare now." He pointed at her with his stick. "She's had at least one bad experience in a trailer, and likely a few more with humans in other circumstances. She's afraid of being trapped, and you're pressed for time and need to get to work or wherever you're going, but the mare doesn't understand that. All she knows is pain and anxiety, although I reckon with her there's some attitude that needs adjusting as well, but that's for another day. First, we need to deal with her fear."

I stared at the old man, amazed at his simple wisdom. I'd been around horses all my life, and the truth of what he'd said resonated.

"Would you spend the rest of the day here if that's what it took to make her load easy for the rest of her life?"

"No, I guess not. I have to be at work in an hour."

"I thought as much. Would you be willing to leave her with me? By tomorrow, we'll have a horse that loads when you ask her to get in the trailer."

I shrugged. "Sure." I could hardly turn down a genuine offer of help. I held out my hand. "My name is Dina Rodriguez."

"Just call me Merle."

His big-knuckled fist had uncommon strength, more than I would have thought for an old guy that packed a walking stick. "I don't have much money, but I'd like to pay you for helping me."

"No, I don't want your money. The horses pay me."

"The horses?"

He ignored my question, but his gnarled old hand patted my arm. "Let's start, and then you can go and do whatever you need to do, while the mare and I get acquainted."

Merle walked up to Piñata and slipped the halter off her head. Crusted blood from yesterday's wreck-stained the nylon straps. "If you would step outside the alley, she'll focus on me better. That's what I need. She needs to know it's just her and me."

I climbed over the fence, and he walked toward the mare. She eyed his approach, and when he got close she dashed past him, away from the trailer. He hobbled toward her and bounced the long lead rope off her hip. She tried to scoot further away, but she had nowhere to go other than back toward the trailer. Merle gave her room to make whatever move she wanted. The mare faced him, her eyes wide, nostrils distended, but she had no choice. She dashed past him, toward the trailer. Each time the mare moved in the right direction, Merle would back away from her. Her flanks heaved. Sweat dripped off her belly. Though she obviously had no intention of putting one foot in that trailer, she eventually faced it. At that point, Merle allowed her to rest. Merle asked nothing more from her. That would come later. I understood. Hopefully by tomorrow, she—and I would understand as well.

When I stepped into the mare's pen the next morning, she seemed less skittish, but that might have been because she was tired and sore. The stiff, dried hairs covering her chest were mute testimony to a strenuous day after I'd gone to work.

"Mornin' to you." I whirled. Merle was standing outside the fence in the same spot I'd first seen him yesterday.

"Good morning, Merle. How did it go with the mare?"

He never answered, only stood and squinted at Piñata. Then, like my question had just registered, he looked at me. "Oh, she did fine. Put a halter on her."

I slipped through the narrow gap between the fence and the back of the trailer and pulled her halter out of the trailer tack compartment. Pinãta stood quietly while I buckled the nylon strap behind her ears.

"Now lead her around a bit, then walk her up to the trailer."

The mare quietly followed me, her head even with my shoulder, which was no surprise. The only lesson she'd apparently learned before I bought her was to lead. I stopped her at the trailer and glanced uncertainly at Merle.

"Now, loop the lead rope over her neck and tell her to get in."

Piñata walked into the trailer like a twenty-year veteran. "Wow! I'm impressed. What did you do with her?"

"We'll discuss that later." he replied grumpily. "Now, tell her to get out."

The mare backed out of the trailer and stood quietly beside me. I couldn't resist petting and praising her.

"Walk her away and then bring her back and load her again. This time, snap the butt chain behind her and . . . well, take her wherever you want to go." The left side of his mouth twitched upward, and his blue eyes twinkled.

I closed the trailer door and turned back to Merle. "I can't thank you enough. What you have done is such a huge help and encouragement, and I would like to pay you." At least now, if I had to get rid of her, I could haul her to a sale.

Merle had started to hobble toward the back fence. He turned and grasped one of the rails with his arthritic, bony fingers before he answered. "No, we already talked about that. You can't pay me. Maybe sometime I'll need a cup of coffee."

"Please let me know. I work at the Spur. May I call you if I have more problems with her?"

"You will have more problems. This mare carries a lot of baggage, and you'll have to re-program just about everything she thinks about humans if you intend to make anything of her."

We both stared at the trailer. "Do you think she's worth it?"

He turned and spit in the dusty alley before he answered. "Yeah."

That single word was enough for me. I wanted to somehow thank him, but no words seemed appropriate. For a moment, our eyes met, and I knew he saw what was in my heart.

I jumped in the pickup and a few minutes later led the mare into the pasture at Mrs. Riddler's. The old woman shuffled out on the deck to look at her.

"A nice-looking mare. Is she any good?"

"She's not much—at least not yet."

"Hmm. It's nice to have somebody in the house that likes horses."

I gaped at her. Wasn't this the woman who had insinuated my morals were questionable, that is if I had any? Didn't this same lady accuse me of having designs on her grandson?

Was this some kind of apology? Whatever it was, I was glad if even for one day Mrs. Riddler had sheathed her sword.

# Chapter 21

The rest of the day, I waited tables and worried about how to start Piñata's training program. What had the man said? Five trainers had failed with her. Why did I think this time would be different? She was big, fast, and dangerous. I chewed my lower lip until it was raw, worrying, wishing I could have found a way to buy the gorgeous, already trained palomino mare. But forty thousand dollars was an impossible amount to raise without Papa's help, and that I would not do. I needed to make a complete break, live my own life free from my father's criminal activities.

The next morning when I went to load her, Piñata hesitated as if she had to think about her lesson. Then she walked into the trailer the same as she'd done the day before. We set off for the fairgrounds. When we arrived, I unloaded her and tied her to the arena fence. The first ride could be in one of the smaller pens or out in the big arena. It seemed prudent to choose the confines of a smaller area.

I'd no sooner unloaded the mare than Merle hobbled over from somewhere behind the chutes. He must have been waiting for me.

"Good morning, Merle. I'm so grateful for your help."

"Mornin'. So, you're going to start her new life today?"

"New life?" I chuckled. "What do you mean?"

"Oh, I figure horses are given a bit of the same privilege humans are blessed with. Every morning when we wake up, the Creator offers us a chance at a fresh start. It's the only thing He's given us to control. We can't do anything about the mistakes we made yesterday, and we sure don't have any hope of controlling tomorrow. The only place He gives us any loose rein is today. It's the same for that mare. We can't undo the bad experiences in her past. And we don't know what's going to happen tomorrow. But we can give her a brand-new way to look at life—for today."

Piñata's ears switched direction as Merle talked. I glanced over the fence to the grandstand, once again spotless, free of Styrofoam and assorted paper debris. Merle was only half right. Both of us had to start over. This mare wasn't the gentle, talented Chiquita. But maybe . . .

"You were going to try to ride her?"

"Yes, I thought I'd ride her and see if . . . well, if she's any good, I suppose." It was a lame answer. Could I even put a saddle on her? If she allowed that, I would then have to decide whether I had the nerve to get on her. Obviously, she bucked very well or the man in Kansas would never have hauled her eight hundred miles to the most famous bucking horse sale in the world.

"There's a decent-sized corral right behind the bucking chutes. I found some old rails kicking around and filled in the corners, so you'd have a round pen. Might be best if you started her there."

When I saw the square pen where Merle had rounded the corners, I turned to him. "You have already helped me so much, and I really appreciate it." I exhaled nervously. "Probably I shouldn't have bought this horse. She may be more than I can handle."

Merle nodded but didn't look at me. "Possibly." He eyed the mare, the way she moved, what she did with her head, her tail, her eyes, and ears. "Horses communicate. You just have to learn their language." He seemed to be speaking to himself, or more likely to Piñata, because he paid little attention to me. "You're afraid of her, and she doesn't trust you. She's afraid of what you'll do or try to make *her* do. If you're going to succeed, you will have to commit to working with her every day. First thing you'll need to do is learn mutual respect."

"I think she would have to trust me first, before I can gain her respect," I said timidly.

"You could think that if you want, but you'd be wrong. Respect is the most important—for both your safety, and for hers. You need to figure out what she can process and understand how much she can learn in a day, but most of all—respect her fear. That means we never push her past what she can tolerate. Do you understand what I'm saying?"

"Not really."

"What's your greatest fear?"

"Snakes. I hate them."

"But what about bull snakes? They're harmless. They won't bite you."

I shook my head. "They're still snakes."

"So, if I had a whole nest of bull snakes in a cave and I pushed you down there so they crawled all over you, that wouldn't cure your fear?"

"No! I'd be even more terrorized." I shivered, just thinking about it.

"And when I started pushing and shoving at you, trying to get you down that hole, what would you do?"

"I would scratch and punch and kick with everything I had in me."

"Exactly. And that's what that mare's been doing for as long as she can remember. So we will never put her in a situation where she can't handle her fear. And, I might add," he winked, "we will never put you in a place where you aren't comfortable. You are not going to get on that mare until it is as natural as swinging your leg over the most broke horse you ever rode. Agreed?"

I swallowed and nodded. "I'm all for that. This morning when I thought about trying to ride her, it was sort of like—well, like looking into a nest of bull snakes."

"Okay, let's get started. First, I want you to ask the mare to lope around the pen. If she refuses or shows a wrong attitude, you speed her up by throwing the end of this rope at her. Then make her turn and lope the other direction. After a while, we'll ask her to turn into us, rather than away. That's important. One of the things we'll want this mare to do the rest of her life is to respectfully walk up to us when we enter the pasture or corral. That lesson starts today."

For nearly an hour, I moved the mare around that corral. Sometimes, I ran faster and farther than she did, but eventually she did turn toward me. Though Merle praised my efforts, I knew she'd only figured out what was expected of her because she'd eliminated all other options. I'd spent most of my life with horses, but I found out that day I had a lot more to learn. What I did understand was that this mare had unusual intelligence.

At one point, Merle's wheezy chuckle broke through my exhaustion. "That's a good place to stop." The mare had just followed my command to walk up to me, her head level with my shoulder rather than elevated toward the sky. She'd come a long way. Both of us had lost a lot of our fear.

I loaded Piñata and promised to meet Merle at the same time the following morning. At Mrs. Riddler's house, I backed the trailer into the driveway, unloaded the mare and turned her loose in the pasture. She ambled over to the rusty bathtub water trough I'd pulled out of the weeds. I shook my head in frustration after she'd nearly drunk the water tub dry. Drinking and eating were the only normal behaviors I'd come to expect from this horse.

So many times, I'd implored God to help me find a horse to replace Chiquita. He'd not sent me forty thousand dollars to buy the palomino mare. All He'd given me was this messed up crazy mare and an arthritic old cowboy. I scowled. Neither the cowboy, nor the horse seemed like much of a gift.

Wearily, I clumped down the stairs to my suite. My cell phone sat on the kitchen counter. The flashing light showed I had voicemail. Probably Frederick? I pulled up the number. The call had come from my parents' phone in Sonora. A foreboding of disaster rolled across the pit of my stomach. This could not be good.

# Chapter 22

I called Mama on my way to work. As I'd suspected, the news was bad. My grandma had passed away, and she wanted me to come for the funeral.

"Families should be together at times like this. Get the ticket, Dina, and I will pay for it. Please, come home."

I wiped at the tears on my face. Grandma had so often been a stabilizing influence in my life. "Mama, I would like to come, but I'm not sure I can get time off work."

"This is family. It is important. Your boss will understand."

"No, Mama. He's American. He probably won't understand."

"You need to come." Mama's voice was quiet, in control, not at all like I had expected.

"Okay, I'll talk to my boss and call you in the morning."

When I told Trent the situation, even though he had a steak flipper in his hand he reached over and gave me a one-armed hug.

"Sorry to hear that. Take whatever time you need, but come back as soon as you can." He grinned. "I'm starting to depend on you. You've done an excellent job, and the customers like you."

I blushed at the praise. I'd tried my hardest to give good value for what Trent paid me.

Next morning, I made flight reservations, then texted Mama with the details before I loaded Piñata and headed for the fairgrounds. Shortly after I arrived, Merle crawled through the fence. It was uncanny the way he seemed to appear from nowhere, like he'd dropped out of the sky.

"Mornin', Dina."

"Good morning. I have to leave for a few days," I blurted.

"Well, that's not good. It's better for the horse if you can work with them every day, especially for the first ten days or so."

"I know. I hate to stop her training, but I have to go home to a funeral. My grandma died."

"Folks get born, married, and buried every day of the year. If you let that get in the way of training this mare, you'll never get anywhere."

"I feel bad Merle, but I need to do this—for my family."

"Well, then go do it. If I have nothing else to do when you think you might want to start again, I'll help you. Then again, I might not." The old man stomped out of the pen. He crossed the coulee and disappeared while I stood in the middle of the makeshift round pen. I needed him to help me, but I also needed to be with my family. How could someone who understood horses so well be completely unreasonable when dealing with human issues?

There was little to do but carry on from where I'd left off the day before. Merle's rejection hurt, and Piñata picked up the anger in my voice. Her reaction was precisely the fear Merle had talked about. After a few more minutes, I loaded her in the trailer and drove home. The mare and I had made no progress.

The rest of the evening, I packed the few things I'd need for my trip home. Apprehension over a meeting with my parents, competed with the excitement I felt when I thought of the reunion with Raoul, and all the people who worked for my family. They were trusted friends more than servants or employees.

Though I'd hoped he'd send one of the men, Papa met me at the airport in Tucson.

"Welcome home. We've missed you." He reached over to hug me.

I stiffened, wanting only to pull away and scream accusations. No excuse or apology would ever heal the bitter anger I held for the terrifying ordeal I'd endured. I'd come home for my grandmother's funeral out of love for her and respect for Mama. When that was over, I would leave.

The desert I loved so well fell behind us as we drove toward Douglas and the Mexican border. Few words had passed since the airport. Once, I glanced furtively at his weak face. Silhouetted against the tall saguaro and spreading yucca, it didn't look weak. Really, it looked sad.

"Can we talk, he asked?"

"Talk? Why would we, Papa? Is there anything you can tell me that will make up for the terror I went through? What can you say that would atone for what you have done to us? No Papa, thank you for the money you gave me when I left. I *am* grateful, but please—stay out of my life. I want nothing to do with what you stand for."

Out of the corner of my eye I glimpsed a dark shadow spread over his face, but I refused to let it bother me. Several times during the silent trip, I thought he wanted to say something, but each time he seemed to think better if it. The border crossing into Mexico was uneventful. As darkness tucked a soft blanket over the land, we pulled through the ornate wooden gates of my parents' Sonora ranch. Mama and I hugged and cried together over my grandma. We retired to the *sala* to be alone and talk. Several times she mentioned Alejandro's noticeable absence. I'd thought he might actually make an effort to come to the funeral. Obviously, he didn't think Grandma was important enough to warrant a trip home.

Mama nearly swooned when she learned that a daughter of hers worked in a *cantina*. Of course, it wasn't. The Spur was a steakhouse that served drinks, but to Mama it might as well have had a lewd, red sign outside advertising sexual favors.

Grandma's vigil was held at our house with many prayers for her—in case she was in Purgatory for a short while. I couldn't imagine my *abuela* there, but perhaps she had committed a sin of which none of us were aware. The requiem mass at our white adobe church in Agua Prieta started late because of the large crowd of people. Even more elaborate than most, the service seemed to go on forever. Then the priest led the procession to the cemetery where he blessed the ground before he scattered incense over the earth and my grandma's casket. I wondered during the burial what Frederick would think of this, but then who cared what he thought? This was our custom, a time-tested rite of the church. It was the kind of funeral my grandma and Mama would want, and I didn't really care what Papa wanted. He would spend a thousand years in Purgatory for his sins.

Eduardo's family, as our neighbors, naturally attended the funeral. In a rare moment without well-wishers in front of me, he suddenly appeared. He'd waited for an opportunity to catch me alone. His hug wasn't entirely unwelcome, though his hands lingered on my shoulders.

"Dina, I am so sorry about your grandmother, but it is wonderful to see you. How long are you going to stay?"

"I am flying back to Montana day after tomorrow."

"I'm sorry to hear you're leaving so soon. I've missed you."

"You are a good friend, Eduardo." I patted his arm, placing particular emphasis on "*friend.*"

"Dina, forgive me if this isn't the place to talk, but there may have been a small misunderstanding that day at your house. Is it possible for us to start over? I would like to have the chance to make you happy. I have always—"

"Eduardo—no! I am not the girl for you. I would like us to always remain friends, but I am sorry. We are not meant for each other."

"Dina, I would wait . . ." His brown eyes pleaded for me to change my mind.

"No.There is no future for us." Though I'd not wanted to cause more pain, the hurt instantly flooded across his tortured face, along with a new arrogant anger I'd not seen before.

"Goodbye, Eduardo."

Eduardo's jaw hardened, and he strode out of the room. After he disappeared, a sense of foreboding evil raised goose bumps on my arms. Something had happened while I'd been away. This was not the same boy with whom I'd gone to school.

The morning after the funeral, I arose early and tiptoed down the stairs. Papa's office was kitty-corner to the bottom landing. The door was always locked, and from our earliest childhood, Alejandro and I were never allowed inside, so my curiosity was piqued when I walked by and noticed the door ajar. My jaw clenched with a rebellious anger, a delayed reaction for all the years I had lived with my father's duplicity. Now things were different because I didn't care what he thought.

My stomach churned with righteous contempt as I pushed the door open. Papers lay strewn over the top of his desk as if he'd hurriedly searched for a document before being called away. The papers were the usual; bills of sale for cattle or horses, receipts for purchased supplies and a new lease agreement with a neighbor. I stepped around the corner of the desk and shoved the ornate leather office chair aside. More ordinary ranch book-work lay in neat piles. Nothing interested me until I noticed the upside-down sheet of paper stuffed under his laptop, as if he'd made a hurried effort to shelter the contents. I slipped it out. At the top of the page, instructions were underlined in bold italics. I scanned the single page. By the time I'd finished, I knew my father was worse than I'd imagined. The document carried detailed transport instructions on the coming shipment of a product they only identified as "C-157." Whatever "C" was, it must be significant. The instructions were to be memorized and immediately destroyed. Probably that was why I ran the sheet through his copy machine. I stuffed the copy inside my jean jacket, returned the original to his desk and hurried out the door. Should I close it or leave it ajar as he must have done when he hurried out? I decided to leave it. He would have no reason to suspect I had violated his sinister privacy, especially at this early hour.

No sooner had I turned away from the door than I heard footsteps in the hallway. I tiptoed toward the kitchen to escape through the outside servant's entrance.

"Good morning, Dina." I froze at the cheery greeting. Though it was barely past sunrise, Lupita, our cook was also out of bed. Breath whooshed out of my lungs. Thankfully, she hadn't seen me in Papa's office.

"Good morning, Lupita. I was just going out to the barn." I opened the door to the outside veranda. Heaps of onions, squash, tomatoes, and peppers, a cornucopia of produce blocked the exit.

"Lupita, what is all this?" I gasped.

"Oh," she waved a hand at the pile of vegetables, eggs, and other assorted foodstuffs. "That sometimes happens. People leave food as a thank you to your father."

*"Papa?"* My voice was a squeaky scratch.

"Yes, he is always so kind. When someone is sick or wants to start a business, it is always your father they ask for help. If one of the old ones from the village needs a dentist, or perhaps to contact a relative in the United States, he always arranges it."

I shook my head. "This can't be, and besides—"

"But of course. Often this is the only way they can repay. We can't use all the food they bring, so your father gives much of it away to needy families. One never has to look far to find those in our country."

I stumbled off the porch, a misty film clouding my eyes. *My* father? Ricardo the coyote, who spirited terrorists across the border to kill and maim those who were now *my* people? I shook my head, trying to process what she'd said, completely at odds with years of evidence, corroborated by the very papers I'd hidden inside my jacket. And yet my mind drifted back to several incidents that had left me puzzled, times when people had greeted Papa on the streets of Agua Prieta, and I glimpsed the deep love and respect in their eyes. How did that fit?

I scuffed through the sandy dirt to the quiet, high-walled barn, wanting desperately to dismiss a father who made no sense. My beautiful Chiquita mare was in her stall, her eyes still full and intelligent, but the disease had taken a toll. She'd lost weight, and her coat didn't shine the way it used to. I fought back tears, knowing this would be our last visit. When I reached her, she rubbed her head against my shoulder. She hadn't forgotten me. I slipped a halter over her ears and led her into the alley.

"The *Señorita* has come home to stay?"

I turned at the familiar voice. "Raul. I am so glad to see you, but no, tomorrow I have to leave."

"Ah, such a short visit?"

"I must be back at work day after tomorrow. I have to leave right after Grandma's funeral."

"Yes, it is a sad time." He shrugged. "We must all go when it is our time."

"Raul, I thought I might ride Chiquita. How is she?"

"She is failing, but I think a short ride would be fine. She will tire easily, so be gentle with her."

"We will only walk. Perhaps we'll take the trail down to the river. I wanted to ride her one more time before . . ." I couldn't finish the sentence, and Raul nodded. He understood.

When I came home again Chiquita would either be gone, or so emaciated from the disease that riding would be out of the question, so I took extra time, just talking to her and enjoying her presence. We picked our way down the well-worn rocky trail to the dry riverbed. The odd stagnant pool of water, interspersed with long stretches of sandy gravel made it easy going for her. After a few hundred yards, we stopped to rest. I held her reins while I sat in the shade of a juniper and stroked her neck and head. It was our goodbye, and there in the river bottom, shielded from any other humans, I cried for my beautiful Chiquita and what might have been. She wasn't supposed to be here in Mexico. She should have been the horse in the little pasture behind Mrs. Riddler's house, not that crazy Piñata. Chiquita was the one with perfect breeding, hundreds of hours of training, and most of all, a huge heart that would have taken her to the top. All Piñata had was an athletic body, and a whole wagon load of fear.

# Chapter 23

Frederick strode out of the Phoenix airport, not at all sure Adrian would have approved this trip. Everything about Dina sent up screaming yellow flags. Beyond the obvious security issues of becoming involved with her, how could they ever reconcile their different cultures, never mind bridge the cataclysmic divide separating their faiths?

After leaving the rental car center, Frederick drove south on I-10 toward Tucson. The miles and towns passed behind him, almost too quickly. Three hours later, he idled through the serpentine streets of the venerable mining town of Bisbee. Sidewalk signs announced coffee shops, cafés, and clothing stores, most decorated with a prospecting or mining motif to attract the burgeoning tourist trade. Midway through the main block of town, a barn-board-fronted café with a half-dozen tables on a front patio drew his attention. He parked down the block, then walked past the café on the opposite side of the narrow street. A couple ate at one of the red-and-white checkered tables. At another, a lone man idly toyed with a cup of coffee. Frederick studied him out of the corner of his eye. A slight frame, thinning hair, the eyes unreadable behind dark glasses. Perhaps Mexican but could be any of a dozen other nationalities. After crossing the street, he walked back, satisfied that the man at the corner table was the one he'd come to meet. At the café entrance, he took a deep breath, then stepped over to the stranger's table.

The man glanced up. "Mr. Roseman, I presume?" He removed the sunglasses and set them beside his espresso cup.

Frederick nodded politely. "And you are Señor Rodriguez?"

The man chuckled. "Oh, I don't know about that. Ricardo will do. I'm not really a Mr. anything. Would you like something to drink?"

"A cup of tea would be fine."

No waiter was immediately available, so Ricardo walked inside to procure the asked for tea. Frederick watched every move, even skidding his chair back a few inches to see through the open door and observe what went into the cup. The man took short, feminine steps, arms held close to his sides, his head in a perpetual questioning attitude. There was nothing masculine about him and Frederick would have disliked him instantly—except, he was Dina's father. That changed everything.

Ricardo returned with the tea, slid the cup onto the table with his long slim fingers and slipped into his chair. His eyes exhibited a sardonic, vacant humor. Clearly, he thought no deeper than the moment required—unless it was perhaps how to milk another dollar out of al-Qaida.

Frederick pulled the tea bag out and placed it on the edge of the saucer. "Mr. Rodriguez, thank you for meeting me. I understand this is not an opportune time for you to be away from your family. May I offer my condolences?"

"Condolences? They're not needed. She was the classic mother-in-law. My life will be easier with that cackling old crow in the grave. She wasted no love on me." The man chortled foolishly, and Frederick's dislike escalated. Dina's grandmother had apparently been more perceptive of men than her daughter. He sipped at his tea while he tamped down his disgust. He needed to be civil. As unlikely as it seemed, this *was* Dina's father.

"Mr. Rodriguez, I've been privileged to become acquainted with your daughter—sort of by default. She rents an apartment from my grandmother."

Ricardo appeared to be half listening, his attention taken with clipping his perfectly manicured fingernails.

"She was kidnapped—because of your activities. You endangered her life, and Mr. Rodriguez, she may not mean much to you, but she does to me. Your associates turned her loose the first time, I presume because you provided whatever they wanted. At least, I hope you did. They're still hanging around, possibly ready to pick her up again if—"

"Mr. Roseman." Ricardo leaned forward. "Frederick, wasn't it?"

Frederick nodded.

"Why do you imagine these men have anything to do with me? You seem to have acquired a lot of information for someone who works as an accountant. That is your line of work, isn't it?"

"No."

"My mistake. What was your employment?" The man fired the question, then sat back in his chair. For a moment, the vacant gray eyes had . . . had what? Frederick was sure the man's eyes had hardened, a brief character anomaly only a seasoned intelligence officer would notice.

Frederick leaned forward. His eyes searched Ricardo's face. "I work for a government services contractor."

"Sure, and you supply toilet paper and pencils to the army, I suppose?"

Frederick could think of no suitable reply to the lightly-veiled insult. Ricardo's eyes remained the same vacuous gray, with a hint of derisive hilarity. Often, they slid away from Frederick's toward the now shadowed street.

"What government services contractor do you represent? Not that I'd recognize the name. My ranching affairs are far removed from your line of work."

"Stirling Associates." Frederick watched the man carefully, but the mouth and eyes betrayed nothing.

"And you are dating my daughter?"

"No, not really, but I would like to—with your permission."

Ricardo chuckled, and again leaned forward. "I'm flattered you would ask. Permission to court a man's daughter is one of the old-world courtesies we have foolishly abandoned. Her mother had long ago picked an eligible young man from our country for her to marry. He was from a good family, and they knew each other from childhood. They would have been married in the church, however, I'm so glad Dina declined to marry him, though at the time I felt different. And what about you? You are Catholic?"

"No, Protestant."

The man slowly spun his his now empty cup on the table while he gazed at the sporadic passing of tourists and shoppers. "That will be something you and Dina will want to discuss thoroughly, before you let your emotions become further entangled. A divided home, if you get that far, would cause difficulty and much unhappiness."

Frederick's eyes narrowed. "I understand, sir." The wisdom Ricardo had just offered was again out of character. His reply suggested he might be more aware of Frederick's involvement with his daughter than he knew. He could recite word for word Adrian's long-ago command. "Never, under any circumstances will you become romantically involved with a woman during an operation."

Frederick tried to justify this trip to meet with Dina's father. This was company business—wasn't it? Ricardo's involvement with al-Quaida . . . but that wasn't really why he was here. Every excuse he offered sounded lame. Nevertheless, whatever Ricardo was involved in could prove to be more sinister than anything they'd ever dealt with. That salved his conscience for a moment, but the tragic stories marched one after another through his brain. Agent after agent who had been compromised or killed during an operation, the victim of a beautiful woman.

Ricardo picked up his dark glasses and slipped them on, his next sentence pitched low and quiet. "If my daughter has chosen to date you, then you are an exceptional young man. However, Dina has always had a mind of her own. That likely won't change. So yes, permission is given, if you're of sturdy enough character to interest her."

"Thank you, sir. I am truly honored."

"And thank you for being courteous enough to ask my permission." Ricardo pushed his chair away from the table.

"As to the other? Many things in life are not as they seem. What happened with Dina was unfortunate." He chuckled derisively and held out the slim, manicured fingers. "And now I must return to my grieving family."

Frederick rose to his feet, angered by the man's cavalier attitude. "I will do whatever is necessary to protect Dina. Obviously, you won't."

A fleeting shadow crossed Ricardo's face, but his words were measured, and carefully bland. "Her protection has been assured. Good day to you, Mr. Roseman."

With steely control, Frederick took the limp hand the man offered, then returned to his chair and watched Ricardo disappear around the corner. Moments later, the waiter scurried over. "Are you ready for the check, sir?"

Frederick examined the handwritten bill with an instant grimace, followed by a slow grin. Ricardo the coyote had scammed everybody in his life, including his family. True to form, Dina's father had stuck him for dinner. Frederick handed the waiter a credit card and frowned.

"Is there something wrong, sir?"

"No . . . no, everything is fine. My friend ordered filet mignon?"

"Most certainly, sir. He finished it moments before you arrived. Have you changed your mind? Would you care to eat as well?"

"No, thank you. I must be on my way." Frederick added a tip, punched the four-digit security number into the card processor, then stood and glanced at the street. A late-model, white Ford pickup with Sonora plates turned the corner and idled southward toward the edge of town. An anonymous color and model, chosen by a brilliant and mysterious man. He frowned and stuffed the receipt into the inside pocket of his sports jacket. Ricardo's meal was at least partially a business expense. Frederick stared at the retreating pickup. He had no doubt Ricardo was an agent. The unanswered question? Who did Ricardo work for?

# Chapter 24

On the first leg of the flight from Tucson to Denver, I scrunched into a middle seat between a business man with a full-size laptop, and a mother who needed to enroll in a degree program on early childhood management. Her three-year-old shrieked and tried to spit on everybody around him from the time we left until the wheels hit the pavement at Denver International. By that time, I'd become a rabid fan of the automobile, no matter the price of gas. God be praised; I escaped the spoiled little brat without a scene. I had twenty minutes between flights so had to hurry to the departure gate for the next leg to Miles City. The plane had already loaded when I arrived, and I was glad I'd only taken a carry-on bag. Any checked luggage would have stayed in Denver.

The flight attendant at the front of the plane smiled a welcome, but then I guess they're supposed to do that to make up for the seatmate lottery and cramped conditions. I crab-walked down the tiny aisle, so intent on finding my assigned scrunch-space at the back of the plane that I nearly missed the familiar blond head in an aisle seat. He was bent over a magazine, and I made a point of jostling him with my bag. He politely moved his oversize shoulder inward without looking up.

"Hey you, get out of the aisle." His head jerked upward, and I laughed. "You weren't going to say hello, were you?"

"Dina, I didn't even see you. What are you doing here?" His face flushed, and he looked at least as glad to see me as I was him.

I glanced around the packed plane. "If we can find two seats together, I'll be glad to tell you." Though it had only been a few days, it seemed like forever since we'd talked. What would I do when this man returned to Omaha? Panic surged through me. Even if all the trouble with al-Qaida was over, life would be a bleak experience without him to . . . to argue with? Because mostly, that's all we ever did.

The middle seat next to me stayed empty. Frederick turned around, and I crooked a finger at him. He grinned, pulled his bag out of the overhead, and walked back. I scooted over, and he took the aisle seat. I squeezed his arm. "Great to see you. Where have you been?"

"I had business in Arizona," he hedged.

"Huh, so you're not telling." I raised an eyebrow. "More spy business?"

"Uh-h, not really. Well, part of it."

"You're always so definite. You don't have to tell me if you don't want to."

He sighed. "Okay, little Miss Detective. Among other things, I met with your father and we reached an understanding—I hope."

"With Papa? About what?"

"His friends. And you."

"What about me? Obviously, he hasn't time to be worried about my safety."

Frederick shook his head. "Don't be so hard on him. I honestly think he didn't foresee them messing with you. He seemed upset over that and assured me you were safe."

"Right," I scoffed. "Like when is this 'safe' supposed to start?"

He scowled. "I guess I had a little trouble with that one as well. Anyhow, tell me what you're doing. You went home to see your folks?"

"Yes, my grandma died. I went for the funeral. My father told you?"

"No, I called Gram yesterday, and she said you had gone. I'm sorry for your loss." He reached over and encased my hand in his, and it made little arrows of fire skip through my arm. "How was it?"

"As good as funerals ever are. She lived a long, productive life. I loved her dearly, but I guess there's a time to move on—for all of us. I think she was ready. Her faith was important to her, and she always gave liberally to the church."

Frederick stared his disapproval. "That's what gets you Catholics to Heaven?"

I frowned. "We've already had this argument." I leaned back in my seat and thought about our constant disagreements. Would our differences blow our relationship apart?

"The problem," he emphasized each word with his hand, "is the difference in our interpretation of salvation. You may believe in salvation by faith, but it's all the extras you tack on that makes it incompatible with Scripture."

"And how is that?"

"Salvation has to be by grace alone—"

"Frederick. We could scatter the New Testament book of James all over this plane and get nowhere. Isn't that what this argument is about?"

"No, it's more than that. Your church has convinced you that working your way into heaven is a viable option."

I'd had enough. "And yours? Go ahead, tell me about your three easy steps to salvation, about the same as a Monopoly 'get out of jail' card.

Frederick's jaw hardened. He didn't reply, and his frustration indicated he thought my opinion way off base, which made me angry. Why couldn't we agree on anything, least of all this issue of faith?

The last leg to Miles City was, as Raul would have said—*muy tranquilo*, very peaceful, because neither of us said another word. Frederick's car and my pickup were both at the airport, and by ten-thirty, we were home. Frederick offered a stiff goodnight. I nodded coolly as I brushed past him and down the steps. I had nothing to say to any man as stubborn as him?

Later, I tiptoed up the stairs and over to the pasture to check on Piñata. She ambled over to greet me, which was a first. I talked to her and scratched her ears with the same hand that had touched the dying Chiquita. How I wished some of Chiquita would rub into this mare's pores. Tomorrow we would start again, only this time, I would have no Merle to help me.

THE NEXT MORNING WHEN I unloaded Piñata and led her into the round pen, a steady drizzle fell from a leaden sky. Without a slicker, the rain soon soaked through my jacket, but we needed to make up for lost time. Piñata seemed to pick up right where we'd left off. A half-hour into the session, I decided it was time to move on to greater, or perhaps more dangerous activities. I pulled my saddle out of the trailer and threw it over the top rail. Then I asked the mare to stand in the middle of the pen without being tied. She did that okay, even though she hardly appeared to be relaxed and comfortable. The session before I'd left, she'd followed me as if I was her security blanket. According to Merle, she needed to understand that the safest place in the pen was right next to me. Much of her fear revolved around having her head touched, so I spent what I thought was adequate time rubbing her face and ears. She still wasn't perfect, but good enough I could bridle her without her jerking away. We were making progress.

She stood quietly while I saddled her. After five trainers had saddled her, I didn't think that would be a big deal. I wasn't. Once, she started to move away, but as soon as I asked her to stand, she froze. Her eyes showed more white than usual, and when I tried to slip the bit between her teeth, her neck went stiff. She refused to drop her head, every muscle tensed. No big deal. I'd lead her around. She'd loosen up. We were comfortable with each other. It was time we moved forward. I gathered up the reins and stuck my foot in the left stirrup.

"I wouldn't do that if I were you." Merle's voice came from outside the pen.

"I have to get on her sometime." I swung my leg over and reached for the far stirrup with my foot. Suddenly, everything exploded. Three jumps later, my face plowed into the wet dirt. The mare bucked and bawled around the pen as I pushed myself to my knees, spitting out sand and possibly some words for which I would have to ask God for forgiveness.

Merle slid through the steel pipes and hurried over to me. "Are you okay?" He slid one of his gnarled hands under my arm and helped me to my feet, then brushed the worst of the mud off the sides of my jacket.

The rain still pelted out of the sky, harder now, and I shivered in my mud-soaked clothes. Sand and water dripped from my fingers as I walked over to catch the mare. She stood quivering on the other side of the pen. Steam rose from her heaving flanks. Raindrops dripped from the ends of her mane and mixed with the sweat that ran down her brown legs. I caught her and led her to the center of the corral.

"You're going to get back on her?" Merle asked.

"Of course." I shivered out the words.

"Well sure, you go ahead and do that. That's what they do in the movies and cowboy storybooks, so if that's what you're trying to write, then that's surely what you ought to do." He turned and crawled through the bars of the corral.

I stood in the middle of the pen, the muddy water running off the edges of my now crinkled, rain-soaked straw hat. "Well then, what do *you* think I ought to do," I yelled. "I want to do it right. I want to win with this horse."

He hunched against the now driving rain and shook his head. “You did everything I told you not to do. What did I tell you about fear? Do you even remember?”

“That we would respect her fear.”

“Yes, I said you need to know what she can tolerate, understand how much she can learn in a day, and most of all—respect her fear. You did none of it. You thought you were ready, so she must be as well. She hadn’t told you that she respected you as her leader, or that she trusted you enough to be on her back.”

“Merle, then help me. What should I do?” Tears mixed with the mud and rain on my face.

“Take your saddle off. Spend as much time as you can with her. Try to make her forget you violated what little trust you’d built. And then—we’ll start over tomorrow.”

# Chapter 25

Piñata and I spent another fifteen minutes in the downpour, but I was shivering and cold, and she only wanted to hunch up and stand with her tail to the wind. Finally, I gave up and pulled the rain-soaked saddle off her. She was more than happy to walk into the warm, dry trailer.

When we got home, I led her into the pasture, then slogged to the house, my wet feet scrunching against the waterlogged leather in my near-ruined boots. Inside the door of my basement suite, I peeled off my dripping, muddy clothes and emptied the pockets of my pants and jacket. That's when I discovered the pages I'd taken from my father's office. Briefly, I scanned them. Their contents sickened me, and I flung the pages on the kitchen counter with my pickup keys, determined to deal with them right after a hot shower.

As the warm water washed the mud and goosebumps away, I wondered how best to handle the explosive intelligence revealed in the papers I'd taken from Papa's office. To my shame, my first thoughts were for myself and whether revealing them to the authorities would affect me. They couldn't deport me. I was an American citizen, born in Douglas, Arizona. But what about that FBI detective? He'd suspected something. If he discovered what I had, he would think I'd been withholding information. Probably that was a felony of some sort. I turned the shower off, stepped out and hugged a towel in front of me. How could my father have done this? It seemed every muscle in my body tensed with either bitterness or fear, which had pretty much been the story of my life since I'd taken those papers. I needed advice. Quickly, I dried off and pulled on jeans and a sweater. My bedside alarm, the only clock in the house informed me I had an hour before I had to be at work. That was more than enough time to talk to Frederick.

The front door jammed when I tried to open it—which was about right for *him*. If the man couldn't even fix a door, how was he going to help me with something as complicated and dangerous as the papers I held in my hand? I pulled harder until the door finally scraped far enough back to allow me to exit. I ran to the top of the stairs and groaned. No car, which probably meant the guy had a girlfriend who kept his pin head in the clouds. So typical. He was *never* around when *I* needed him. I stomped down the stairs and threw on my green uniform blouse. I'd try to talk to him tomorrow morning—or not. Probably, I should just go find that nosy detective. At least *he* wanted to see me.

Mrs. Riddler tottered onto the veranda when I walked up the stairs. We chatted for a minute, and I asked her if Frederick would be so kind as to have another look at the defective basement entry. She informed me he'd gone out south of town to help a friend brand some calves. That made me even angrier. Why hadn't he invited me? Sure, I would have had to pass because of work, but he could have at least asked. But at least he was in town. That was important, because the more I thought about what I'd taken from my father's office, the more I trembled. This was too explosive, way beyond my ability to handle.

Except for one table of four, the Spur was deserted when I arrived for my shift. Occasionally that happened. It was as if all of Montana had suddenly decided steak was bad for the waistline. Susan and I were on together as usual. I doubt Trent made enough to cover our wages, but it gave us a chance to catch up on the cleaning. Trent was the greatest boss ever, but he quickly turned into a tyrant if the place wasn't up to his standard of cleanliness. He insisted that floors and furnishings be spotless.

At the end of my shift, I cracked the screen door and peered out into the gloomy parking lot. Susan's venerable Chevy Sprint sat next to my pickup. Only one other vehicle sat in the lot, and a customer in the bar probably owned that. Nothing indicated my father's friends were still around. I dashed to my truck and drove home, confident they'd left—at least for now.

Dark storm clouds scudded across the midnight sky when I pulled into the driveway. Frederick's car was once again in its usual spot which sent a thrill through my veins. I determined to be up early in case he had plans to leave. I needed to ask his advice. What should I do with the papers?

When I reached the bottom of the stairs, my door wouldn't open, though I tried the key twice. I rammed my shoulder into it. Still, it wouldn't budge. Angrily, I trudged up the stairs to the living room door, wondering why I'd chosen this dump, all the time knowing I wouldn't move—for a hundred reasons.

Thankfully, Frederick answered my knock instead of his grandmother. Made decent by a red robe, his blond hair stood on end. Bleary-eyed, he peered at me in the gloom. "Dina, what's wrong?"

"The door you did such a great job of fixing won't open."

To his credit, or perhaps because he was too sleepy to think of an appropriate answer, I was spared one of his sarcastic replies. He tightened the belt on his bathrobe, slipped on some shoes and clumped down the gloomy stairs. I handed him my key. He turned the knob, and of course the stupid thing almost flew open. He looked at me as if I had an IQ of forty or less and motioned for me to enter my castle. I flicked the light switch on—and froze. "Frederick!" I screamed.

He'd started up the stairs, but the panic in my voice instantly brought him back to the landing. We both stared at the upended drawers, the clothes, female necessities and makeup that littered the room. The mattress lay on the floor. I stepped inside. The bathroom door stood ajar. Inside, three words scrawled in crimson lipstick on the bathroom mirror froze every capillary in my quivering body. "DEATH TO INFIDELS!"

My head swiveled to the kitchen counter where I'd left the rain-soaked papers I'd photocopied in Papa's office. Nothing remained. They were gone. They'd found what they wanted, and they had still torn my apartment to shreds? The meaning was chilling, made doubly so by the scrawled message on the bathroom mirror. I'd messed with the will of Allah. Besides, I knew way too much. For that, I would pay with my life.

Frederick slipped and arm over my shoulder, then gently pushed me aside. He stepped through the carnage, tight-lipped. "Give me a minute. I'll find some clothes and help you clean this up." I considered telling him I was too scared to stay here alone, but then I remembered he was leaving. It wouldn't be long before I wouldn't have his help.

While Frederick dressed, I shuffled from the bathroom to the main room of the apartment, took a deep breath and crossed my arms tightly over my chest, trying to contain the panic that threatened to overwhelm me. Five minutes later, he came downstairs wearing a T-shirt and sweatpants. Together, we slid the mattress onto the bed. I scanned the feminine apparel all over the floor. "Uh, why don't you work in the kitchen, and I'll deal with this."

"Okay. But holler if you discover anything unusual. It may be significant."

A half-hour later, everything was as normal as we could make it at one o'clock in the morning. Frederick perched on the end of my bed. "Do you have any idea what's going on here?" he asked.

I considered a no, but not for long. This was now too dangerous to hide. "Yes, I do. I copied some papers in my father's office. I haven't a clue how these people found out. Likely, Papa told them? No, it couldn't be him. Surely he wouldn't . . . but how else would they know?"

"Where are the papers?"

"They were there." I pointed to the spot on the counter where I'd flung them, then pulled the only chair I owned away from the rickety little card table. I turned the back toward Frederick and straddled it. "Do you know anything about C-137?"

Frederick's eyes narrowed. "Depends. Can you be more specific?"

"No. The note talked about a coming shipment of a product. That's how they identified it."

"Oka-ay?"

"What is it?"

"If you're referring to Cesium-137 it's a radioisotope. For terrorists, it would be a sought-after substance to build a dirty bomb. They would use something simple like dynamite as a detonator, or possibly ammonium nitrate fertilizer. Either one has the force to scatter the Cesium pellets over a wide enough area to cause significant contamination. The resulting panic and economic disruption would be devastating."

Frederick stood and paced around the room. "Dina . . ." he raised both hands to the sky. "Why did you take the papers? These are dangerous people."

I leaned my chin over the back of the chair. "I went into my father's office because I despise what he's doing. What I did was an act of—well, I suppose delayed teenage rebellion." I stuffed my hands in the pockets of my jeans. "The papers were in plain sight on his desk, so I copied them. I didn't even think about the consequences."

Frederick scowled. "You've got that right."

I glared right back at him, though he didn't seem to notice.

"So that's what this is all about—a shipment of Cesium-137 into America?"

I shrugged. "I'm just telling you what was in the paper. They gave detailed instructions where my father had to make the delivery." I threw up my hands, all the bitterness from my childhood carried in my voice. "Who better than Ricardo, the coyote?"

"What's the destination?" Frederick asked wearily.

So, I told him what had been on the paper, and then thanked God in heaven that this man was here. He seemed to know exactly what to do. At least he made me think he did.

# Chapter 26

When I awoke the following morning, Frederick sat on the step, his body blocking the sunlight from filtering through my kitchen window. For all I knew, he'd been there all night.

"Hey." I waved through the curtains, then walked over and gave a mighty reef on the door. It wouldn't open, so I banged on it until he shoved from the outside and broke it loose. "How about having another go at my port of entry, Mr. Fix-it Man?"

"Good morning to you, too." His deserved sarcasm turned to instant concern the moment he saw my face. "What happened?"

"I'm okay, and yes, good morning. I got bucked off."

"You shouldn't be riding that goofy—"

I'll decide that. And would you please fix this door. If anyone tried to get in here, even Trent would hear them clear down at the Spur."

"Put on something more than a nightgown. I'll take care of it this afternoon. Now, we need to discuss a few things."

"Can't. I need to be at the fairgrounds in a half-hour. After that, I'll be at work."

"Then when can we talk?"

"Come to the Spur at eight. I have a short break—unless we're exceptionally busy."

"How about now? Forget that horse. This is about your life."

"No, I won't forget that horse. And it's important that I work with her every day. We can meet for a few minutes after I come back from the arena. That is, if you're here. You were gone yesterday. Your grandma said you went to a branding, and you didn't even invite me. Nice guy!"

He spread his hands in resignation. "I thought you had to mess with that crazy mare and then go to work."

"Well, I did, but you could have at least asked."

His blue eyes softened. "I promise, you will never get to make that accusation again. I won't miss another opportunity. See you tonight at the Spur."

My face warmed as I watched him take the steps, two at a time. My only experience with love had been a schoolgirl crush on the class president in my junior year. Somehow, that didn't compare with the high-octane jolt that went right down to my toes every time this man was in sight, never mind the constant thoughts about him when he wasn't around.

Hurriedly I dressed, loaded Piñata, and headed for the round pen. At least today it wasn't pouring rain. While I drove, I planned what we'd try to accomplish. When I'd caught her, she'd seemed normal. I hoped that meant she wasn't holding a grudge for my having barged into her fear zone.

When we arrived at the fairgrounds, Merle waited in his usual spot, one foot cocked onto the bottom rail of the pen.

I unloaded the mare and led her into the pen. I hadn't long to wait for Merle's scathing review of yesterday's events. The short of it was he made me start with all the basics again like it was the first day.

"Today, you'll make an unbreakable contract with her—another one." He paid no attention as I probed at the gravel rash on my cheek. "Your part is that you will never again push beyond the fear she can handle. Hers is to stand and face her fear, not run from it; so to succeed, you need to make a huge effort to understand this mare. You need to figure out what new experiences she can handle each day. Take that saddle blanket and put it on her."

Carefully, I slid the blanket onto her back.

"That's great. You know what it felt like to her?"

"No."

"Like you were sneakin' up on her with a rattlesnake. Now, jerk it off and throw it back on as if you'd saddled her a thousand times. Then do it at least fifty more times over every inch of her body. If she steps away from you, then you make her move out fast. After a few rounds, her lungs will tell her it's easier to stand and face a little bitty snake than to run until her tongue's hangin' out."

The amazing thing is that everything Merle told me was right. He read horses like they were a first-grade Primer. They were to be respected, but in return, he demanded the same level of consideration from them. Though yesterday had been a disaster, within minutes I saw the rebuilding of the trust I'd broken with Piñata. She was comfortable because she knew what to expect, and by the end of the day, I had saddled and unsaddled her a dozen times from both sides with little tension, and no fear. I wondered if tomorrow I would have to put a foot in the stirrup and get back on. I hoped she was afraid because I was, and the gravel rash on the right side of my face still burned. Perhaps Merle would put it off for a few more days.

When I arrived at the house, Frederick had fixed my door. It didn't work like it should, but if I used both hands it would open, and most times it would close it if I stuck my hip into it. He wasn't much of a carpenter.

I donned my green uniform blouse and dashed on some makeup for my shift at the Spur. Frederick's car sat in the driveway, and I heard the rise and fall of his voice upstairs as he spoke to somebody on the phone. I waited to talk to him as long as I could, then gave up and left for work.

Frederick walked into the Spur at five minutes to eight. Wednesdays usually meant a light customer load, so I was able to take my scheduled break. We sat at a corner table close to the kitchen. He ordered a steak sandwich, and I hurried through a taco salad and iced tea.

He wasted no time on small talk. "Dina, how did al-Qaida discover you had that document?"

My eyebrows shot upward. "You don't need a master's degree to figure that out. My father—who else?"

"No, I don't think he would have told them."

"And why not?"

Frederick chewed on a bite of tough flank steak. I should have warned him we'd had two customers tonight who had complained. It was simply a bad cut of beef. After the second complaint, Trent had taken it off the menu. Unfortunately, Frederick had ordered it before the menu change.

Frederick gave the flat-lipped shrug I'd come to know so well. "Just something your father said—about you."

I raised an eyebrow. "Probably, I don't want to hear it."

Frederick ignored my snide comment. "Back to the question. I think you're right. Nobody else could have known you took the papers. Al-Qaida would not take the chance of bringing in other people on something this big. If I'm right, this may be the biggest play they've made since nine-eleven. Your father is likely the only person outside of their organization who is in the loop." He tapped a finger on the table and stared out at the listless evening traffic on Main Street. "Does he have a security camera in his office?"

I faked a non-committal shrug. "How would I know? We weren't allowed in there." I rubbed my suddenly sweaty palms on my jeans as my heart sank.

"With an office full of covert documents, it makes sense that your father would take that kind of security precaution."

"I suppose." Momentarily, I was distracted as Susan seated a couple at one of my tables. In five minutes, I had to be back on the floor.

"If your father had a hidden camera, he knows you took those documents."

I gripped the table trying to contain the sudden, choking fear. My eyes darted around the room.

Frederick reached over and patted my arm. "Your father is the least of our problems. The bigger issue is the other hidden camera in the room. That one belonged to al-Qaida."

My face blanched. Why had I done something so foolish?

"After talking to your father, I have to believe either he is the biggest bungler west of the Mississippi, or he . . . well, we won't go there yet. But I *will* say, . . . I'm convinced he's a very intelligent man."

"So, what are you saying?"

"Only that he knew they'd bugged his office. The problem is he didn't dare touch it, because he would have wanted them to think he didn't know. And that all worked well until you walked in and filched the most important document of all time."

My hands trembled. Why had I been so foolish? I pushed to my feet.

Frederick held up a finger. "Give me one more minute."

Nervously, I glanced toward the couple to see if they were ready to order, then reluctantly dropped back into the chair.

My fingers worked at each other as my eyes darted around the room. Frederick didn't give me time to respond. He spelled the situation out well enough that the fear I'd carried instantly multiplied.

"Now they have that document back, they have to do something about you. When or how they will strike is the question, but what you cannot do is walk out that back door—or go home."

"What—what am I going to do? I have no other place to go."

"I'll take care of that." Frederick's jaw clenched as he pulled a phone out of a holster on the left side of his belt, a distinctively different one than the one I had seen him use so often.

"Who are you calling?"

"Dina, this isn't something we can do alone. What we're dealing with involves national security—and your life." Frederick started to punch numbers into his cell.

"Wait." I reached over and covered his hand. "Let's at least talk about this."

He stopped the call but held the phone ready. "Talk about what? This is about your life." He grabbed my hand and gently cradled it between his. "I'm not going to take that risk. His eyes held mine. "You mean too much."

I could have drawn my hand away. Instead, I slipped my fingers into his strong ones. My emotions were scattered all over the place, and I didn't even want to think about where this would lead, but for that moment, I appreciated his strong male presence.

After a few seconds, Frederick released my hand. "We need to leave—now. And I need to make that call." His eyes moved to the phone still in his hand.

"To whom?"

"This is FBI territory. They can hide you. They're set up for this kind of thing."

"No, I won't do that, at least, not yet. We don't know for sure that they know. Besides, I will not let some Muslim terrorist ruin my life. When I go, Piñata is coming with me. I'm not quitting on her. She's just started to really—"

Frederick rolled his eyes. "Don't you understand? Having to put a horse on hold is only an inconvenience. A bullet wrecks your life."

I tossed my hair back. "You may be right, but I still think we should wait. Isn't there some place I can disappear to for a few days where I can take her? How about that friend of yours, the one with the ranch down on the Tongue River?"

Frederick tapped the table with an index finger while he scanned each entrance into the building. "I'll think of something. Start work again. Do the same things you always do. He glanced at his watch. It is now eight thirty-five. At exactly nine-twenty, give no warning but run for the front door. I will be parked outside."

"What about Trent—my job?"

"I'll take care of Trent."

"Okay." Reluctantly, I rose and hurried to take care of the guests at my tables. Then, I cleared a table that had just emptied. Fear turned my hands into buttery appendages, unsteady enough I could manage no more than two plates at a time. When I set a couple on the long counter by the dishwasher, Frederick was on the other side of the room talking to my boss. Trent looked at me and smiled. I nearly broke into tears. He didn't deserve all my problems. By now, he must wish he'd hired someone who was less trouble. The rest of that hour went by in a blur. Once, I dropped a plate, but at least it was in the kitchen—and empty.

Susan walked in with an armful of dirty dishes as I was sweeping the shards into a corner. "Wow, you're really falling for that guy, aren't you? You haven't dropped anything in weeks." I tried to smile, but it didn't come off well. She must have seen the fear and uncertainty scrawled across my face. She slid her armload of dishes roughly onto the counter. "Did he give you the runaround tonight? If he did, he'll never know what hit him."

"No, it's not that," I replied. "Some other stuff."

"What—are you pregnant?"

"No." I blushed. "We're not that close, and even if we were, I wouldn't sleep—"

"What do you mean? You're a virgin?"

The color rose in my face. "Well, I just don't think it's right—"

"You sweet kid. Where did you pick that up in this day and age?" She gave me a quick hug.

"Thanks, Susan. You've been such an inspiration to me. You work so hard, and I have appreciated your help so much."

Susan's order came up, and she left with three plates and several bottles of condiments. When she returned, I was just leaving with fresh silverware and plates, but she squeezed my arm. "Go for it, kid, but don't do like I did. It's a dismal future when you get knocked-up when you're seventeen. You have a lifetime of hard work in front of you. Not that I'm sorry about having my Nathan. He's in high school now. It's just—there's happier ways to raise kids than doing it alone."

I blinked the sudden mist from my eyes. What I was facing would have the same result. Always alone, hiding from terrorists, constantly looking over my shoulder. There would be no barrel horses, and I certainly wouldn't be able to attend college. A husband and a family? That would always be out of the question.

# Chapter 27

The clock on the back wall of the Spur seemed to have stopped. I checked my cell phone twice, just to make sure it hadn't. Every time a customer opened the door, I froze. Squeezing tentacles of fear threatened to choke off every breath of oxygen in my body. Three minutes before Frederick's deadline, I finished cleaning a table and started working closer to the front. On my last trip to the kitchen, I grabbed the few necessities I needed; my bank card and the cash I had left in my purse. I stuffed it all in my pockets, picked up a couple of clean glasses and some silverware and headed for the last table before the door. Susan looked at me strangely because that was her area.

"I'll get that in a minute, Dina."

I mumbled a response, my hands shaking so badly, I didn't dare trust my voice. What would happen when I ran out that door? What if they'd anticipated that? I glanced at the clock. What did it feel like to have bullets tear through your body? How much did it hurt? What if Frederick wasn't there? Should I run into the darkness, or back into the lighted restaurant?

When the minute hand rested at the bottom of the clock, I moved toward the street entrance as if I were walking to the other side of the room to clear a table. Abreast of the door, I dropped the dishrag on a table and made a hard right. Hardly breaking stride, I pulled the door inward and sprinted the few steps to the sidewalk. Air whooshed out of my lungs. Frederick's Mustang was at the curb, and as I ran toward it, the passenger door cannoned back.

"Quick! Get in." I'd barely hit the seat before he floored it and barreled down the street as fast as that Mustang would accelerate. By anybody's books, that was first-class flying. I guess the police car that threw his lights on thought the same.

"Of all the luck," Frederick groaned. He peered into his rearview mirror at the cruiser now a block behind us. "I'll bet Doug saw it was my car, but we're not stopping."

"Doug?"

"The sheriff. We're pretty good friends—at least we were. I'm sure it was him." The big engine reverberated with a throaty baritone which failed to cover the screeching soprano of the tires as Frederick muscled the car through the last curve and dove for the approach to the westbound interstate. At the bottom, he wrenched the steering wheel into a skid, crossed the median underneath the overpass and accelerated onto the eastbound pavement while the sheriff's car was still out of sight on the ramp. Both of us breathed a sigh of relief when no flashing lights appeared. The feint seemed to have worked.

I leaned back in the seat. "Where are we going?"

"Friend of mine has a ranch out on Boulder Creek. He and his wife run a bunch of cows and do a few other things to keep starvation at bay. I think they can find a place to keep you safe for however long we need."

"And what about Piñata?"

Frederick sighed. "Piñata the renegade should have been on a meat truck before she was lucky enough to find you."

"Oh, is that right. Well, look here, Mr.—"

"Calm down."

In the dim light of the instrument panel his crooked grin was like cool water on my fear-induced anger.

"Hey, I'll have somebody pick her up tomorrow. That doesn't mean you will get her immediately. We'll take her to the fairgrounds. She can stay there for a day or two. Then when it's safe, I'll bring her to the ranch. We don't need these guys following her to you, so you'll have to leave that one in my hands. I'll do the best I can."

I reached over and patted his arm. "I'm sorry. I shouldn't have snapped at you. And thanks, that means a lot."

My watch showed midnight when we pulled off the county highway. Frederick bounced the Mustang over a cattle guard and down a half-mile of gravel road. An outside porch light illuminated the yard as well as a thousand voracious mosquitoes. Inside, a light cast a soft glow from the wagon wheel shaped glass at the top of the door. I thought the people must have gone to bed, but as soon as we stopped, a middle-aged man in a checkered shirt and the same jeans everybody wore in this ranch country, stepped outside. He tucked his thumbs under a pair of bright red suspenders and waited.

Frederick opened the car door and looked at me. "This is home."

"Don't you want to see if we're welcome?"

He smiled gently at me. "Let's go. With Bud and Lorie—it's okay."

"Well, you should ask."

"I already did, but only because we'd arrive in the middle of the night. Otherwise, I wouldn't have bothered. That's the kind of friends they are—so come on. You're arguing again."

I glared at him, but it carried little effect, especially in the dark. Obediently, I trailed behind him.

The man's voice floated down to us. "About time you got here. I was ready to leave the porch light on and go to bed."

We stepped up on the spacious veranda. The man walked forward and stuck out his hand. "You'll be Dina. I'm Bud. Lorie has to work tomorrow, so she turned in a bit ago. Come on in. We've got a place for you as long as you need it, though I can't say much for the company you keep." He inclined his head toward Frederick and grinned.

Frederick punched him playfully in the arm. "Don't you be telling any stories now."

Bud chuckled. "Grab Dina's bag, while I show her downstairs."

I spread my arms, embarrassed at my vagrant standing. "I'm sorry. I don't have—"

"Yes, you do. I'll get it." Frederick vaulted off the porch and into the darkness as I followed Bud to a bedroom at the bottom of the stairs.

"Here, Dina." He opened the door. "I hope you'll be comfortable." He pointed across the hall. "There's a bathroom right next to your room, and if you need anything, just holler. You make yourself at home, and I mean that."

I tried my best to thank him for their wonderful hospitality. A minute later, Frederick crabbed through the door and into the room, laden with a couple plastic shopping bags, and of all things—my suitcase. Bud again graciously offered whatever I might require to be comfortable.

"Anyhow, goodnight Dina. We'll see you in the morning. You get up whenever you want, and if nobody's around, just find the kitchen and fix whatever you'd like."

After I'd again thanked Bud for his generous reception, he left us and tromped up the stairs. I turned to Frederick. "You have amazing friends.

What's with this?" I pointed to the suitcase.

He shrugged, a half-guilty look on his face. "Your clothes and other stuff. I just tipped bathroom contents and dresser drawers into a heap and jammed it all into your bag. I hope I got everything you need."

"When did you do that?" I asked indignantly.

"Between the time we talked at the Spur, and when I picked you up."

I unzipped the suitcase and looked at the jumbled contents. Toothpaste smeared one of my favorite blouses.

Frederick spread his hands. "I'm sorry. I had about eight minutes to pack, so if things aren't as neat as they ought to be, I apologize."

My face reddened. "You were in my room, in my personal—"

"Dina, if there had been any other way, I would *never* have done that." His face was now redder than mine, and suddenly we both laughed because he was right. There hadn't been any other option. For him to bring me anything after tonight would be too dangerous. I was now in hiding. For how long, I didn't know.

# Chapter 28

On the way back to town, Frederick scanned every side road for a parked vehicle, but so far Dina's pursuers hadn't surfaced, which might mean nothing. When he idled past the park on his way to Gram's, he glimpsed the familiar gray Audi inexpertly concealed on a side street. Instantly, he realized his mistake. They would know exactly how long he'd been gone. His grip tightened on the steering wheel. Tomorrow they would start a grid, working outward until they found where she was hidden. But he would be the first target. They would try to get information from him, by whatever means necessary. His face turned grim, and under his breath he muttered, "Bring it on, boys."

When he got to the end of the street, the gray Audi had fallen in a block behind him. Instead of turning in to Gram's driveway, he floored it, which meant something with the Mustang. Even if it failed to be the hottest car on the market, it was snappy. The headlights behind him faded into the distance. He'd caught them off guard, but it didn't take long before they closed the gap. He made sure they were within a quarter mile before he again punched the accelerator to the mat. He just hoped nobody's cows were on the highway. If he hit one at this speed, there wouldn't be enough left of the cow or the car to scrape into a burlap potato sack.

Six miles out of town, he'd lengthened the distance between them to at least a mile. Perfect. The big sweeping Ferguson Corner ahead swung to the left, passable at eighty, but the sharp right-hand corner after that was a killer, even at fifty. Two hundred yards before the second corner, he slammed the shifter into park, jumped out, and sprinted around the front of the car. The forty-year-old sign, loose in the ground, moved easily, not that it mattered.

Frederick hugged the square post and bent his powerful legs. It seemed easier now than on those long-ago Halloween nights when as a teenage kid his strength had bought him the acceptance his poor riding skills had failed to deliver. He squeezed and lifted, then got another grip and heaved the post nearly out of the ground before twisting it a quarter turn. He ran back to the car, dived in and drove to the end of the corner before spinning around and parking on the inside of the turn. The scream of a high-revving engine reached his ears, seconds before the wavering headlights broke through the night, searching for the road ahead. But at that velocity, and with no warning of the dangerous corner, the result was inevitable. The pavement disappeared in front of them, and Frederick followed the screeching brakes and dust as the car careened off the road and bounced through the sagebrush. He stepped out of the Mustang, jacked a shell into the Beretta and sauntered across the road. Miraculously, the Audi had stayed on its wheels. The passenger door inched open. Frederick crouched and put a bullet through the back side window. Both occupants dived for cover on the far side of the car. It gave him time to flatten one tire. That was enough. He loped back to the Mustang and sped toward town. The message might suffice. He would and could fight. It might give them something to think about other than Dina.

Ten minutes later, Frederick parked the Mustang on a quiet side street, then hiked back to Gram's. There would be no further trouble tonight. The war would start tomorrow.

Morning dawned bright and clear, typical for the semi-desert Miles City climate. After two cups of coffee, Frederick dragged out his cell and called Hardy to ask him if he would haul Dina's mare to the fairgrounds. Hardy would be unknown to the al-Qaida men, and it seemed doubtful they would have any clue about the horse. He would have liked to deliver her saddle and more of her horse gear, but it wasn't safe. Better if after things settled down, Hardy delivered the horse. He'd figure out some other way to transport the saddle.

It was still early when Gram toddled out to the kitchen where Frederick sat mulling through options. "Do you want a poached egg?"

"I would love one, but I can get it."

"No, let me do it. I'm going to have one myself, so I might as well fix yours."

"Thanks, Gram." He dialed a number, the same one he'd started to dial last night at the Spur. "Pete Sardinha, please."

After countless minutes of canned music, a secretary put him through. Pete's faint Italian accent growled in his ear. Like Frederick, Pete had been a high school immigrant to America.

"Fred, how are you doing?"

"Fine. I have a big one for you."

"In Montana?" he snickered. "Let me guess. Horse thieves?"

"No, seriously, Pete, this is heavy-duty. Who runs your Billings office?"

"We don't have an office in Billings, or anywhere else in Montana. Nothing has happened there since the Unabomber, that Kaczynski guy. If anything ever did break loose, we'd split it between here and the Salt Lake office."

"Then you better send somebody out here."

"Why?"

"Al-Qaida."

The instant silence trumpeted Pete's astonishment louder than any words. Seconds passed before he spoke. "I'll fly into Billings day after tomorrow. Can you meet me at the airport?"

"No. You need to be here now. Come straight to Miles City—tomorrow."

"I'll be there. Where can we meet?"

"I'll be at the Spur Bar on Main Street at seven."

"The Spur . . . what?

"They have the best prime rib in the state, but if you don't—"

"I'm in."

Frederick snapped the phone shut and turned his attention to Gram as she laid two pieces of toast onto plates. "Thanks, Gram. You spoil me rotten. I could have done that."

"I know, but I like having you here. I'm not too old to poach a couple of eggs."

Frederick went to the fridge and poured a glass of orange juice before moving back to the table.

Gram ladled the eggs onto the toast. "How are you and Dina getting along? And that reminds me; I didn't hear her come in last night."

"Dina's going to be gone for a few days, so don't worry about her."

"You seem to be well-informed about that young lady's schedule."

Frederick smiled sheepishly. "I try to be. She's kind of special."

"So . . . that's the way it is?" Gram turned from the stove, one hand on her walker, the other holding a plate.

"Afraid so. It . . . well, it just happened."

Gram set the plate in front of Frederick. "The girl does have some attributes. She seems to understand horses, and that's not a bad thing."

Frederick chewed on an overcooked egg. A swallow of orange juice helped the bite slither down—along with Gram's backhanded compliment.

"Gram, how long has it been since you've seen your sister in Sturgis?"

"Oh, I don't know. I guess it's been a year or two, but it's unlikely I'll see her again. I'm getting too old to travel that far."

"What if I took you over there?"

"No, you don't have time for that."

"Well, it just so happens that I do. Would you go if we could leave in the morning?"

"Hmm, that's short notice. I'd have to call Doris and see if she can handle company. After all, she's not much younger than me."

"Call her and see if you can stay for a week. Then I will drive over and pick you up. Would that work?"

Gram's smile was as wide as the Missouri river in flood. "Well, I suppose . . . if you have time."

Frederick patted her shoulder. "Gram, we're going." All morning he'd stewed over the danger he'd brought to Gram through this mess. Al Quaida knew this was where he lived. After last night, what they would do now was anybody's guess.

# Chapter 29

When I tiptoed upstairs, the lack of any sound meant Bud and Lorie had long ago departed for work. A hint of shame washed over me that I'd not been up at first light. After all, that's what I'd been used to before I started at the Spur. It would be nice to become an early riser again.

I shuffled into the kitchen in the clothes and slippers Frederick had provided from my meager wardrobe. The refrigerator yielded apple juice and a bottom drawer contained a blueberry bagel. That seemed perfect, so I stuck the two pieces of bagel in the toaster. While I waited, I wandered through the living room, a glass of apple juice in hand. Rodeo action pictures were scattered over the walls. Most appeared to be Bud in years past. Obviously, he had been a bareback bronc rider and a good one because there were two or three from the National Finals in Las Vegas. But it wasn't those that interested me. One wall overflowed with pictures of barrel racers. Some of the names I'd heard and followed—women who were at the top of their profession, but most of the pictures were of five-time world champion Lorie Linder. I peered at one of the shots. It was a close-up of her turning a barrel at the Pendleton Roundup. Her face, silhouetted against the vast grandstand carried a frozen, intense concentration. But why would there be so many pictures of Lorie Linder? Lorie, . . . no, it couldn't be. Had Frederick mentioned Bud's last name?

Slowly, I walked to the counter and looked out the kitchen window. On the far side of the yard, an extensive set of working corrals sprawled next to a barn. At the end of the corrals, three barrels were placed in a big outdoor arena. A rider loped a black horse in slow circles. Even from here I recognized her, not only from the pictures on the wall, but all the others I'd pored over through the years. Here I was standing in her home. Lorie Linder's job wasn't in town. It was out there in that arena, training some of the most talented barrel racing horses in the world.

While I ate the bagel, I stood over the sink and stared out the kitchen window. Lorie rode so gracefully, every move like ballet, the black horse reaching for new heights as he scampered around the barrels.

I brushed the crumbs off my hands and pulled my boots on. To watch somebody like Lorie was a dream come true. Probably, she wanted to be left alone. Nevertheless, I had to find out. Like a hummingbird drawn to a petal feeder filled with sugar water, I made a beeline toward the arena. Lorie now worked the colt slowly around each barrel. She made him change leads, drop his front end and pull through the turns, bending and building that supple responsiveness into his body, but most of all, forming a foundation for his mind. I stood with my face tucked between the pipes that formed the arena fence.

Lorie hadn't seen me, and I guess the black colt hadn't either until she loped him past me and he suddenly skittered away from the fence.

Lorie stopped him and rode back. "Ah, you're Dina. Welcome to our ranch."

I stammered. "I'm sorry. I didn't mean to startle your horse. I just wanted to watch you. I'll leave if you want."

"No, please stay. I wish there were a hundred more of you. Barrel horses are like people. They need to get used to crowds, and that is something I can't simulate here at the ranch."

"Oh, thank you. I would so much like to see you train."

"You're welcome to watch me. Frederick told Bud you have a horse you're training to run barrels. Tell me about her."

"Well, I just bought her. I don't know if she's going to make it. She has a lot of bad history."

Lorie continued to work the colt back and forth in the arena as she talked. "Why don't you bring her to the ranch, and we can work on her together?"

"Oh Lorie, that would be wonderful. I would stay out of your way, and—"

"Dina, you're welcome to bring her. You're trying to make her a barrel horse?"

"Yes, but it isn't going as well as I'd hoped. She's nervous and flighty, and sometimes, she just loses it."

Lorie side-passed the black colt over to the fence. "Barrel horses, because they're bred to run, can get crazy real fast. At three or four years old, they have a super-athletic body, but without the brain to go with it they are nothing more than a barely-controlled runaway. Sometimes it's important to let their mind catch up with their body before we push them for speed."

I climbed up and sat on the top rail of the fence while I thought over what Lorie had said. Was that what had happened to Piñata? Had somebody pushed her until some fragile circuit in her brain had snapped?

Lorie moved the black colt back and forth. Through the whole time we talked, she continued to work on his responsiveness to her feet and hands.

"How far along is your mare?" Lorie asked.

I sighed. "She's a five-year-old, but barely started. I think she knows more than what she shows. Something must have happened in her past to cause all the resentment and fear. Every step is a major issue."

"Hmm, I might be able to help. When she comes, we'll go to work on her. Who knows? Under all that baggage, you might have a world champion."

I smiled and bit my tongue, wondering how to respond. There had been no hint of sarcasm in Lorie's words, but anything I wanted to say about my crazy Piñata did not have world champion attached. I just hoped Lorie wouldn't send me and my psycho mare back to wherever we'd come from.

LATE THE NEXT MORNING, Hardy rode into the yard on his big Badger horse, leading Piñata.

"I rode over from the Peterson Ranch. It's only about five miles cross-country. That's what Fred told me to do, so here she is." Hardy peered at my face. "Are you in trouble? How come you're out here?"

I struggled with an answer. "No, I'm not in trouble—well, perhaps a little, but trust me, you don't want to hear it, at least for now."

Hardy shrugged, still curious. "What're ya' going do with the mare?"

"Barrel race on her." My voice exuded way more confidence than I felt.

Hardy eyed her as he handed over the lead shank. "Didn't she come from the bucking horse sale?"

"Yes, but she didn't buck. I think she just needs a new start."

Hardy pursed his lips. "That's a hard way to go if you want to barrel race, but good luck—and don't get hurt. You wouldn't be near as pretty in a hospital gown." He grinned at my discomfort. "Come and rope again if you'd like."

"I will—and thanks so much for your help."

Hardy turned his horse and rode back the way he had come.

Piñata walked quietly beside me as I led her to a corral. The next few days would be all mine. Lorie had left to compete in some rodeos in the Midwest and now there was no Merle to mentor me. I stroked the mare's neck and face, smoothing her silky mane. I tried to remember what Merle had told me about fear, and not pushing the mare past her comfort zone. I studied Piñata's alert brown eyes, waiting for whatever came next. For now, her body showed no tension, but only because I wasn't asking her to do anything. I slipped the halter off, and she trotted to the far side of the pen. I stood in the middle and clucked at her. Piñata turned and walked toward me, though her eyes announced a wary caution. Somehow, I had to make this mare understand that the safest place in her world was right beside me, or better yet, with me in the saddle. I'd been close to that, but then I'd tried to ride her before she was ready, which had destroyed everything.

For two long days, I did nothing but work in the round pen. Piñata and I were both exhausted, but by the time I led her outside, she hugged me like a shadow. To her, I now represented safety. We also had a beginning mutual respect, and hopefully even a thimbleful of trust. I'd started to understand what Merle had tried to communicate. Respect had to be the foundation. Everything else was secondary, a lesson I would not forget.

A week after I'd arrived at Bud and Lorie's ranch, the morning dawned brassy and hot. I'd heard nothing from Frederick, which probably meant his spiriting me away at midnight had worked. Quietly, I dressed and tiptoed up the stairs. Lorie already sat at the kitchen counter.

"Good morning." She took her glasses off and set them on the well-marked Bible in front of her. "I was going to scramble some eggs. Want some?"

"Sure." I glanced at the pages. "What are you reading?"

"Psalms. I love the poetry—and the comfort. Trust God. Righteousness will prevail. That's really the whole message of the book."

"Sometimes that's hard to believe."

"Yes, I suppose it is." She stood. "How many eggs?"

"Just one. So, you're Protestant?"

"Hmm." Lorie cracked three eggs into the skillet. "You're throwing a big loop. Protestant includes a whole bunch of folks with whom I would have little in common, but if you mean Protestant as compared to Catholic, yes, I am. Why?"

"I just wondered. Protestants always have their Bibles out. I'm Catholic." A defensive note crept into my voice, and I hadn't meant that to happen.

The spatula paused. "No, I didn't know. That is so interesting. I'm embarrassed to tell you, but I don't think I've ever had any close Catholic friends, other than Bud's family."

"Well, I am," I finished lamely.

"Good. You'll be my first truly Catholic friend. Sometimes we build pretty high walls with our differences, but we may have more in common than we think."

I smiled, happy to agree as I basked in Lorie's unassuming friendship. However, today I had to face the roiling fear that was making my stomach do flip-flops. The time had arrived. I had to again step into the saddle. What would Lorie say? I didn't know. She was a thousand miles away. I walked back and forth through the pen. Some day in the future would be a better time to move forward with Piñata—wouldn't it?

Lorie dropped the religion conversation, which was fine by me. When I shuffled out to the corrals, the mare eyed me from the safety of her feed pen. However, when I stepped inside, she walked up to me and stuck her head almost under my arm. I haltered her, then led her into the round pen. For a while, I petted and talked to her, trying to decide whether she was ready to ride? What had Merle said? You're not going to get on that mare until it's as natural as swinging your leg over the most broke horse in the country. My face tingled where the scraped skin had healed. I stroked Piñata's ears, and suddenly I understood. My fear had stopped our training program from moving forward. She was ready to trust me for one more step. Now, I had to trust her.

Piñata stood with ears at half-mast, idly swatting at flies with her tail while I saddled her. She'd been used to the equipment long before we'd met. Her trust issues were with humans, not the saddle. After slipping the snaffle bit into her mouth, I flipped the cotton one-piece rein over her neck and walked away. My stomach tightened. I wasn't ready. This was crazy. But the mare ambled over and stood next to me with her nose nearly touching my chest. Would she be as comfortable with me in the saddle as she was with me close to her on the ground, or would it be like before? I walked to the middle of the pen. She followed. I grabbed the saddle horn and stepped into the saddle. Her eyes widened, and her muscles bunched for action, but by that time I was already back on the ground. She let out a big breath of air as if to say, "If that's all you want, I can handle it."

So that's what we did. Each time, I would stay a few seconds longer. After an hour, she stood with a foot cocked, her eyes half-closed, clearly bored with the whole process. By now, I was sitting on her for five or ten minutes at a time, petting and talking to her. Occasionally, I would ask her to give to a light pressure on a rein, which again, she knew well. A hundred times we did it. Left and then right, get off and back on. Only one baby snake at a time. Then Piñata sighed and suddenly moved forward. Fear sluiced through me. This was it. I clutched the horn with both hands to stop myself from dragging at the reins. She'd told me I could sit up here, not give her any orders. She ambled around the pen, and slowly my muscles relaxed. She wasn't going to buck me off. We had passed a milestone. I just didn't know which one.

By the end of the next day, Piñata and I were in the big arena. She even loped, and when I felt her smooth power, I knew I'd not been wrong. This mare had talent. Somewhere, in the back of my mind, Merle's voice cautioned me. Today, you'll make an unbreakable contract. You will never push beyond the fear she is capable of handling. But her fear was gone. I laughed with the delight of success. I had her trust. And that's when she bucked me off.

# Chapter 30

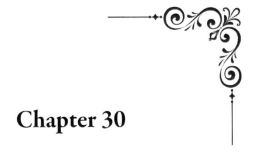

The two-hundred-mile trip from Sturgis back to Miles City gave Frederick ample opportunity to plan for the evening meeting with agent, Pete Sardinha. Trent waved from the kitchen as he walked into the Spur.

"Hey, come in here for a minute."

Frederick pushed through the batwing doors and stood a respectful distance from the huge grill.

"Tell me, what's going on with Dina? Do I need to find a new girl?"

Frederick sighed. "Trent, I can't tell you how crazy this is. All I can say is that this isn't her fault. Can you manage until the end of the week?"

"I guess so. But after that I have to hire somebody else, not that I want to. Dina's great help, but I need her here."

"You and I both know that's what she wants as well. I promise. Three more days. Then, she'll either be back, or you can go ahead and fill the vacancy. Is that okay?"

Trent shrugged. "Yeah. I'll manage. Susan can handle it for a while."

"Thanks, and I owe you a big favor. I'll spread the word about your culinary abilities to the ends of the earth. I'll even take a chance and eat here." Frederick chuckled at Trent's scowl.

"Get out of my kitchen," Trent growled, but the twinkle in his eye took any sting out of his order.

"I'm gone—at least out of your kitchen, but I really do have to eat your cooking tonight."

Frederick snickered at Trent's testy reply. He turned in time to watch the front door open and close. A slight, dark-haired man stood in the entry while his eyes swept the restaurant. He never moved until he spotted Frederick. Both nodded an acknowledgment. The man strolled toward the weathered-wood greeting desk where credit-card scanners fought for space with menus and various other restaurant necessities. Susan smiled and ushered him to a table—or tried to.

"May I sit over there?" He pointed toward a table at the back, the same one Frederick and Dina had used.

"Certainly." Susan set a menu in front of him and took his drink order.

"That man will join me." He pointed at Frederick.

Susan pursed her lips, displeasure scrawled over her finely chiseled face.

Pete glanced up in time to see her disapproval as Frederick slipped into the chair on the other side of the table. He reached across and shook Frederick's hand.

"Frederick, great to see you again."

"You too. How's life these days in the CIA?"

"Same as always. How come that waitress doesn't like you?"

"Hmm." Frederick fidgeted in his chair. "We both admire a young lady, if perhaps not in the same way. I suspect she feels I am not quite suitable, and also that I may be responsible for some of the young lady's troubles. She may be right as to suitability, though I plead innocence in regard to her trouble."

Pete gave him a sharp glance. Frederick pretended not to notice, but the message in Pete's eyes had been unmistakable. A romantic entanglement?

Frederick stared at the ceiling. He couldn't agree more, but it changed nothing, and tomorrow he was going to see her—if he had to crawl through five miles of sagebrush on his belly.

Susan returned to take their orders. Frederick ordered the prime rib, baked potato, Thousand Island dressing.

Pete looked over the menu. "Double it, except I want French fries and Italian."

Alone once more, Pete leaned forward. "It's good to see you. How long have you been in Miles City?"

"About two weeks. Had to come see how my old Gram is doing."

"And?"

"She's going strong. Eighty-nine years young. I just took her over to Sturgis to see her sister."

"That's great. She'll enjoy that."

The conversation stopped while both men scanned the newest customers at the door. A few seconds later, Pete turned back and spoke. "So—what's this about al-Qaida? And where did the information come from?"

> Frederick drummed his index finger on the wooden table top and stared across the room. "The girl."
>
> Pete leaned back in his chair and crossed his arms.
>
> Frederick stopped tapping. "Look, what you're thinking is obvious. Forget about whatever relationship you think I might have with her. She has overwhelming evidence that al Qaida is inside the country."

"I'm listening."

"Nobody knows better than you guys what a disaster our Southern border has been. All of us worried about what could occur if Hamas, al-Qaida, or any of a half-dozen other Muslim radical groups decided to take advantage of our porous Mexican border, and so far, Washington has done nothing to plug the holes. Now, what we feared has happened."

Pete played with the straw in his Coke while he surveyed the nearly empty restaurant. "Why weren't we involved—before they got into the country?"

"Maybe you are."

The straw froze in his hand. "You're saying we have people who know about this?"

Frederick tapped nervously at the table top with an index finger. "I'm almost sure of it, though I can't prove it.

We did have evidence that suggests al-Qaida has smuggled in enough Cesium-137 to make a dirty bomb."

Pete leaned back and raised an eyebrow. "What do you mean you *had* evidence?

"The papers the girl took from her father's office are now gone, stolen from the girl's basement suite."

Pete's mouth tightened, his eyes never leaving Frederick's face. "So what was their target?"

"Originally, Denver. There's reason to believe that's no longer the case."

Pete twirled his straw again and stared at his glass while Susan put down their plates. "Interesting. Why would they have picked Denver?"

Frederick shrugged. "Does it matter? The important thing is that we discover the new location." He leaned forward. "Pete, you've been down this trail before. What will they use for a detonator?"

Pete rubbed at the dark stubble on his jaw. "I would guess plain old nitrogen fertilizer. It's inexpensive, and easy to get. TNT would also work. With the fission material you say they have, detonator material is not a problem. Either one will scatter the Cesium over a significant area, enough to cause panic and deaths far worse than nine-eleven." Pete picked away at his salad. "Any identification on the bomb maker?"

"The document identified the man only as Ibrahim."

Pete's hand paused halfway to his mouth, the succulent prime rib poised on the end of his fork. "You're ruining a really good steak", he growled. He set his fork back on the plate in front of him. "Though there are about a million Muslims with that name, I think we have to presume this is important enough that it could be *the* Ibrahim. His last name is Asiri. He's the best bomb technician al-Qaida has, and this is big enough they may have shipped him over."

"I can't believe they would take that chance. Wouldn't they just train a few goons to follow instructions and—"

Pete shook his head. "I doubt they would. This isn't the same as putting a few wing-nuts through a third-rate flight school until they can jockey an airliner into a building. If they've spirited Asiri into the country, they're deadly serious. That also gives us a pretty good idea of the detonator. His specialty is pentaerythritol tetranitrate."

Frederick leaned back and crossed one leg over the other. "Good old PETN?"

"Yeah, actually it's the same stuff that fried the underwear bomber's privates. That was a botched Asiri job—fortunately for us and everyone on that plane. Since then, Al-Qaida has kept him safely tucked away in Yemen with one of Osama bin Laden's lieutenants."

Frederick eyed the door as Susan seated another group of diners, while his index finger again tapped a nervous pattern. "Why would they use PETN. It's great stuff, but it's hard to transport and dangerous to handle. Why wouldn't they go for something simpler? Sure, nitrogen fertilizer is bulkier, but it's less volatile and doesn't leave a trail. Any farmer can buy it, and when you have a combination as valuable as Cesium-137 and Ibrahim Asiri, keeping an operation simple is important."

Pete shifted forward in his chair. "You're right, but if they actually sent Asiri over here, I'm betting he's going to use the same ingredient he's used in the last three operations."

Susan scurried over and cleared their plates. "Can I tempt you gentlemen with dessert?"

Both declined. Frederick met her hostile eyes and grinned. "Just the bill, please—and compliments to the cook." If she cared that much for Dina, he decided he liked her despite what she thought of him.

Pete pulled out his wallet. Frederick snatched the bill off the tray. "Nope. Miles City is my town. This one's on me."

Pete shrugged. "If you insist. I'm sure the agency would be glad—"

Frederick waved Pete's protest away. "Let me buy the steak. Just give me some direction—better yet, take it out of my hands."

"Tell me about your source?"

Frederick took a deep breath. This would be tricky.

"Dina is the daughter of a small-time smuggler who owns a ranch at Agua Prieta—across from Douglas, Arizona. His name is Ricardo Rodriguez, and I think if you talk to the right people in your organization, they're going to have something on him."

"What makes you think that?"

Frederick held up a hand. "It's only a hunch. I've met the man once. Mostly, we talked about his daughter, but there's no doubt in my mind the guy's an agent. He's working for somebody."

"Oh, no." Pete's eyebrows reached for the sky. "And you're having an affair—?"

"You know better." Frederick's lips formed a hard line. "The young lady rents a suite from my grandmother. I have a high level of respect for her, and if she would have me, that could indeed lead to . . . well, other commitments, but so far, she's kept me at arms' length."

Pete waved Frederick's protestations away. "Fair enough—just checking."

Frederick handed a credit card to Susan, who ran it through her portable machine. He punched in his security number and added a generous tip. She deserved it, and besides, it might raise her opinion of himd.

Pete winked at Susan as she turned to leave. Frederick made an effort not to grimace while he tried to remember whether Pete was between his second and third, or third and fourth wives.

For the next half-hour, Frederick filled in every detail about Dina, her father, and the stolen papers. By the end of the conversation, the responsibility for finding the Cesium had passed from his hands to the CIA. They could battle with the FBI over jurisdiction and protocol.

At 7:35, the two men strolled toward the front doors. On the sidewalk, they paused, hands tucked in the pockets of their jackets to ward off the chill desert wind.

"Thanks, Frederick. I owe you. I hope somebody in the agency has their finger on this. This will shatter some cherished perceptions of America's safety."

"Pete, you're welcome. This is dangerous, and I don't envy you guys."

Pete scowled. Worry etched over every line of his face as they strolled to the side lot where he had parked. "Yeah, I hear you. Let's have a quick coffee in the morning—say, 6:30 in the dining room at the hotel?"

"I'll be there."

They shook hands, and Frederick walked to the back lot where he'd parked the Mustang. Again, there was no sign of the gray Audi. Since Dina had disappeared, the two al-Qaida men seemed to have gone underground. He unlocked the car and idled toward the street. Suddenly, the rental car in front of him erupted in a fiery yellow volcano. He slammed the shifter into Park, jumped out and sprinted toward the blazing inferno of gasoline and metal. Thirty feet from the car, the heat drove him back.

"Pete!" His tortured voice, consumed by the searing flames did nothing for the inert body inside the molten inferno now halfway into the street. Pietro Mattias Sardhina had embarked on a journey to a place far different than the planet called Earth.

Numbly, Frederick trudged back to his car, fumbled the key into the ignition, u-turned, and bounced over the curb at the back of the Spur. Tumbleweeds and discarded coffee cups crunched under his tires as he idled through a vacant lot. Hanging around would only complicate matters. Doug would still be looking for him, and he wasn't ready to face that. Far bigger issues must be addressed first.

A tentacle of fear churned through Frederick's veins, not for himself, but for Dina. Had Ibrahim Asiri already slipped into the United States? Was he here in Miles City? The fear, quickly replaced by burning anger spread like volcanic lava to every muscle and bone in his body. Whoever had done this knew their trade. Mercury fuses weren't complicated, but they were too technical for most garden-variety terrorists. This had been the work of a craftsman. When Pete's car had dropped from the parking lot to the pavement, the mercury bubble had shifted enough to close the contacts. This may have been a test-run, a warning. Whoever had killed Pete Sardinha would be preparing for bigger game, which meant—there was no time to lose.

# Chapter 31

Piñata and I spent day after day building bridges of trust—and smashing them. Her whole life with humans had been one big disaster after another. Everything I thought she should learn, she already knew, once I got past the fear. That's where everything slowed to a crawl. Regaining her trust had to be taken a baby step at a time. Often, the old panic would explode through her body, and though she never bucked again, she often threatened to turn into an uncontrollable runaway. When she grabbed the bit and ran, her ears flattened against her neck, and I realized I'd pushed too hard, broken our contract. After spending hours calming her down, we moved back to the level where she could handle her fear.

By the end of the week, we'd progressed to spending time in the surrounding hills, trying to deepen the level of trust. She understood what I wanted. Somewhere in her past she had spent time with an excellent trainer, but then something happened that blew her mind into a thousand twisted pieces.

I had not seen Frederick since the night he'd dropped me off at the ranch. Once, I'd tried to call him, but he never answered, and I didn't dare try again. He'd warned me not to use a phone—for any reason. Bud and Lorie had been gracious beyond belief, but I chafed under the enforced confinement. Even though Lorie had helped me immensely with Piñata's training, I couldn't stay here forever. It was time to move on.

Frederick must have read my mind, because that afternoon he drove into the yard. Instead of the Mustang, he was driving my pickup, pulling the single horse trailer behind, which seemed a good sign.

I eased the mare down to a walk and watched him stride into the arena. My heart did a little flip, which forced a big smile onto my face. I'd intended to show my displeasure at being left here so long, but I was so glad to see him the frown wouldn't stick.

"Looks like you might have a barrel horse." He grinned up at me as I stopped Piñata in front of him.

"It's too early to tell yet, but every day, she loses more of her fear." I dropped the reins on her neck. "And, it's about time you showed up. Do the pickup and trailer mean what I hope it does?"

"No, but I wanted you to have your saddle and gear. When it's safe, which shouldn't be long, you can just load up and come home."

I stepped off the mare and led her out of the arena. "How much longer?"

"Give me a few days, just to make sure."

I slipped the bit out of Piñata's mouth, haltered her, then tied her to the hitching rail. "Have you talked to Trent?"

"Yes, several times. Don't worry, you still have a job."

"I can't believe he hasn't fired me and hired somebody more dependable. I'll have to work for him the rest of my life, just to make up for all I've put him through."

Frederick chuckled. "Well, he is a little exasperated, but right now your absence is one of his smaller problems."

"Why, what's wrong?"

Frederick sobered. "Last night, a CIA man was killed as he pulled out of the parking lot."

"Them?" Fear trickled through my veins.

"Yeah—a car bomb." Frederick swallowed and looked away, but not before I saw the lines of tension around his mouth. His next words were hard, and he spat them out like loaded shotgun shells. "He was a good friend of mine. One way or another, they're going down."

"So, there will be lots of CIA guys in town now. It should be safe to go home?"

"No! Wait a couple more days—just to be sure."

If he hadn't snapped at me, I wouldn't have acted so much like a spoiled teenager. Angry words boiled over. "Hey. Before I met you I had a life, Frederick Roseman. Is this compulsion to control everyone around you part of your Protestant heritage?"

Frederick's face stilled, then darkened with building anger. "I think control fits more with your Catholic dogma. Your church tells you what to do and how to do it from the moment you're born to the day you die." His voice cut like an ice-coated machete. "Just in case you haven't noticed, my life was also much simpler before you came along. Please, do as you think best. I'm sorry for meddling in your affairs. It won't happen again." He whirled and stalked to the house.

I wanted to call after him, to tell him I was sorry, that I hadn't meant what I'd so foolishly said. I hadn't even asked him if anybody else had been hurt in the explosion, or if there was any damage to the Spur. My mouth opened. I stuttered a few words, but he was already too far away, and the breath escaped from my lungs without making my vocal cords work. Stubborn and stupid pride had made me look immature, and my petulant outburst had probably cost more than I was prepared to pay.

A few minutes later, Frederick and Bud drove toward town. I stomped to the house kicking rocks out of the way like they were al-Qaida agents. Why had I argued with him? I had everything I could want here, and *he* had made it happen. Nevertheless, I tore blouses off hangars and stuffed them into my suitcase. When I'd finished, I sat and tried to formulate a plan. I thought about going back to Mrs. Riddler's. Wouldn't that be fun. I would have to walk right by the upstairs living room window. Worse, he might be on the front step. I wouldn't be able to ignore the carefully masked hurt in his eyes, which meant I would have to apologize. That would serve me right. Perhaps the next time, I'd put my brain in gear before my big mouth.

Upstairs, the automatic garage door opened and I heard Lorie's car tires squeak on the concrete floor. I ran up and met her. She had a load of groceries in her arms.

"Hi. Can I help?"

"Sure. There're two more bags in the back seat."

"I'll get them." I set them on the counter in the kitchen.

Lorie opened the fridge, took out a soft drink and strolled over to the living room picture window. "How's Piñata coming along?"

I slid onto one of the kitchen counter bar stools. "Today? Really good. She seemed to turn a corner. It's like she let go of a huge part of the fear inside her. She's starting to trust me."

Lorie's face lit up. "Dina, that's wonderful. Do you think she has the speed?"

I nodded. "She might. We were up on the flat this morning—you know, that big one over by the Bar O Ranch?"

"Sure, it's about two miles long."

"Well, I've always been afraid to let her really run. The most we've done is a very controlled gallop, but today I didn't hold her back. If it hadn't been so fun, I would have almost been afraid. She is faster, I think, than my Chiquita mare."

Lorie took off her sunglasses and absently tapped the frame against her teeth. "She's that good?"

I shrugged. "It's difficult to tell unless you're clocking her, or you have another horse running beside you, but she felt like she had wings."

"Oh, that is so exciting, to think you found this crazy bucking horse and made something out of her." She patted my arm. "I'm impressed."

"Well, we're not there yet."

"You're going to be. I've watched her, and I agree. She's special. Hey, how about a celebration. I'm taking the day off tomorrow. Want to go shopping in Billings?"

Momentarily, I considered whether to ask Frederick if that was safe, but after our stormy parting I was sure he would tell me to do whatever I wanted—because he couldn't give a rip.

"I'd love to go. I have enough days riding Piñata that she won't forget anything now. In fact, after what I put her through today, it may do her good to have a day off." I pushed the safety issue to the back of my mind. After all, we weren't going to go anywhere near Miles City.

"Great. We'll spend the day shopping and do lunch. Oh, I almost forgot to ask. How did your truck and trailer get here?"

"Frederick."

Lorie frowned. "I thought it wasn't safe to bring it."

I rolled my eyes and shrugged. "Apparently, everything's changed."

"Does that have to do with the big explosion in front of the Spur Bar?"

"Apparently, it does."

"Part of Main Street was still cordoned off this morning. Miles City never had anything this crazy." Lorie leaned against the counter and slurped the last swallow of Coke through her straw. "So let me guess. Bud took Frederick back to town?"

I shrugged as if I couldn't care less. "As far as I know. They left here together."

"Oh-h. It's that way." She gave me a sharp glance. My lack of Frederick knowledge had been self-explanatory.

# Chapter 32

Frederick clenched his teeth, trying to concentrate as Bud rambled on about the cattle market and the dry conditions on his upper range. Any other time, he would have listened attentively, but all he could think about was Dina. Why had he been so pig-headed? He should have backed off, instead of making the stupid, insensitive remarks about letting her live her own life. What had he said? "My life was much simpler before you came along." Yeah, it sure was. In fact, it had been downright dreary. And now it would be that way again. Hope you like it, Freddy boy, because, she's gone. The thought sent panic rushing through every vein. Some things were negotiable. Dina wasn't. He couldn't imagine going back to whatever existence he'd led without her.

"You didn't even hear me, did you?"

"What was that? Sorry, my mind was elsewhere."

Bud snickered. "You're finished, aren't you? That dark-haired little Dina has got you good."

"What are you talking about?" Frederick growled and stared out the side window.

"Listen, my friend. I don't know what happened back there, but I'd bet ten head of cows she told you to shove off."

"You better not bet because you might lose your cows."

"I doubt it." Bud punched him playfully in the arm. "Get over it. She's a sweet little gal. We've enjoyed having her, and she can stay with us anytime. But Fred, there's about three-billion other women in the world, give or take a few. Don't hang your hat on Dina if it isn't going to work."

"Uh-h sure. I'll do that, because I know I'm getting stellar advice from the guy who all through high school would have jumped into a pool of liquid cow manure to even kiss Lorie Nygard's hand. Three-billion other women in the world? Yeah, that's classic. I'll really think about that, Bud Linder, just before I tell you you're a senile hypocrite."

Bud laughed and held up a hand in surrender as they pulled into Gram's driveway. "Okay, I have a short memory. Go for it. You can come and cry on ol' Bud's shoulder after she breaks your heart."

"Not going to happen," Frederick growled as he closed the pickup door and stood with his arm propped on the sill. "Anyhow, thanks for being there, for your hospitality to Dina—everything. You and Lorie are special, and I appreciate what you've done. I don't even know anybody else I could dump a guest on for weeks on end."

"Oh, get out of here. That's what friends are for." Bud's brow wrinkled. "But Fred, one other thing. Lorie says Dina is staunch Catholic. If this was to work between you two, how are you going to handle that?"

Frederick stepped back and ran his hand through his hair. "Bud, I don't know. I hoped there would be a way, but like everything else, that hasn't gone well either."

Bud stared at him for a moment. When he answered, his voice matched Frederick's disappointment. "So, I keep my cows? Well, it might be for the best." He backed out of the driveway. Frederick waved, then swatted a mosquito as he watched Bud turn onto the street.

Before walking up the steps to the house, Frederick surveyed the sidewalk, the windows, each detail of the old building. Before he touched the door, he peered at the lock. No marks, nothing that looked like a forced entry. The back door also showed no signs of tampering. He fitted the key into the lock and eased it to the right. As the key turned, the cell phone at his hip vibrated. His heart skipped two beats as he clawed at the holster. When he had the phone in his hand, he walked into the yard. "Yeah."

"Frederick?"

"Yes." His heart rate returned to normal as he shoved the house key back into his pocket.

"Don Barker, CIA. I spoke to you this morning."

"Yeah?"

"Would you be available for a meeting sometime this evening?" The raspy voice sounded like thirty years of unfiltered Camel cigarettes.

"When?"

"Whenever it suits you?"

"Let me grab a bite. Where do you want to meet?

"You know the town. Where would you recommend?"

"In twenty minutes, I'll be in the park on North 7th Street. What do you look like? Never mind. I'll recognize you."

"It won't be me. It will be Thomas Mann." The line went dead. Frederick snapped his phone shut. Granted, Pete's death was tragic. Agents usually didn't get blown up, at least not inside the country, but that still wasn't enough to call in the heavy artillery from McLean Headquarters. Only one man in the agency had more authority than Thomas Mann. This could be a very interesting meeting.

Frederick went back to the door and cautiously pushed it open. Nothing. Had al-Qaida moved on? If they had, where had they gone? The paper Dina had taken from her father's office had made it clear. Denver was the target. But nobody knew the timeline. And that was critical.

He wolfed down a ham and mustard sandwich, shrugged into a worn sports jacket and walked south toward the park. A completely secure place for an intelligence meeting didn't exist, no matter the operation. But a public park at dusk with an open field at his back and the sun behind him would hamper the vision of anyone approaching from the street. That probably was as good as it would ever get.

Ten minutes later, he sat on a bench as far away from the street as he could get. The newspaper he'd brought held no interest, but newspapers were convenient props.

Promptly at seven-fifteen, a muscular black man with thinning gray hair stepped out of a car on the far side of the street. He might as well have had a badge branded across his chest in thirty-six-point font stating he was big-city CIA. Frederick scowled. Why was Thomas Mann here? He scanned the park as the man approached. Two agents strolled back and forth on the sidewalk. There would be at least one more behind him. He didn't need to turn around and look to know that. Frederick folded the newspaper. No need to play hide and seek. Thomas settled on the end of the bench and scanned the park. When he was comfortable with the setup, he turned. "Good evening, Frederick. You're looking well."

"Thank you. And you as well, sir." Frederick momentarily considered whether to reach across and shake hands. He didn't. Neither did Thomas. Security trumped friendship or camaraderie.

Thomas jammed his hands deeper into the pockets of his jacket. "Pete Sardinha came to see you. Why?"

Small talk was over. Frederick replied carefully. "I stumbled onto some information that seemed vital to national security. I trusted Pete to take it to the right people."

"And?"

"Al-Qaida has smuggled enough Cesium-137 into the country to make a sizable dirty bomb." From the corner of his eye, Frederick scrutinized Thomas's face. Other than a noticeable tightening of his lips and facial muscles, no emotion played over his stoic features.

"How did you access this information?"

"In a roundabout way, from a small-time border smuggler by the name of Ricardo Rodriguez."

Thomas's jaw imperceptibly tightened at the name.

"I became acquainted with his daughter after she rented a suite from my grandmother.

"Here?"

"Yes."

The crickets had started their nightly mating calls before Frederick finished the details of Dina's kidnapping and the stolen paper she had taken from her father's office.

Thomas listened politely, then sighed. "And you say they continued their surveillance until three days ago?"

"Yes. Tuesday, the car, a gray Audi disappeared."

Thomas chewed at the knuckle of his index finger, then spoke. "You are involved with the young lady?"

"We have become friends."

"Your reputation is impeccable. I will not question your judgment." He sighed. "What you have told me tonight about al-Qaida we already know. If someone outside the agency had to find out, I'm glad it was you. If it had been another law enforcement group, or . . . well, we don't need those complications. I talked to Adrian earlier this evening. He felt you should remain a part of this operation, that is . . . if you agree." He peered across the bench, his dark features further muddled by the darkness that now surrounded them. "Your company has made life easier for us in a hundred ways. There probably will never be a time when we won't depend on undercover people to take care of vital American interests." Thomas reached inside his coat and pulled out a badge. "Sometimes though, it is helpful to have official status." He held it toward Fredrick. "This can remove obstacles and at times protect against consequences. Consider yourself CIA on this one."

Frederick reluctantly slipped the badge into his shirt pocket.

"You will continue to work independently. Just keep me informed."

"As you wish." Frederick nodded, barely able to cover his distaste. The badge would hardly be a help, and the price tag was a veiled attempt to buy loyalty. After tonight, the whole alphabet soup of agencies would weigh in. The FBI, because it was within the continental U.S., ICE because somebody had probably smuggled a bomb that technically could be construed as contraband, and of course the DEA because drugs or some other illegal substance might be present. It was important for the teams to have picked their players before the war started.

Thomas waited for the blasting bass from a kid's car stereo to fade down the nearby street before he again spoke. "Ricardo is dead."

Frederick sat straighter, glad the darkness masked the sudden shock. "How do you know?"

"Because he's one of ours."

Frederick thought back to the meeting in Bisbee, Ricardo's slim, almost feminine hands and hooded eyes. Then there were the puzzling words, vague hints that there was more to this man than he was willing to show. "Many things in life are not as they seem. I love my daughter." Ricardo had pushed away from the table and held out the soft, manicured fingers. Frederick recalled the jolt of recognition when he'd glimpsed the fleeting moment of steel in Ricardo's eyes that moments before had been vacuous, sardonic, and empty. He'd suspected, but now he understood. That day, he'd met one of the greatest agents the CIA had ever produced.

Frederick's jaw muscles tensed with a building anger. "What happened?"

"He delivered the Cesium to Henderson, Nevada. As soon as his contacts took delivery, it appears they killed him and dumped his body down an abandoned mine shaft. We have rescue people at the site, but so far they've been unable to recover his body."

"And his family? Dina? When will you notify—?"

"We have a large quantity of Cesium-137 floating around that needs to be secured. The news will have to wait, at least for now."

Frederick bit off the answer he wanted to give. "Fair enough, as long as it's soon."

Thomas glared at one of the agents who had moved too close. Anger sharpened his voice. "It's all so frustrating. Ricardo worked undercover for years. He was an absolute genius, and we had no warning anything was wrong." He rose stiffly to his feet, hunched his open coat tighter around his shoulders and buttoned it. "Believe me, if there had been any hint, we'd have never let him go to that abandoned mine site. We'd have secured the Cesium and stopped the operation."

Frederick took a deep breath of the chilly night air. Whatever had happened could not be changed. "If I can be of any further assistance—"

"Ricardo's killing was unexpected. The Cesium was not. Thomas's voice failed to filter the irascible anger in his eyes. "I like to think we can trace a package at least as well as FedEx, but I do want you to stay involved." The palm-sized screen in Thomas's hand suddenly lit up. He peered at the message. The blue light briefly illuminated the deep tracks that radiated from his eyes and mouth, the cumulative war wounds of a thousand wrenching decisions that meant life or death for agents around the world.

"The package seems to be on schedule." Thomas held out his hand. "Thank you again. Call me if there's anything else critical. Otherwise, we'll talk in the morning." He handed Frederick a card with a number scrawled on the back. For a few seconds he blended with the night before the lamp on the other side of the street picked up his moving figure.

Frederick watched as Thomas slid into the back seat of the waiting car at the edge of the park. He wondered what "staying involved," meant. This was technically FBI turf. However, nobody in Washington would protest if the CIA carried the ball to the finish line—as long as there were no complications.

When Frederick walked out of the park and back toward Gram's house, he instinctively held to the back side, far from the lights that illuminated the street. At the far edge of the park, he paused in the shadow of a small grove of juvenile aspen while he carefully surveyed each car in the surrounding neighborhood. Finally, he shrugged. The whole mess was now out of his hands. Federal agencies would have downtown Denver sewed up tight enough a pregnant mouse wouldn't squeeze into town. They would take no chances.

Frederick's soft-soled shoes made no noise as he stepped out of the grove and onto the sidewalk, but a nagging premonition continued to dog each step as he made his way to Gram's. He'd forgotten something. A piece of the puzzle had escaped him. How he wished he could sit and talk this over with Adrian. He padded along the darkened street, every sense alert to danger. As he neared the house, the answer came to him. Al-Qaida had left town because the documents Dina had taken were now unimportant. Denver was no longer the target.

# Chapter 33

Lorie and I left the ranch before eight on our shopping trip to Billings. Bud grumbled about how many calves he'd have to sell to pay for this crazy shopping trip. Despite his griping, as we went out the door, he planted a tender kiss on Lorie's lips and told her to have a good time. Surreptitiously, I studied every move they made. How they related to each other was important, though if someone had asked why, I couldn't have enunciated a reasonable answer. It wasn't as if I had any future with Frederick. That egotistical control freak and I were not on speaking terms.

During the two-hour trip to Billings, Lorie quizzed me about what it was like living on a ranch in Sonora. It was fun talking about home, but of course, I didn't tell her about my father's other profession. That would not enhance my standing with her, or for that matter, anyone in this ranching community.

"And your family—they're Catholic as well?"

"Yes, I grew up with the church being an important part of my life. We attended Mass every Sunday."

"Bud would like it if we did that. Occasionally, we do. Other times we attend a little non-denominational church out in the country."

"What's non-denominational?"

"We're not affiliated with anybody—you know, like Baptists or Presbyterians. We just don't think belonging to an organized group is all that important."

"So, what do you do when you have an argument over scripture or some church sacrament—say, like communion?"

"We get together and discuss the issue, then we pray about it, and God gives us guidance."

"But what if you still can't agree?"

Lorie chuckled, then raised an eyebrow. "If the disagreement is serious enough, we have a church split and one more Protestant denomination. Ever since Martin Luther, we Protestants have a poor history of agreeing on Biblical issues. There is something to be said for having a final arbiter on church doctrine and discipline."

The miles passed almost too quickly. I hadn't made the effort to develop new friends, and it was fun to get to know Lorie better.

"So, you and Frederick seem to spend a lot of time together. Does that have a romantic side to it?" Lorie asked.

I sat with my hands in my lap, nervously rubbing my thumb against an index finger while I tried to verbalize what was in my heart. "Yes. It didn't begin that way, but now I care a lot about him—even if we're currently having a war."

"And what about your faith differences?"

"I'm not sure. Is that a big deal? It seems to work for you and Bud."

"Hmm. We're still married, and yes, we love each other deeply. If I had it to do over again, the same thing would happen, but if I knew then how much we would disagree on items of faith, I'm not sure I would have dated him."

"Why?"

"Because that man is wonderful. I would fall in love and marry him again. But our differences are part of the reason we haven't had children. We're still arguing whether they would be raised Catholic or Protestant. Bud is insistent that they would have to be baptized in the church. I'm not sure I could do that."

"I think Frederick and I could solve those church issues." The moment after the words rolled out of my mouth, a lead weight rolled around in the pit of my stomach. Would our ongoing arguments never end? What would that be like for a lifetime? No, it wouldn't be that way for us. Faith was an issue we had to work out, no different than who did the laundry, mowed the lawn, and dried the dishes, a housekeeping thing. True love could overcome those differences. But as the silence lengthened, and the white lines passed beneath the humming tires, I remembered Bud and Lorie's tender kiss at the door. It was plain to see they loved each other, but having different faiths hadn't worked. I glanced sideways at Lorie, at the firm set of her mouth, and knew she was mulling over her own marriage problems.

The thought of losing Frederick brought stinging tears. I loved him. If I hadn't known it before, I did now. We could do it. Surely he would see that I couldn't walk away from the church that formed the very core of who I was as a person.

As we neared Billings, the sugar beet fields and irrigated pastures that drew life from the meandering Yellowstone River gave way to the first subdivisions. Occasionally, I checked the rearview mirror. Nothing seemed unusual. No suspicious cars tailed us. As usual, Frederick had overreacted.

Twenty minutes later, we dived off the interstate and headed for the downtown shopping area. For an hour, we strolled through dress shops and clothing boutiques. After a couple hours, neither of us had found any clothes worth buying.

"Let's go to the Primrose Mall," Lorie said. "We can eat lunch, and then shop for another couple of hours before we have to head home."

"Sounds good." We packed our meager purchases into the trunk and drove the few blocks to the eighty-five-store mall. It was Saturday, and the parking lots were jammed. Eventually, we found a parking spot and rushed inside, Clothing and shoe stores slowed our progress, each one providing more shopping delights. A small Vietnamese restaurant seemed the perfect place for lunch. We found a quiet corner booth and talked clothes and shopping until we had stuffed ourselves with flavors of lemongrass and lime.

"How about Victoria's Secret next?" Lorie asked.

"Super. I love going there—when I can afford it." I grimaced. "That didn't used to be an issue, but now there's no more Papa's credit card."

Lorie laughed. "It seems you're adjusting well."

"That's only because I've been so busy. When we walk out of Victoria's Secret and my hands start shaking, you'll know I'm going through withdrawal." We both giggled while we made our way through the Saturday crowds toward the store. I soon realized they had everything I had ever found in Tucson. This would be hard. If I spent more than twenty-five dollars, I wouldn't be able to pay the rent. I doubted if Mrs. Riddler would accept some trumped-up excuse about having to buy new underwear.

When I walked to the till, the bill came to twenty-eight dollars and ninety-five cents. If I could go back to work, I could handle that small over-budget amount and still keep a roof over my head. I counted out the money to the cashier, then strolled out into the mall to wait for Lorie while she paid for the bras she'd bought. I glanced at my watch. Two thirty-five. Soon, we'd have to start for home. People streamed by, some with clear purpose, others shopping or ambling along, doing nothing more than killing time. A dark-complexioned man in a black leather jacket hurried past me. Quickly, I averted my eyes. His eyes left my face and flickered sensuously downward. Fire alarms clanged across my brain. A faint smile broke over his ebony-whiskered features as he slowed. The face seemed vaguely familiar. Was his sudden interest in me overblown testosterone, or was he one of *them*? An icy finger traced down my spine. I didn't know, but neither was I sticking around to find out.

"Dina, what's wrong?" Lorie stood in front of me.

"We . . . we have to get out of here. Now." The man's eyes turned toward me one last time before he disappeared into the crowd of shoppers. My hands shook as I clutched at my bag of merchandise, and it had nothing to do with credit card withdrawal.

# Chapter 34

Sleep wasn't an option, so Frederick paced the living room floor. If Denver was no longer the location, where was it? Thomas had said an hour ago that the Cesium had just crossed the Colorado border. Maybe, but he doubted it.

He scrolled through his contacts to Thomas's name, pulled up the CIA man's number on his phone and waited.

"Yeah."

"Frederick here. They removed your transmitter."

"Who said we had one?"

"Nobody, but you never would have sent that valuable a package without direct contact and supervision from Langley."

"Okay, so we did. What makes you think they found it?"

"Because they've left town. They're no longer interested in killing the girl."

"And the transmitter?"

"Oh, it's still going to Denver. The Cesium went somewhere else."

"Come down—no, I'll have a car pick you up. He'll be there in ten minutes."

When they escorted Frederick into the room, his eyes scanned the occupants. Two agents and Thomas sat at a conference table on the far side of the room.

Thomas nodded to him. "Frederick. Carla Monroe. She works out of our Minneapolis office." The Afro-American woman with the multiple shoulder-length braids stood and shook Frederick's hand. Thomas pointed to the other silent figure. "This is Bill Collins. Bill flew out from Langley." The short, blond man at the end of the table acknowledged Frederick's presence with a nod, then turned away.

"Okay, let's get started." Thomas flicked a switch and pointed to the screen on the wall. "This is where Ricardo delivered the Cesium." He stabbed at a point on the lower left of one of the pictures. It's an old mine northwest of Henderson, Nevada.

Frederick studied the group of photos. One of the closeups showed a few ramshackle buildings haphazardly grouped over a rock-strewn mountainside.

"Ricardo drove straight through from the Mexican border. We had good contact with him at all times. "Here." Thomas indicated a squat, sunbaked building. "Ricardo backed the SUV into this old shed. A half-hour later, another vehicle arrived. From the satellite photos, it appears to be a white Chevy Tahoe, the same make and model as Ricardo's. It also parked inside the shed. Within minutes, one of them left and headed back to Las Vegas, then hit I-15 east. An hour ago it turned on I-70 towards Denver. We have agents on it. Two men are with it, neither of them Ricardo. Nor did Ricardo appear with the other Tahoe which drove to the downtown Marriott in Henderson then also left on I-15. We immediately sent agents up to the mine."

"And he's there?"

Thomas nodded. "We're ninety percent sure they killed him and dumped his body down one of the abandoned mine shafts."

"And the vehicles?"

Carla turned in her chair. "Here, I can show you. Let's start with the Marriott parking lot. We even have drone photos."

Frederick stared at the parking lot picture. The lot contained a few scattered vehicles, but there was no white Chevy Tahoe.

"Twenty minutes ago, the transmitter put the first Tahoe twelve miles west of Grand Junction, Colorado, so we are still going with a Denver target." Thomas eyed Frederick, his whole body challenging the assumption that the bomb had disappeared.

"So, where's the second Tahoe?" Frederick asked.

Bill leaned back in his chair and pointed at the screen with the pen in his hand. "My guess is they dropped the assassin off at the Marriott. He then caught the hotel shuttle to the airport. He's already on a plane out of the country. I don't think it matters where that vehicle is at. Our focus should be the first, the one heading toward Denver."

Frederick scrutinized the detailed photos, ran a hand through his hair and turned away. Suddenly, he whirled and pointed at the top right-hand picture. "Zoom in as close as you can get on that one." The agent brought up the single picture. Thomas stared at him, before turning back to the screen. A clear top-view emerged of the white Tahoe in the Marriott parking lot. Frederick pointed a pen at the numbered stall. "Either that's a different vehicle or they changed parking spots. Before, it was in stall two-fifteen. Now, it's in two-sixteen. Scroll back. Let's look at every bit of footage since he pulled in there."

Carla fiddled with the mouse.

Thomas glared at the screen. "Go ahead. Say it. We're all thinking it anyhow."

Frederick resisted the urge to smile at Thomas' discomfort. "The camera will tell us what we need to know."

No one spoke as the next video image reeled through on the screen, verifying that the Tahoe had indeed parked in stall two-fifteen. Not only was two-sixteen empty, it had three orange traffic cones in front of it. Twenty minutes after the first Tahoe parked, another identical one pulled into the lot. A man stepped from the passenger side, removed the cones and parked beside the first one. Two men exited the newly arrived Tahoe. One of them transported an elongated suitcase with all the care of a newborn baby. After they'd transferred the extra luggage, they left the lot in the identical vehicle parked in two-fifteen.

Thomas growled softly and turned away. He paced the room while Frederick and the two agents stared at the screen. "The perfect shell game, a ruse I've used a hundred times, yet I fell for it." He turned away and wiped at his forehead. "How many thousands of people will die because I missed—"

"Sir, we need to stop the one vehicle you have tracked." Frederick continued to scrutinize the screen.

"I'm aware of that." Thomas's voice carried the causticity of too little sleep and too much stress. "Bill." He turned to the agent beside Frederick. "Make that happen. Hold those men in Grand Junction. We don't have time to fly them around the country. We'll interrogate them there. Do whatever you have to do to make them talk." He set his jaw and met the startled looks of the others in the room. "It's their constitutional rights against the lives of thousands. For that call, I take full responsibility."

No one spoke as Bill left to give the orders that would stop the two al-Qaida operatives.

Frederick walked to the four-inch slit some bureaucrat had thought sufficient for a window. For a moment he stared at the field across from the parking lot as his mind clicked through each possible scenario.

Thomas glanced at Frederick. "Give me your thoughts. Up to now, we've done everything wrong. Already, it's cost the life of an agent. We can't afford any more mistakes." He turned to Frederick. "You're still convinced the Cesium is not in the Denver-bound Tahoe?"

"Absolutely. The Cesium went somewhere else, which means it has disappeared."

Thomas swore under his breath. "Losing that package is not an option."

Carla swiveled her chair around and stared into the distance while she chewed a fingernail. "Let's do a grid."

Thomas glanced up at the wall clock. "It's midnight. That Tahoe left the Henderson Ramada parking lot around four, so they've had eight hours." He groaned. "They could be anywhere in a half-dozen states, but what if . . .?"

Frederick and Thomas locked eyes, both their minds following the same tack. Thomas shook his head. "No, we can't do it."

"Why? It's a Chevy Tahoe—probably new." Frederick's voice cracked across the silent room.

"The FBI already lost a case involving OnStar. The ninth circuit appeals court slapped their hands hard. If we do it . . .? No, we can't, but we do need plate numbers. Thomas peered at the screen. "Carla, can you get a license plate number off the screen?"

Carla shook her head. "It's doubtful." Her fingers tapped at the keyboard, changing the angle and distance. Seconds later, her mouse stopped. The three of them hunched toward the screen. A slight rise into the parking lot tipped the nose of the Tahoe up just enough to reveal a Nevada plate. The last three numbers were barely visible. Seven, six, six. Either the first digits had mud on them, or the picture quality was such that they were unreadable.

"So, gentlemen, we have something. We know it's a white Chevy Tahoe. Now, what year is it?"

Frederick pursed his lips. "Give me fifteen minutes." He punched in a phone number on his cell, looked at his watch and shrugged. "What good is a hometown if you can't call a car salesman buddy in the middle of the night?" He waited for an answer on the other end. Thomas and Carla listened to the one-sided conversation.

"Arnold, how's it going?"

"Yeah . . . yeah, I'm fine."

"Hey, glad you're still up. Got a quick question. What's the difference between a new Chevy Tahoe and last year's model?"

"No, I don't want to trade in my Mustang—at least not right now. And yes, I do know what time it is and that you've probably never sold a car after midnight on a Friday night."

"I know you'd give me a deal. When I make the move, you're my man—absolutely."

"The bumpers are different? Like how?"

"That's enough. I just needed to know . . . yeah, okay. Lunch, but not this week. I'll call you in the next few days to set up a time—for sure. Good talking to you again."

Frederick snapped the phone shut and slipped it into its case. "It's this year's model. The trim is a little different from last year, and so is the bumper design." He pointed to the computer screen. "Yes, that's definitely it."

Thomas was already on the phone. He paced around the room as he waited for the call to connect. "Seth? Thomas here. Get a hold of somebody in our Las Vegas office. I want the agent in charge there to call me within the next twenty minutes. Here's the number." Thomas rattled off the Miles City Sheriff's Office phone number and extension.

Ten minutes later, the phone rang. Thomas punched the speakerphone button and picked up the handset.

"Thomas Mann here."

"This is Ethan Chaudhry in Las Vegas."

"Thanks for returning my call, Ethan. I need you to run a trace on every white Chevy Tahoe in Nevada with a plate number ending in seven, six, six. How soon can you get back to me?"

"Give me forty-five minutes, sir. I could do it faster, but the late hour . . ."

"Yes, I understand. I will wait at this number."

"We'll get on it. Any idea of the year?"

"New—this year's model."

"No problem. I'll be back to you within the hour."

"Thank you." Thomas set the phone down and collapsed into the office chair in front of the desk. "Any ideas?"

Frederick stared out at the pavement. Moths flitted around the streetlight at the entrance to police headquarters. No other movement broke the stillness. Miles City had long since turned in for the night.

"What if it isn't a conventional bomb?" Frederick's question permeated the room as if he'd breached one of the social graces.

"You have a different theory?" Carla's voice was testy.

"Not yet. But I think it could be beneficial to examine whatever presumptions we're relying on." He shrugged.

Thomas eyed each of them warily before he spoke. "Let's wait and see what DMV in Nevada gives us."

Twenty-five minutes later, the desk phone rang. "Thomas here."

"Sir, we have seventy-three white Tahoe's with those specs. Three of them have plates with numbers ending in seven, six, six. Two of those were sold in Clark County. That's Las Vegas. The other one was bought in Reno." Ethan rattled off the plate numbers for all three. "Is that sufficient?"

"Absolutely. We can run with it from here. But stand by or have somebody available. I may need to get hold of you again before morning."

Frederick watched Thomas slump lower into his chair. With so many unanswered questions, did they still have time? Was the target now Las Vegas or some other close western city? If it was, would they detonate the bomb as people arrived for work in the downtown area? That seemed likely. He glanced at the black and white wall clock. Nearly two a.m., which meant they might only have a few hours. And the toughest hurdle was still ahead.

Frederick stopped pacing and shoved his hands into the pockets of his windbreaker. "Are you going to call them?"

Thomas tapped a pen on the edge of the desk. "The minute we bring in the FBI, the war will start. They'll want to know why they haven't been informed. This is inside the country—their turf."

Frederick tapped a finger on the tabletop. "Onstar is the only hope we have."

Thomas's shoulders slumped. "They will demand control of the whole operation, even if they don't have squat for information. They're about cops and robbers," he growled. "All they know is, 'slam 'em against the wall and put the cuffs on.'" He stood and kicked the chair away. "But we don't have a choice."

Frederick stared silently at the computer screen, still zeroed in on the plate numbers of the missing Chevy Tahoe. He waited for the CIA man's decision.

Thomas paced around the room, then dialed a number. Frederick watched him punch the privacy button. "Carl? Thomas Mann here."

"I'm well aware of the time in Virginia, but I wanted to talk to you rather than someone on the duty desk. We have a situation where we need to bring in your people. It's one of our long-term operations that started offshore. Al-Qaida—with a dirty bomb."

"Yes, that's what I said. They are already in the country—apparently with enough Cesium to do the job."

Thomas's next audible sigh needed no explanation. "Is it productive to argue jurisdiction at two in the morning, or do we move forward?"

"No, I'm not giving you control, but I will share everything we have. We need to find the vehicle with the radioactive material. It's a Chevy Tahoe equipped with OnStar."

"I know all about the ninth circuit appellate judge, but there isn't another way. Can we work together on this?"

"Neither of us have any choice. How soon can you get your people on it?"

Frederick listened as the second highest bureaucrat in the CIA rattled off the vehicle identification number and the last three numbers on the license plate. Whether Thomas liked it or not, the FBI was now involved. Division of responsibility was secondary. The important thing was to find the Cesium.

Thomas slipped the receiver into the cradle, his hand immobile while he focused on the desk. Frederick waited, his arms crossed. Carla stared at the screen, trying to get a better shot of the Tahoe east of Denver.

Thomas wearily sighed, and pulled out his cell. Again, Frederick tried to follow the one-sided conversation.

"Did you find him yet?"

"You're sure he's dead?"

"How deep is the shaft?"

"Okay. Get a civil team to help—do whatever is necessary. Call me when you know anything definite." Thomas snapped the phone shut and gestured with it as his weary voice crossed the room. "It's two hundred and eighty feet to the bottom, and the shaft is caving in on their rescue people. They may not be able to get anybody down to bring up Ricardo's body."

Carla leaned back in her chair. Thomas continued to stare at the screen. "I can't get a good picture of the occupants of the Denver-bound vehicle, but there are still at least two of them."

Thomas scowled, clearly displeased with the slowness of the apprehension. He stepped away from the screen and turned to Frederick. "There's no need to stay longer. Come back in the morning. By then, we'll either have news—or it will all be over."

Frederick nodded, understanding the curt dismissal. Seeing the interagency rivalry play out through the rest of the night would make for frustrating theater. Having an outsider in the room would only make matters worse. Ten minutes later, one of Thomas's security detail dropped him at the house. He paced back and forth in the darkened living room, glad that Gram was still at her sister's in Sturgis. At least five hours stretched in front of him before he would be allowed to rejoin the party. He slumped into the recliner, the phone at his elbow, but sleep refused to drive away the hooded, sardonic eyes of the man he'd met in Bisbee. Nor would it erase the vision of the dark-haired girl, her back to the setting sun as she flung the accusing words he would never forget. "I had a life before I met you, Frederick Roseman."

# Chapter 35

Frederick strode through the doors at police headquarters before seven. Two strangers had joined Thomas and Carla, the four of them hunched toward the computer screen.

Thomas turned as the door clicked shut behind him. His jaw clenched for the briefest moment before he introduced the man and woman beside him. "Frederick, I would like you to meet special agents Wesley Dunn and Ronnie Regier. Both are terrorist experts with the FBI." The two agents turned to shake hands with the newcomer. Both either missed or chose to ignore the thinly-veiled condescension in Thomas's voice. Frederick eyed each of them, more than familiar the politics of interagency rivalry. Wesley was short, fiftyish, his dark eyes and skin color suggesting Oriental heritage. Ronnie's bulky frame appeared to be at least ten years younger and three inches taller than her male partner. Nobody sported black eyes or bruises—yet.

Thomas continued. "And this is Frederick Roseman, *our* special agent." Both FBI people eyed him with the expected distrust reserved for outsiders before they turned back to Carla's computer screen.

"Just to bring you up to speed, Frederick. Thanks to Wesley and Ronnie, we have located the missing Tahoe."

"OnStar?"

Thomas rolled his eyes and nodded. "Yes, as of five o'clock this morning we have stepped into sketchy legal territory. That aside, our missing Tahoe went north. Presently, it's a few miles west of Butte, Montana which makes me think we're following the wrong dog—that is if they're actually going to use the Cesium."

"They're here in Montana?" Frederick's voice trailed into a whisper.

No one spoke until Wesley cleared his throat and walked over to pour another cup of coffee. "It doesn't make any sense to me. Why would Al-Qaida smuggle something as valuable as Cesium-137 into the country to blow up the Bozeman feed store? Los Angeles or Seattle, yes. Even Denver I can buy. They're not going to waste it in a state with more cows than people. They're either moving it here to hide, or it's going through to a larger Midwestern target. It may be Minneapolis or Chicago Who knows?" His glance pinpointed Thomas. "You shouldn't have stopped the vehicle in Grand Junction last night. It would have been more constructive to let them continue—with adequate surveillance, of course."

The corner of Frederick's mouth tightened. Adequate surveillance could only mean FBI personnel.

"So what evidence do you have that the canister is in this vehicle?" Ronnie pointed to the computer screen.

An uncomfortable silence filled the room. Finally, Thomas spoke. "We have eliminated any other possibilities. We know it isn't in the one headed to Denver."

"What about the other Tahoe that matched the records?" Wesley asked derisively. "The one in Reno."

"We've checked it," Thomas said. "It was bought by the maintenance supervisor at the Blue Bay Casino. He still owns it, and he doesn't fit the profile. Besides—"

Ronnie broke in. "Thomas is right. The Tahoe in Montana has the Cesium. When they stopped for gas north of Pocatello, they pulled into a full-service bay. Neither man left the vehicle. They were glued to those seats, and after that many hours, that's not natural. No snack, no trip to the bathroom—nothing."

Frederick stared out the window, deep in thought as he listened to Ronnie's gravelly voice.

"That's still not a positive. You're guessing," Wesley grumbled. "How soon before the Task Force is in place?"

"Another three hours, which will put them close to Billings, if the vehicle continues west on I-90." Thomas's words were clipped and controlled, despite the dark circles under his eyes.

Carla swiveled in her chair. "Is it possible to do a takedown as soon as our guys are in place?"

Wesley crossed his arms and stepped away from the screen. "We have to do it. There's too much risk if we don't secure the Cesium."

Frederick turned from the window to watch the three agents and Thomas. All were at least twenty years senior to him, but this was going the wrong way. His voice cracked across the room. "No. You cannot do that. It's too dangerous. People are still dying in the Ukraine from the Chernobyl disaster. Even the small amount of radioactive material they're carrying could contaminate hundreds of square miles of crops, livestock, and people."

Thomas spoke without looking up from the pad of paper where he drew tortured configurations. "What do you base that on?"

"Say we took them down east of Bozeman. These guys will be nervous. If something goes wrong they will pull off the grandest jihad suicide of all time. A few thousand will die, but a hundred thousand people will have to be evacuated, and it won't be for only a few weeks. It will be for two or three lifetimes. We don't have the scientific evidence to even know how long the contamination would last."

"Which means we have to get them to leave the vehicle with the Cesium in it before the Task Force can move?" Thomas asked.

"Anything else is out of the question," Frederick answered. "They may not give us that opportunity, but it's what we have to hope for."

Another hour of surveillance passed. The Tahoe made its way steadily eastward. Everyone held their breath as it approached the college city of Bozeman. Three exits later, the group breathed a collective sigh of relief as the vehicle climbed the mountain pass, then wound its way down the other side to windblown Livingston. Frederick stared at the moving vehicle. A faint dread built from the tips of his fingers and through his arms until it filled his whole chest cavity. He tried to project himself into the bodies of these two warped terrorists. How would they think? What governed their actions, other than the desire to deliver the penultimate blow against the great Satan—America? Had Wesley assumed correctly that the Cesium's ultimate target lay in one of the larger cities to the east. That seemed more likely, because nothing else made sense—unless . . .

"Thomas, I need to make a couple of phone calls."

Thomas peered over the top of his glasses, his eyes now even more bloodshot from the all-night vigil. He rose from his chair and followed Frederick into the hallway. "You're not buying this, are you?"

Frederick's lips formed a straight, hard line. "This whole scene should be playing out in New York or Los Angeles, not here. We're missing something."

For a moment, Thomas searched Frederick's face. "Do whatever you think. Just keep me posted."

Frederick nodded and strode out the front door. He stood beside the Mustang, his hand poised on the door handle. Personal matters should never interfere with business. Despite his misgivings, he grabbed his phone and pulled up Dina's number. No answer. Momentarily relieved, he shoved the phone in his pocket. The relief lasted no longer than a minute. If he didn't talk to her now, he'd lose his nerve. Then the process would be even harder. He took a deep breath and punched in Bud and Lorie's house number.

"Hello?"

Frederick grimaced. Why had Bud answered the phone? He was never in the house at this time of the day. "Hey, Bud. How are you?"

"Good. You caught me having a mid-morning cup of coffee. What's happening?"

Frederick shifted his weight from one foot to the other. The sun seemed scorching hot. He wiped the sweat away from his brow. "Is Dina around the house?" he blurted.

"No. She and Lorie went to Billings."

Frederick's chest tightened. "Any idea where?"

"How do you expect me to know? I can find my way to Western Ranch Supply and not much else. However, I do know that Lorie always goes to that big mall over on the south side of town, the one just off the interstate."

"The Primrose?"

"Yeah, I think that's it."

"Okay, talk to you soon. And Bud—thanks again, for everything."

"For nothing. Having Dina has been a pleasure. But if you don't hustle a little harder with this girl, she's going to get away."

"Goodbye, Bud." Frederick stared down the street. His fingers clenched the phone in a death grip. Dina in Billings? Al-Qaida there with enough radioactive material to kill thousands of people? And if Wesley was wrong? What if for some crazy reason, Billings was the target? Frederick jammed the phone in his pocket. Panic washed over him, as if he'd just shut the Mustang's door with the car keys lying on the driver's seat. Would al-Qaida really use something as valuable as Cesium-137 in a pint-sized city like Billings?

He dialed a number as he strode to his car. "Mario?"

"Of course. It is my old friend, Frederick?"

"Yes, Mario, it's me."

"How are you? Are you so busy you cannot find time to have one small cup of tea with a friend?"

"Mario, I am sorry. The company has kept me on the road for many months. Are you well?"

"I'm fine. How is it that I have the pleasure of a call from the greatest spymaster in America?"

"You flatter me, and there is no need for that among friends. I have a question. Tell me Mario, if terrorists had a bomb laced with Cesium, how would they use it most effectively?"

"Oh-h, serious stuff. People think if that happened in America, they would use it in a large city like New York or Washington, but that is not necessarily so. You of course know the devastation a dirty bomb would leave in an urban area. First responders deal with blast casualties, the injured and dying. Emergency rooms fill to capacity with bleeding, traumatized people. Then a second wave of victims who were only close to the blast arrive at area hospitals with nausea, vomiting, and diarrhea. Within the first twenty-four hours, hundreds more follow. Then the "R" word is heard, and thousands more find out they've been exposed to massive quantities of radiation. Authorities are confronted with mass panic. So yes, that brand of terrorism works well in an urban area."

Frederick gripped the phone as he tried to picture an explosive device that could obliterate an American city, not for a week, but for two centuries.

Mario interrupted his thoughts. "Though it has never happened, another scenario worries me, one that can conceivably be even more devastating. If a dirty bomb is detonated near one of your prime agricultural belts, the same immediate injuries and mass panic would occur, though on a smaller scale, but if a part of the nation's food supply becomes contaminated, the problems compound, simply because the results aren't immediately visible. Cesium doesn't have to be used in a bomb. It can be distributed in powder form so fine that it can conceivably be pumped through an air-conditioning system. Say it was employed in a large indoor venue, at one of your American football games or shopping malls. Minute particles of that dust would land on every person and they would not even know it. A few would feel ill in the first twelve hours, others, not for weeks, but they would all carry it from the building to their homes and workplaces. In an agricultural belt where the food and water supply are affected, the resulting devastation would be more long-lasting, and conceivably much larger."

Frederick stiffened. "So, terrorists could use this powder in virtually any place that has central air-conditioning?"

"Of course. The important thing is that they pull the attack off without discovery to allow people to mingle and spread it further. If they can do that, it is much more dangerous and demoralizing than a bomb."

"Thank you, Mario. I must go. Say a prayer for me—for America. We will visit over a cup of tea, soon I hope. You have done me a great favor. May I call you if I need more technical data?"

"Of course, my friend. Always."

Frederick jammed the accelerator to the floor at the on-ramp to the interstate. What had Mario said? Something as simple as an air-conditioning system? People would carry it to their homes? If that was right, the results would resemble the Russian disaster at Chernobyl. People would succumb to the effects for years?

Frederick's mind ricocheted from one possibility to the next. The target must be some large city to the east. Minneapolis? Chicago? Surely not anything in Montana. But Mario had talked about the devastation that could occur in an agricultural area, which meant Billings made perfect sense. There wasn't a larger city for at least five hundred miles, and the area had significant agricultural production. Frederick scanned the cars ahead, then glanced in the rearview mirror. No visible terrorists, but then he knew there wouldn't be. He fell in behind a white Ford Taurus. Supposing they'd chosen Billings as the location, where would they target? The city water supply? Or would they use it, as Mario had said, in a large building's air-conditioning system? If so, where would that be? On this hot August Saturday afternoon, there was only one place that fit—the eighty-five store Primrose Mall.

# Chapter 36

Three miles west of downtown Billings, Frederick pulled onto a frontage road. Higher than the interstate, it gave him a good view of passing vehicles. A hundred yards ahead, the first streetlight would with any luck slow traffic for an even closer look. He pulled out a phone and dialed a number. The answer was immediate.

"Thomas here."

"What's the location of the target?"

Silence, while Thomas peered over Carla's shoulder to check the screen. "They're east of Laurel, about ten minutes from Billings. Where are you?"

Frederick started the Mustang. A white Chevy Tahoe had stopped in the middle of a line of traffic at the red light ahead. "Maybe looking at them. I want to tail them through Billings, to make sure this isn't their—"

"Do it. The SWAT guys are within ten minutes of them, but if you think the target is Billings, then tail them."

"I can't believe this would be it, but we shouldn't take any chances. I'll talk to you if there's any change." As Frederick eased into the traffic, he disconnected. Neither time nor adequate phone security allowed him to carry the conversation further.

Six cars ahead, the suspect Tahoe took the exit north toward Roundup and Lewistown, both small towns with long stretches of nothing in between. Thomas had been right. They were headed for a carefully chosen remote ranch property to store their deadly cargo for some future event. He sighed with relief. It still wouldn't be easy. Without a doubt, al-Qaida had spent millions of dollars to purchase the Cesium. It would be well-guarded. But a storage site would give the SWAT team options, and more important, time. The odds of disaster and carnage were unacceptably high if they had to act in the next two hours.

On the north side of the city, instead of continuing on the Roundup highway, the Tahoe turned right onto one of the last industrial streets. Frederick followed at a distance past a row of trucking companies and wrecking yards. Ten blocks down the street, a dilapidated block building with peeling paint huddled between an electrical supply company and a FedEx warehouse. As Frederick idled by, he glanced at the commercial sign in the front window. Merit Plumbing and Heating. An electric overhead door opened and swallowed the Tahoe. The car and its contents disappeared inside.

At the end of the block, Frederick turned left and then into the alley. Two additional overhead doors gave access to the back of the building. He winced as he idled past them. In this industrial area of town, the Mustang stood out like a flower child at an Amish picnic. Where the alley met the street, he crossed and tucked the offending car between two warehouses. It was the only place where he could see both the back entrance and at least some of the street. What now?

Wait—or call Thomas? Move the SWAT team in and do a takedown?

Ten minutes later, his phone rang.

"What happened?" Thomas' voice cracked across the miles.

"The Tahoe is still in the building."

"Then I think we should move the SWAT guys in."

"No, it's too risky until we know more about the building layout. Hold it . . ." Frederick watched both back doors open. The front one clattered up as well. Three identical white vans emerged, all decorated with Merit Plumbing & Heating logos, roof racks, and ladders. At the street, two of them rapidly accelerated on different side streets. The third one turned and sped by the Mustang, headed for the downtown area. Sunglasses obscured the driver's eyes. A baseball cap covered his dark hair. His bronze skin could have passed for Hispanic, but Frederick knew it wasn't. He reported each van's movements over the still live connection with Thomas.

"We've lost the Cesium." Thomas's hollow voice ground out his misery. Frederick heard him relay the news to the others in the room. Everything they'd hoped for had gone wrong. Each of those vans had been large enough to easily carry a half ton of explosives. Did that mean the Cesium now had a detonator? Acid leached from the lead weight in the pit of his stomach. Whatever happened from here—they were no longer in control. Al-Qaida had allowed for every eventuality, and Frederick knew he had underestimated them. Whoever drove the van with the Cesium would undoubtedly detonate it immediately if he felt threatened. But what if Mario's other scenario was real, and a major Billings venue like the Primrose Mall was the target? That possibility galvanized him into frenzied action. As the Mustang went airborne over the curb he clawed for a cellphone. What Mario had warned against, was very close to reality for Dina, and the hundreds of others who would be trapped in the coming rain of death.

Frederick weaved in and out of traffic along Grand Avenue. Occasionally, he glanced in his rearview mirror. A patrol car would complicate matters. At the corner of 43rd and Carson, the light turned red. The Mustang's tires howled as he edged past a long line of cars and slid into the right-hand turn. Way behind him, the flashing lights of a police cruiser slowed the traffic around him. He cut around three cars and hit the yellow light on Broadview at seventy. The city cops could nail him later, if there actually was a later to worry about.

At the entrance to the Primrose Mall, he scanned the two sides of the building he could see. The white Merit Plumbing van, wedged between a service door and a loading dock sent an instant lightning bolt of adrenaline through his veins. Any official warning to mall security was too late. The plan must be exactly what Mario had surmised. A soft hit, unknown to anyone until the damage had been done. But no ladder stood against the building wall to access the roof-mounted air-conditioners. Would the blast obliterate most of the mall and spread radioactive material over a good part of the city? Frederick clenched his teeth. All he could hope was that there might be time to defuse it. Much of that would depend on the sophistication of the detonator system. If this was an Ibrahim Asiri bomb . . .? He refused to finish the thought as he bounced the Mustang partly onto the sidewalk and slammed it into park. Dodging shoppers, he ran inside. The place overflowed with shoppers pursuing America's national pastime.

Frederick sprinted through the food court. A security guard trimmed his fingernails next to the doorway of a Chatters store. As Frederick closed the space between them, the guard slid the penknife into his pocket. He sauntered out into the stream of shoppers, the boredom in his stance mute testimony to the quiet safety of this small-city shopping mecca. Frederick's eyes flickered down to the man's belt. A baton hung on one side, a holster on the other. He never even slowed. At the last moment, he moved slightly to the right and clotheslined the guy, caught him in a chokehold and pulled him upright before he hit the floor. The nine-millimeter Glock in the guard's holster slid out easily, and he shoved the man away. Fear transfixed the security guard's face as Frederick cocked the revolver. He scrambled backward, wanting to run from the bullet that would end his life. Frederick raised the gun and fired three times, with a measured space between each shot. The bullets thudded through the acoustic tile in the ceiling and lodged somewhere in the roof structure, doing little permanent damage. The guard stared, uncomprehending.

"Where's the nearest fire alarm?" Frederick barked.

Relief followed by anger washed over the man's features. "Why?"

"Clear this building as fast as you can. Don't ask questions, just do it, then get out yourself." Another security guard slid around the corner and into a crouch, gun drawn, eyes searching for the shooter.

"Deal with him." Frederick pointed at the uniformed guard. "We have three, maybe four minutes to clear this mall before it blows into a million pieces."

"Hold it. Who are—?"

"Here." Frederick flipped the CIA badge in its plastic folder open and jammed the gun, butt first into his belly. "Do it now. And send a couple more rounds into the ceiling. Pull the fire alarm. Do whatever it takes to empty this place in a hurry. And help people get to the doors."

The other security guard strutted forward, stiff-legged, like a whiskered mongrel circling an alley cat. Frederick ignored him and ran down the mall. Toddlers to grandmothers scurried or were carried to the closest exit, various levels of panic etched across each face. Frederick glanced at his watch. How long had he been in the building? They would give their cargo of death no more than a five-minute fuse. There could only be a few moments more.

An open service door led to the loading docks. He ducked outside and scanned the area. A blue dumpster hugged the side of the building in front of him. The white van, nearly hidden from view was nosed in next to the dumpster. The back doors were both open, but no half-ton of nitrogen fertilizer or dynamite lay among the tools. A telescoping metal ladder now leaned against the wall of the building. There would be no explosion. The only sound that would break the pulsating conversation of shoppers would be the steady drone of the giant air-conditioners turning a hot Billings afternoon into cool shopping comfort—and death.

# Chapter 37

Frederick sprinted for the metal ladder and climbed high enough to peer over the vast expanse of roof. A hundred feet to his left, two coverall-clad workmen with swarthy features huddled over the fans that sucked hot Billings air across the coils of pipe. He ducked below the roof-line and scrambled back to the loading dock. He had lost. The CIA had lost. America had lost, but he would save as many lives as he could. He ran back into the mall, dialing numbers, barking orders, talking to the SWAT team now only seconds away. They could take down the terrorists on the roof. He would save as many lives of those inside as possible.

People continued streaming for the exits, young mothers holding babies close to their breasts, hurrying beside dozens of teenagers, all musically-unwired but still texting in an attempt to appease the gods of Facebook and Twitter.

Frederick stopped to help an elderly gentleman. He shouted in his ear, tried to tell him to leave the building as quickly as possible. It did no good. The screeching guitars from a rock band in the center of the mall drowned out any possibility of conversation with an old man who had turned off his hearing aids. Frederick pushed him gently into the seat of his walker and wheeled him to the exit, or at least as close as he could get to it. Crowds of panicked shoppers clutching bags of merchandise elbowed their way through the glass doors to the street. He left the old man and ran further down the north wing of the mall. The air ahead had a colored tinge, already contaminated with the radiant blue dust. The Cesium-137 had started its deadly work. He skidded to a stop. It was time to get out, and as far from here as possible. But at the end of the corridor, hundreds of people milled around like blind monkeys, trapped with no adequate exit. For a minute, he watched. Had these people not heard the shots? Why had they ignored the clanging fire alarm? Only a few scurried through the airborne powder.

Frederick hugged the wall as he tried to move closer. Then he saw her. At the end of the wing next to a boutique store window, Dina leaned against a pillar, Lorie beside her. For a split second, he considered dashing through the deadly powder spewing from vents in the ceiling. Immediately he abandoned the idea and sprinted to the front entrance and around the side of the building. Close to where the Merit Plumbing van was parked, a bald, middle-aged man backed out of a parking spot in a three-quarter ton Chevy pickup. His grim visage telegraphed his desire to escape this madhouse. Frederick ripped the driver's door open. "Get out." The man hesitated, a huge mistake. Frederick grabbed his shirt-front and lifted him to the ground. "Sorry, friend. Consider this your civic duty." He bailed into the driver's seat and slammed the transmission into drive. Three entrance doors were placed evenly into that wing of the building, each labeled with a store name. The third door was the target. Twenty feet before impact, Frederick jammed his foot to the floor. General Motors rose to the occasion. Two tons of energized steel surged forward. The locked door and three feet of the cinder block wall caved in. Frederick backed away from the gaping hole and shut off the severely damaged truck. Antifreeze dripped from the smashed radiator. He slid out from behind the deployed airbags, then clambered over the pile of debris. A sales lady in a skimpy blue skirt stood inside, her jaw still resting on her ample bosom.

"Get out of here," Frederick growled as he raced by her. Inside, a dozen people stood mesmerized, seemingly unable to make a decision.

Frederick reached the first of them. "Go out that way." He pointed to the gaping hole. It was then he saw Dina and Lorie. He ran up to Dina and grabbed her arm. "Follow me."

"Where? What are you talking about?" Dina jerked away.

"For once in your life, don't argue."

She glared at him, but both women did scurry along behind him. He jumped through the shattered blocks, reached back to help them through, then glanced to where he'd last seen the parked van. A SWAT team vehicle squatted menacingly in front of it, blocking any escape. Spread-eagled against the wall of the building were the two al-Qaida operatives. Frederick sighed. They'd been late to the party, but if they did everything right they might contain the holocaust.

"So, would you deign to tell your subjects what is going on?" Dina stood in front of him, her dark eyes snapping with anger.

"Those guys." Frederick inclined his head toward the spread-eagled al-Qaida operatives. "They wanted to kill everybody in the mall. That powder floating out of the air-conditioning system? That is Cesium-137. It's what contaminates the ground at Chernobyl, in Russia."

Dina looked at him for a long time. "Mr. Roseman—you are crazier than a jack rabbit with cooties. You've lost it. That powder was part of a public-relations blast for the British rock band that you must have walked right by. They're called Blue Powder. Remember the canopy over the bandstand?" Dina gave him no time to answer. "They had a compressed air system that blasted out occasional puffs of colored powder. Lorie and I didn't want to get the stuff in our hair, so we stayed down at the end of the mall until they were finished."

Frederick stared at Dina, then glanced at the smashed door, the pile of shattered bricks, the destroyed Chevy Silverado, and finally at the Merit Plumbing workers who were no longer spread-eagled and cuffed. Now they were talking to the SWAT team as if they were old school mates rather than terrorists, and suddenly the realization hit him. Al-Qaida had played them all for fools. The radioactive Cesium wasn't here. It had vanished. The consequences of that blunder would outweigh any of the flak and fallout from today's Primrose Mall fiasco.

# Chapter 38

Two hours after the uproar died at the Mall, a half-dozen FBI agents arrived to join the two CIA agents. What had been a botched attempt to stop a nonexistent dirty bomb, now had to be explained to the media. Both agencies issued standard 'we're keeping America safe' platitudes. The press's skepticism was heightened by the lack of any captured suspects. Thomas hinted to at least one of the newscasters that a large blond man was a person of interest in the investigation, then ordered Frederick back to Miles City—or the Bahamas, anywhere but here.

Frederick knew better than to argue. This was not a time to be in the limelight. The local police refused to give up jurisdiction until federal agents taped the area and more or less told them to get lost. Normally, the FBI boys were more diplomatic, but egos were bruised, tempers were short, and the whole operation needed a cohesive and competent leader to sound retreat. The FBI were not about to admit responsibility and were more than happy to fade into the background and let Thomas continue as agent in charge. Jurisdiction was no longer an issue. According to the FBI, this was simply another botched CIA operation.

The mall evacuation eviscerated the much-hyped concert by the Blue Powder rock band. Their promoters along with the Primrose Mall immediately filed a suit for four and a half million dollars. The owner of the smashed pickup settled on site for a new truck to replace his three-year-old Silverado. All in all, the day had significant consequences for the American taxpayer. The worst was that no one had any idea how to trace the lost Cesium. Neither Langley nor Washington were impressed, and before the end of the week the first whispers would circulate through the halls of Congressional power for regime change in the CIA.

Thomas established the post-op headquarters in a vacant room on the first floor of city hall, though there were now few orders to be given. Nobody had any idea where or when the Cesium had disappeared. After completely unproductive hours of finger-pointing, they agreed to retrace the camera evidence back to Henderson, Nevada. Had the Cesium even left? If so, where had they lost it?

Frederick loitered at the edge of the room, waiting for Carla to arrive from Miles City with her communications equipment and expertise. Again, they scrutinized the switch in the Nevada parking lot, then followed the Tahoe north through Idaho and across Montana. Like a homing pigeon, the vehicle inched toward Billings. Previously, they had skipped parts of the video. Now they peered at each segment, desperate to discover whether the Cesium had actually arrived at the Merit warehouse.

Hours passed. No person or vehicle came within range of the vehicle supposedly carrying the canister. By eight o'clock in the evening, white Styrofoam coffee cups littered the room. Then, less than an hour from Billings near the little ranching community of Reed Point, an identical white Tahoe pulled out of a ranch road exit and fell in behind the one carrying the radioactive bomb material. It inched closer. For a few moments, no other traffic was in sight. The Tahoe in the rear pulled alongside the first one. At seventy miles an hour, the two SUV's inched within a foot of each other. A small suitcase passed from the first vehicle to the second. One of the FBI men gasped at the audacity of the stunt. The two identical vehicles then parted. The first then accelerated and carried on to Billings and the Merit Plumbing warehouse. The second took the Columbus exit and disappeared.

Frederick edged closer to the camera and joined the rest in stunned silence. The Cesium had never reached Billings.

Thomas rose to his feet and paced the room. Both CIA and FBI agents scrambled for their phones, presumably calling for more investigative help. Merit Plumbing Company personnel had been in custody for hours. Now, every paper and procedure would be torn apart to find the location of the radioactive material.

One by one, Thomas scrutinized the players. "So, what do we do now? We've lost the package. Anybody have any ideas—beyond this phony plumbing company?"

Frederick broke the ominous silence. "There may be a way."

Both Thomas and Carla turned uneasily toward Frederick, doubt colliding with the faint hope in their eyes. The FBI agents to a man crossed their arms and stared elsewhere, distancing themselves from this outsider responsible for the bungled mall recovery. However, neither was ready to clash with Thomas over the stranger's presence in the room. That ammunition would be saved for bigger battles ahead. From their perspective, the wreckage was where it belonged—in CIA hands.

"Give me a few minutes." Frederick turned and left the room. After consulting a phone book in the front office, he dialed a number.

"Billings Real Estate—Bobby here."

"Bobby, this is Frederick."

"Hey Fred, good to hear from you. Tell me you're moving back to Big Sky country and want to buy a hideout estate. Come on. I could use the commission."

"Yeah, right. You're the richest agent in the state. You don't need my pennies."

Bobby laughed. "That was two years ago. Now my wallet's flatter than an Iowa cornfield. I've never seen it so bad. But there are a few screaming deals out there, and Fred if you're looking for something, you're talking to the right guy. I've got forty acres down toward—"

"Bobby, I don't want forty acres, at least not today. But I do need some information. Can you pull up all the sales of rural acreages from Columbus south to Red Lodge that have sold in the last six months?"

"Of course. That won't take long. In fact, I can tell you off the top of my head. That's my old stomping grounds. I'll check for more, but I'm aware of three. Two of them were ten-acre parcels down by Absarokee, bare land with no buildings. You want a few acres with a house, or does it matter?"

"Yes, probably with buildings."

"The one that sold with a house was over toward Red Lodge, one of those off-the-grid properties way back in the sticks. You know, the kind of remote ground pot farmers salivate over. A friend of mine sold it to some folks from Yemen, if you can imagine that. A guy and his brother. Neither could speak more than a few words of English. Anyhow, I'm boring you. It sold at a shade over three hundred, which was a steal. The house cost more than that to build."

"You're not boring me. Got an address for that one?" Frederick's response was controlled, but only because of years of training. "Bobby, thanks. I owe you, and when I need that wilderness hideout—you're my man."

"Hey, glad to help. Do you want me to send you some listings in the area?"

Frederick hesitated, not wanting to be disingenuous. Then again, after this disaster it might not be a bad idea to invest in some backcountry Montana real estate. "Yeah, send them, and also any other listings in remote areas that you have on file."

"I'll have them to you within the hour."

"Thanks, Bobby—and take care." Frederick walked back into the conference room. Everyone eyed him as he took his seat.

"There's a better than even chance the Cesium is stored at a remote property down by Absarokee."

"Where's that?" The FBI agent's voice grated through the tension in the room.

"About an hour southwest of Billings."

Thomas sighed and scrubbed at his eyes. "Maybe we've been saved from our own incompetence." He looked around the room, then turned to Frederick. "What's the address?"

"It's coming. Should be here within the hour."

"You're sure this is it?"

"No. Not until I see if there's a white Chevy Tahoe in the yard."

A half-hour later, Frederick scowled as he logged onto an email account on his phone. Immediately, Bobby's listing information flashed onto the screen. He scrolled through the statistics and pictures of the sold properties. The third matched Bobby's description of the Red Lodge "marijuana farm special."

"Carla, could you pull up a satellite image of 1578 Donnelly Creek Road?" Every agent peered at the screen as Carla worked the mouse. Suddenly, the screen blurred, then sharpened as the address came into focus. Hidden in dense pine, the secluded property sported a horse barn, round pen, and some other corrals, in addition to a log chalet-style house. A quarter-mile long graveled driveway ended in an egg-shaped circle in front of the dwelling. Next to the house, an older blue pickup nosed into an open carport. Frederick held his breath. If he was wrong . . .. One of the FBI men stabbed at the screen. "There!"

Frederick let his breath slowly escape. A white Chevy Tahoe sat partially hidden to the left of the blue pickup. Phones again erupted like geysers. SWAT personnel were summoned. Jurisdiction again acquired significance. The remote Red Lodge property suddenly vaulted to the most fought over piece of real estate in America. Frederick sighed with relief, glad to walk out of the room. His role was finished.

# Chapter 39

Lorie and I drove the first thirty miles chattering about shopping and our purchases, which meant neither of us wanted to broach the "Frederick" subject. Lorie wasn't sure how I felt about him, and more to the point, his actions today at the mall. On my end, I felt a strange need to stand up for him, even though his behavior today had been beyond bizarre.

Lorie finally spoke. "It could have been worse. We could have been shot. Those *were* gunshots at the other end of the mall, and we never did find out what that was about."

"No, I guess not." I scrunched down in the seat. Why had Frederick done that crazy number? Who would drive a new Chevy truck through a brick wall? What was he thinking? I turned my face to the window to hide the sudden flush of embarrassment. By now, he was probably in jail, and that made my stomach do even bigger flips.

Lorie glanced sideways at me, disturbed by my silence. "Dina, Bud and I have known Frederick since high school. He's not a fool."

"I'm sure you're right, but—"

Lorie chuckled. "The only book Frederick ever packed to class was a dog-eared green spiral notebook. He had the same textbooks the rest of us did, but I don't recall ever seeing him with one, and he never got anything less than an 'A.'" She reached over and touched my shoulder. "Hey, I'm not sticking up for him, but the man *is* brilliant."

"Meaning what?"

"There may be more to this story. All he told us when he moved you out to the ranch was that some bad people were following you around." She gave me a sideways glance. "I'm sure you know more about that than I do, so . . . let's not shoot him—at least not yet."

"Sounds fair to me." I didn't want to shoot him at all, but what had happened at the Primrose Mall needed an explanation.

After a long silence, Lorie asked, "How is Piñata coming along?"

"Really good. She knows way more than I ever thought. Somebody spent a lot of time training her before something snapped inside her head."

"That's not unusual, especially with barrel horses. They are bred to run, hardwired to win. Our job is only to guide them, but sometimes if we push beyond their capability, they resent it. I know I've told you that before, but I wonder if that's what happened to your mare. Maybe she just needs to be reassured that you're a team, and that you are both working toward the same goal."

"Hmm, I never thought of it that way, but I agree. It's not like I have to teach her to give to the bit or turn a barrel correctly. Somewhere, she learned that. Her issues are about trust. What I have to get across is that I respect her and won't barge into her fear zone."

Lorie slowed for the exit onto the county highway that led to the ranch. "I think what you've been doing, riding out in the hills and running just for the sheer pleasure of it has been a great experience for Piñata. She needs to discover that working together is fun." Lorie glanced in my direction. "And that goes for you as well." After she'd parked the car in the garage, Lorie turned and spoke. "Remember why you started chasing cans. It was because it was exciting—fun. Forget about trying to push her, and most of all yourself to be at the top of the heap. Run because you love the sport and see what happens."

That evening, Lorie and I sat at the counter while we recounted the crazy events of the day to Bud. He shook his head and muttered something about a love-sick bull moose, then yawned, and stumbled off to bed.

We sat in silence while I finished the last of my Coke, then swirled the ice cubes at the bottom of the glass. My stay here had been wonderful, and I'd learned so much from Lorie. Every day, she had taken time out of her busy training schedule to help me, but now I needed to move back to town. I set my glass down. "I'm going home tomorrow. You and Bud have been so good to me. I want you to know how grateful I am."

"We've enjoyed having you." Lorie folded her arms and leaned against the kitchen sink. "Dina, I never take outside horses to train, and only a few students. We're too busy with the ranch and our own horses, but you have a lot of ability and determination. If you'd like, leave the mare here. I can continue to help you, and besides, you need places to ride her away from the arena."

I didn't have to think long before I answered. It would make my day longer, but Lorie's help was invaluable. "How can I ever thank you? I hope I will be worthy of your time." My eyes were moist, and I had to swallow the lump in my throat because, though I didn't deserve it, I knew I had the best teacher in the world.

Sunday morning, I packed my bags and drove back to town. Before I reached Main Street, the red, brick Catholic church came into view. I parked on a side street and slipped through the doors. The font was to the left, and I dipped my fingers into the holy water, made the sign of the cross, then slipped into one of the few empty pews about halfway to the front. It seemed so right to be here this morning, which made me wonder about Bud and Lorie. Did they come here together? Lorie had indicated that coming here was a rare event. Why was there such a chasm between their beliefs?

The first song, filled with reverence, rose to the ceiling high above us. During the singing, the priest and two lay ministers made their entrance. The priest's voice was deep, rich with the significance of words intoned for a thousand years.

Where was Frederick? Was he in a church this morning? He'd never talked about attending any church here in Miles City. I would have to remember to ask him.

The service moved through the scripture reading and the priest's homily. The congregation then stood and recited the Apostle's Creed. *"I believe in the Holy Spirit . . . the forgiveness of sins . . . life everlasting . . ."* My mind wandered back to Frederick, and I tried to picture him standing here beside me. What would he think? Were there irreconcilable differences in our faiths? Bud and Lorie hadn't done well with their differences. I tried to force my wandering thoughts back to the rise and fall of the congregational response, an acknowledgment that seemed as old as time.

After the service, I walked down the solid stone steps and into the bright sunlight, my heart at peace. This was my church. These were my people. Some of them had found salvation and some were still searching, but the same was likely true in every church—even Frederick's.

# Chapter 40

Much to my surprise, Trent said I still had a job. I was glad to be back, but the first bone-weary night of waiting on customers reminded me of Susan's warning. If I wanted a different future, then I'd better think about school.

At the end of my first shift at the Spur, I trudged to my pickup and drove through the deserted streets toward home. When I arrived at Mrs. Riddler's, I parked in my regular spot in the driveway, clicked my pickup door shut with as little noise as possible and trudged toward the house.

"Got time to talk?"

My breath caught in my throat at Frederick's voice in the darkness. I peered at his faint outline on the step as I stuttered a reply.

"For a few minutes, though there's nothing to say. I don't know what you thought was going on the other day in Billings, but—"

"Dina." His voice was quiet and sad. "I don't want to talk about that—at least not now. We need to talk about your family . . . your father."

"What about him?" I stepped back, suddenly anxious.

"He's gone."

"You mean dead?" My heart stopped. "Papa?"

"Yes."

"What happened?" A tortured groan rose from deep inside my chest. Somehow, I'd always known this would happen, and now our family would suffer even more because of my father's lawless border activities.

Frederick stood, reached for my hand, and pulled me down beside him. I laid my head on his shoulder and snuggled into his warmth, trying not to succumb to the storm of emotions in my heart. I wanted to cry, but all I could think of was the hurt and shame for too much of my childhood. Papa's smuggling activities had created a massive chasm between us.

Frederick's arm curled around my shoulder. His other hand worried at a leather key chain in his lap as he stared out at the dark street. "Your father died at the bottom of an abandoned mine shaft in Nevada, not far from Henderson."

"Where's that?" I crossed my arms in a futile attempt to ward off all the mixed-up sadness and anger that beat its way to the surface.

"Close to Las Vegas."

"How did it happen? What was he doing there?"

"As time passes we'll find out more, and—"

I stood, and took both his hands in mine. "Frederick, what happened? Don't lie to me or try to shield me from the truth."

"Really, I don't know any more, at least not about his death."

"But why was he there?"

"That part, I can't tell you, not yet."

I studied every nuance of Frederick's profile. What was he holding back? Why had my father been in Nevada, and why was he so tight-lipped about whatever he knew?

"Then his death *was* a result of his smuggling activities?"

Frederick hesitated. "Yes, but perhaps not in the way you think. Please don't ask anymore. Not now. Just understand that I'm immensely sorry for your loss, and if there's anything I can do to help, please tell me."

Dina stepped back to the edge of the sidewalk. "Long ago, my father chose his work over us." My words carried all the anger and hurt of my childhood. "If he is dead, then I'm sad for Mama, for what might have been. I will attend his funeral, but only for my mother's sake."

"That seems callous."

"I don't think so. Not that he wasn't good to us. He was. It's just that he was never around."

"And you're bitter because of his work?"

"Why wouldn't I be?"

A three-quarter moon beat back the cloud cover long enough Dina could see Frederick's face while he answered.

"Sometimes, circumstances are not as they seem."

Dina's hands clenched into fists in her lap with a building anger. Frederick clearly refused to understand the fear and antipathy she and Alejandro had grown up with. "Has Mama been notified?"

"Not yet. They were waiting until they retrieved the body. It's a long way to the bottom of that shaft."

"So how do you even know he's there?"

"They sent down a camera. A rescue team has made several attempts to retrieve his body, but the sides keep caving in. Bringing him up may not be possible. If you want, I will have someone from the agency notify your mother?"

"No, I will call her in the morning. Our family will have to make the necessary arrangements." My voice grated through a sudden and unexpected cascade of emotion. "He was gone so much when I was growing up, it seems fitting he won't even attend his own funeral. I despised what my father did. Now we must all grieve the consequences." The tears slipped down my cheeks, unheeded. He was my father, and despite everything he'd done, I loved him.

The next afternoon, I called Mama. Strangely, she was rational, which I didn't expect. She heard me out, asked a few questions, and though her voice was quaky with tears, she didn't break down, nor did she go into her signature hysterics. Her words were expected. Her quiet acceptance of her husband's death wasn't.

"When your father never called, I knew in my heart something terrible had happened. You will come home, won't you?"

I sighed, wanting desperately to refuse, but this was not a time for more hurt. "Yes Mama, I'll come as soon as I can get time off work. Perhaps we can find out how to contact Alejandro?"

"I will take care of that."

Her confident reply made me suspect Mama knew exactly where Alejandro's escape had taken him.

"We will wait to have the memorial mass until you can be here."

Mama could orchestrate a crisis at the slightest provocation. Now, at what should be the worst moment of her life, she played the stalwart soldier. It didn't fit.

"Call me as soon as you know when you can come." For a moment, there was silence, and when mama again spoke, her voice carried the huskiness of grief that would not wait. "Dina, I need you."

I bit my lower lip and tried to barricade my own threatening tears. For once, my mother was right. We needed to be together. "Yes, Mama, I will fly home as soon as I can."

After the phone call home, I trudged outside and headed for my shift at the Spur. Weariness dogged every step. The night before, it had been after midnight before my head collapsed onto my lumpy pillow. At six thirty, I'd dragged myself out of bed so I could be at the ranch to ride before eight. If Lorie would take the time to help me succeed with Piñata, I determined she would not find me ungrateful or lazy. After I'd saddled the mare, we jogged up to the big sagebrush flat by the Bar O where I let her run, simply because that was what she loved to do. I hoped that later when we went to the arena where I pushed her for every ounce of speed, the same pure love of running would transfer to scooting around three barrels. A few times it had. When it worked, she was awesome. Other times, the wrecks threatened to destroy her confidence—and mine. Too often, the moment I'd push her for speed, she'd tense, and everything would go crazy. She'd grab the bit in her teeth and run to the fence. Usually, she gave me fair warning if she was going to buck. I'd bail off and lead her around the arena until she calmed down. That strategy wasn't completely successful, but it kept me from getting another gravel rash on my face.

This morning, Lorie had paced back and forth while she watched me coax Piñata into the arena and around the barrels. When I finished my third dismal run she walked to where I was cooling the mare down.

"She's seen all this before."

"I don't know, Lorie. Maybe I was wrong. If she's done it before, she only has bad memories, because she sure doesn't do anything right."

Lorie grinned. "No argument there. She carries some serious baggage. The minute she sees a barrel, all the bad memories come back, her eyes get wide, and she loses it. I've seen this in other horses, and I can tell you with near certainty what happened. She was a big, athletic three-year-old. Somebody pushed her way past what her mind could handle. Three-year-old colts are equivalent to young teenagers. And when you push them beyond what they are capable, they either break down physically or like her—mentally. Once they are injured, they're finished, and it often has nothing to do with tendons or ligaments. Something snaps in their head, and they fight everything they associate with that pressure." Lorie eyed the mare, stuck her hands in her pockets and ambled back to her hip. "The good news is—some of the mental cases can be rejuvenated."

I stopped what I was trying to do with the mare and looked out at the surrounding hills. "So, what do I do to make that happen?"

"You have to help her forget whatever happened in her past. Up there on the sagebrush flat, you've reminded her that running is fun. Now you need to transfer that to the arena."

"I've tried to do that, but nothing has worked." I stepped off the mare and stroked her neck.

Lorie stood in front of us, punctuating each sentence with her hands. "Every morning, you keep riding her outside, but from now on, don't let her run. The only place she gets to do what she loves is in here. Leave the barrels in their usual place. This is a big arena. Open her up around the outside perimeter. Don't even look at the barrels. Continue to work on giving to the bit, creating suppleness in her body, and mostly—learning to have fun."

What Lorie had said made good sense, though I cringed at the countless hours I'd have to spend before I could get back to running the barrels. Weariness had long ago robbed every ounce of strength I had. How many months had I invested in this crazy horse? It didn't matter. I couldn't go back, so I stepped into the stirrup and rode around the perimeter of the arena, too tired to care whether she bucked, ran away, or just walked. For the first time, I felt Piñata relax. What had Merle said? "Sometimes we get in a hurry and start with the end result instead of taking baby steps. We don't deal with the horse's fear." That sure seemed to fit this situation.

A week later, I had even larger dark circles under my eyes from lack of sleep. But I'd kept up at work, and Piñata had pranced her way through the last quarter mile home to the arena she had once dreaded. Inside, we scampered through big figure eights, and then progressed to breaking the pattern and occasionally even rounding a barrel. She took it in stride, her ears flickering forward at the familiar pattern. Every morning, Lorie watched and offered helpful suggestions.

By the end of the second week, Piñata could make one complete run—but no more. If I tried to do the pattern again, she would revert to the crazy, mixed-up mess she had been since we started. That day, when I again made my single blazing run, Lorie sat on a stool in the corner of the arena by the tack shed. I stepped off and loosened the cinch. She crooked a finger at me. I walked over to where she sat, expecting a dose of blistering criticism. Not that I minded. It was always for my benefit.

Her words far from what I'd expected. "Dina. You may not think it, but you're ready."

"Yeah, right." I flipped the rein over Piñata's neck and leaned against the stirrup leather, while my arm rested on my worn saddle. "For what?"

"I'm going to two barrel racing futurities next week. One's in Nampa, Idaho. The other is in Las Vegas. I think you should go with me."

"Oh, that would be fun. I'd love to see all the top racers. Everybody will be there."

"No." She nodded toward Piñata. "I mean, compete."

"Lorie, you have to be kidding. No, I can't do that. She's absolutely unpredictable. One day she's okay. The next—she's a volcano."

"I know, but it's time she had some exposure to crowds, other horses, all the distractions that go along—well, with being a star."

"What do you mean? A star?" I scoffed. "You think her name's Piñata for nothing? Too much of the time it's still the same as the first day, like I'm flailing away blindfolded, trying to find the hidden candy—and getting nowhere." I jammed my hands in my jean pockets. "I've given up on ever going too far with her. If we could win a few local barrel races, and maybe snag a college scholarship that would be enough." I jabbed a finger at the mare. "Her? Futurity material? Hardly."

Lorie just nodded. "Well, you might be right, but don't you think we should give her a chance?"

I scowled at Piñata's sweat-darkened hide. Her flanks still heaved, and suddenly I knew that though her mind could only handle one run, for those few moments she had given everything she had. It only took one run to win a barrel race. I shrugged, then jettisoned whatever good sense I had. "I think it's crazy, but we'll try it."

After I'd unsaddled the mare, I drove back to town to start my shift at the Spur. More time off? That should go over well. I still hadn't asked Trent whether he'd allow me to go home for Papa's memorial. Now, I wanted to take *more* days just to go and play? This time, he would fire me for sure.

# Chapter 41

Trent stared at me like I'd lost my mind, along with my job when I asked him whether I could have four days off to go to a barrel racing futurity. He chewed on his mustache, then poked at the steaks he was grilling while he growled, "Well, I guess so." Then he smiled and patted my shoulder. "A professional barrel racer who wins futurities may be good for business. The only problem is that you'll spend more time signing autographs than serving steak. What am I going to do then?"

I laughed. "I don't think that will be an issue—not anytime soon."

"It better be. We're all cheering for you."

I wanted to reach across the counter and hug him, but it wasn't possible, nor would it have been proper. I didn't deserve this guy for a boss. All I could do was send up a silent prayer that God in heaven would bless him and his business, because my continued absences sure weren't helping it.

Piñata and I spent each day building confidence and trust. That's what was supposed to happen. Too often, those building blocks were bowled over by doubt and uncertainty. We rode outside, but never more than a slow lope. The big run was always saved for the arena, even though one was still all she would consent to do. If I tried to push her into another, she would panic and do her panicked run to a corner. No amount of pulling or prodding could stop her.

The three days before we left for the futurities, I continued to do our single run, though it wasn't enough. She needed to learn to bend better around the second barrel, and she wanted to crowd the third. But nothing worked. The first run, she would scamper like a banshee was chasing her. If I tried to do a second, her resentment was mirrored in every stride.

The morning Lorie and I left for Nampa, Frederick stepped out on the veranda. "Hey, hope you do well. Have a good time."

Have a good time? What was he talking about? We needed to have a serious discussion. I attempted a smile, but it was like I'd just dragged my face out of the freezer. The crazy stunt he'd pulled in Billings needed a major explanation, and until that happened, our relationship would remain in park.

"Thank you. I'll try." I averted my eyes, then realized my voice had been hardly above a whisper, so I had to say it again. Conflicting emotions battered at every defense I'd constructed, and I rummaged in the trailer tack compartment to avoid meeting his eyes. Anything more I might have said would have to wait, because at that moment, Lorie pulled into the yard. We loaded up and left. Frederick waved from the porch. I pretended not to notice.

The trip was uneventful. Late that evening, we conquered the last mile and pulled into the rodeo grounds at Nampa, Idaho. I watered and fed the horses while Lorie cooked supper in the trailer living quarters. We ate with little conversation between us, then fell into bed. Though tired from the long drive, I tossed and turned, unable to sleep. Sometime after midnight, I slipped into my clothes and edged through the door. The grass, soft under my feet, made a swishing sound as I silently passed the dozens of motorhomes, campers, and horse trailers. A hundred yards in front of me, the raised announcer's booth rose stark against the moonlit sky. I pushed through the gate by the bucking chutes and stood in the spongy dirt of the arena. Tri-colored barrels with bold-lettered advertising scrawled across their surface sat like lone sentinels at their respective points in the arena. I stuffed my hands in my jacket pockets and walked out to the first one. How would it go tomorrow with Piñata? Would we make fools of ourselves? Never in my life had I seen this level of competition. I shouldn't have agreed to come. We should have entered a few amateur rodeos, or maybe a local barrel racing jackpot where there weren't any people or the pressure of big money. Lorie wasn't the only world champion here. The prize money was huge, and it had drawn every big dog in the sport, which disqualified me. I felt like a Chihuahua in a fight with a Rottweiler. I trudged to the second barrel and kicked at the loose dirt. True, they were only forty-five-gallon drums, and all we had to do was turn around them faster than everybody else to win, but that seemed so far beyond our level. Fear clutched at my throat, and I scuttled out the back gate. Why had I listened to Lorie? So what if she was one of the great trainers in the sport? This time she had made a big mistake—and I would pay for it.

Before returning to the trailer, I stopped and glanced back at the lonely moonlit stretch of manicured dirt, then shivered in the cold night air. I didn't belong here. However, I'd paid the two-hundred-and-fifty-dollar entry fee. I had to run. But as I tiptoed back into the camper and crawled into my bunk, I knew—there was no way I could win anything in this crowd. The best I could hope for was to avoid embarrassing myself—and Lorie. Eventually, my resentment and fear subsided, enough I fell asleep. I had no business here.

Somewhere in the distance I heard the outside door close. I pried open an eye and stabbed at the power button on my cell phone. Six-thirty in the morning. Time to be up. Lorie would have gone to feed and water the horses, and likely wouldn't be back for a while. She knew nearly everyone here, so she would visit with others who were out early. I pushed the covers off and sat on the edge of the bed, an ominous feeling of dread twisting my stomach into knots. Today was the day I would make a fool of myself. Already, I could hear the comments. "She should have bought something other than a dead-beat bucking horse," or "Why is Lorie Linder packing that loser? She should have stayed home and done a little more training before she threw her money away." My face burned as I pulled on my dark jeans and blue blouse. They seemed right for the occasion. While I brushed and tied back my hair, a multitude of possible disasters paraded through my mind. Fear turned every bone in my body to the same slippery consistency of the eggs I broke into the skillet for our breakfast.

By the time I saddled the mare, I was no help to her. I was afraid—and she knew it. When our turn came to run, her eyes were fixed on the heavens. My trembling hands telegraphed the fear right down the reins. The tension in her body transferred back to me through the saddle. We burst into the arena, turned wide on the first barrel, nearly bounced off the fence on the second and knocked the third over before she made a crazy run for the hole leading out of this scary place. Somehow, I got her stopped before we ran into anything. I jumped off and led her back to the trailer. Tears of embarrassment threatened to spill over, but I held them until I could escape to the camper. Why had Lorie brought me here? This contest was so far beyond us. We were like first graders who accidentally stumbled into a college calculus class. The best thing to do was to see if we could draw out of the futurity tomorrow night in Las Vegas. Even if they wouldn't refund my money, I would rather lose the two-hundred-dollar entry fee than go through that humiliation again.

Swiftly, I wiped at my bitter tears and hurried back to the arena. Lorie would run in a few minutes. The least I could do was be there to support her, instead of sitting in the camper feeling sorry for myself. When I slipped up on the fence, Lorie glanced my way, shrugged out of her jacket and handed it to me. Concentration froze every line on her face as she moved her horse to the gate leading inside.

"Go get 'em, Lorie." That was what I wanted to tell her, but it didn't seem right. How do you offer encouragement to a five-time world champion? They know exactly what they have to do to win. Anything I could say would sound trite, so I clutched at the coat and gave her a petrified smile.

The bay four-year-old ran a picture-perfect pattern. Though it was his first futurity, he handled it like a veteran. On the home stretch, Lorie popped him once with her bat, and that keen little horse picked up another gear and scooted to the finish line. She wouldn't win, but they would definitely place high enough to pay for the trip.

I kept pace with her as she rode back to the trailer. "Lorie, that was awesome. He did so well. I can't believe . . ." Suddenly I stopped. What would she say? Would she be embarrassed that she'd brought me? After all, she had introduced me to several girls as one to watch in the future. I was one to watch all right—and laugh at. For a moment, I hated the mare. It was her fault. She was nothing more than a washed-up bucking horse, and in my conceited ignorance I'd thought I could compete against horses with generations of careful breeding. As Lorie slipped a halter on her horse, my face turned red with another wave of shame. How could my ego have gotten so big?

"Dina." Lorie unbuckled the cinch then reached over and grabbed my shoulder. "Quit beating yourself up."

"It was a horrible performance. I was so embarrassed, and—" I turned away and bit back the angry tears.

"No. Stop right there. Sit down here."

I sat beside her on the running board of the trailer.

"You need to understand something. If you want to go to the top, learning to control your mind is the most important tool you need to master to win. Sure, it's necessary to have the right horse, and you have to learn the fundamental skills so when you have that horse you can put the physical part of it together. But with every performance, there is a time to look back at your run and learn from it. Pick out what you did wrong. But just as important is to identify what you did right. Then, if it's a bad run you stick it in a box and bury it. And don't dig it up, because if you do, not only will it make you a continual failure, it will ruin your horse. That negativity transfers right through you to the mare. Do you think she's feeling good about today? Do you think she doesn't know that you're angry and embarrassed?"

I sat with my chin cupped in my hands. "Yes, I think she does understand. And you're right. But it is so hard to forget a botched-up failure like today."

Lorie put a hand on my shoulder. "If barrel racing was easy, everybody would be a world champion. God has blessed me with some super talented horses, but there are other girls with as good or better, and there are plenty who ride as well as I do. What I've learned better than most is the ability to control my mind."

"If that works, how do you put a disaster like today behind you?"

Lorie absently coiled and uncoiled a lead rope as she gazed across the parking lot. The left corner of her mouth turned upward. "It's a God thing. He allows bad things to happen—for a reason. And those events I see as bad are where I learn the most. Don't get me wrong. They aren't easy, but they are the lessons I always remember."

"I know you're right, but it's *so* hard."

"Yes, it is, but internalizing those principles is important. And Dina—you will learn them on your way to the top."

I glanced at Lorie's face. Surely she was joking. Me—to the top? After today?

She smiled. "Yes, you'll make it. Now, take that mare and ride her around the action. After the arena is clear, spend some time in there, enough to let her know you have the same confidence in her that you had before we left home."

I nodded and got to my feet. "Thanks, Lorie. I will learn—someday."

She smiled. "Don't be out there too long. We have a six-hundred mile run to Las Vegas, so we need to skedaddle."

# Chapter 42

The sun had colored the gaudy landmarks that define downtown Las Vegas a dark pink as we pulled into the South Point parking lot. I gazed in awe at the hundreds of stalls and the vast indoor arena. The mustard seed of confidence I had left, shriveled. Yesterday's problems were nothing compared to this. At least that had been outdoors. Piñata had never run inside a building. For that matter, neither had I. This would blow the last fragile circuit in her mixed-up brain.

Lorie apparently had an inside track on my fears. "Dina, it's okay. Inside that arena are the same three cans you've run around a thousand times. There will be more bunting and hooraw, but that's all it is. The moment they open the gate, we're going in there to ride so we'll have plenty of time to get used to it."

I swallowed the icebergs of fear and nodded my head. "Okay." We watered the horses, then downed some cereal and toast.

"I'm going to sleep for a few hours. I suggest you do the same." Lorie lowered her eyebrows into a severe frown.

"I'll try."

"Do more than try. Remember what we talked about yesterday. Sleeping when you need to is an important part of learning to control your mind. This is a good day to start."

I did try, and after a couple of hours of worry, my cascading anxiety slowed enough I dozed off. I hoped Piñata had followed the same advice.

Lorie shook me awake just before eleven. "Time to ride. They let contestants ride in the arena until one o'clock. That should be enough time for us farm girls to get used to the city lights."

I rubbed the sleep out of my eyes and tried to grin. A week wouldn't be enough to get either the mare or me used to anything as grand as that venue.

We saddled up and led our horses across the pavement to the big doors. An alley, broad enough for a whole herd of horses led into the cavernous building. Piñata's eyes dilated until they resembled old-time Coke bottles. She snorted at the strange scents, the colored streamers, and the rows of plush red seats. Inside, we joined other riders, all of them trying to make sure that when they burst out of that alley and toward the first barrel, everything would be as familiar as home. Most would be successful. I tried not to think about what could happen to us. Piñata would burst into the arena and see the bright lights and all those people. She would swerve toward the wall, grab the bit in her teeth, and bolt for the exit. I knew it. Yesterday's embarrassing fiasco would be nothing compared to this.

For an hour, Lorie and I rode inside the arena. Many of the women rode up alongside us to talk to Lorie. She was a star, which meant everyone wanted to be seen with her.

Some I recognized, girls we'd met yesterday at Nampa who had made the same overnight run as we had. Lorie introduced me to several, again giving me glowing praise, which after yesterday was completely incomprehensible.

Two hours later, we rode back to the trailer. Lorie haltered and tied her horse without comment though I felt her eyes on me. "You're afraid she's going to lose it, aren't you?"

"Yes. When we walked in there this afternoon, she wanted to jump out of her skin. I know she will fall apart. Tonight, there will be lights and noise, and she can't handle that."

"Which is why we're here. She has to get used to those things."

"But she isn't going to even look for that first barrel. She'll do some crazy spook and make fools out of us. I just hope she doesn't duck out from under me. That would be really embarrassing."

"So . . . you'll ride into the arena, expecting her to spook. You're going to sit straight and ready—just in case. And you know what? She will sense you're not riding to win, that you're afraid, that you don't trust her to be on the team."

"Yeah, I guess you're right. I don't trust her."

Lorie jammed her thumbs into her pockets and raised an eyebrow. "So, you're going to safety up, just try to make a decent run and forget about winning. Is that it?"

I shrugged, suddenly deflated. "What would you do?"

"Doesn't really matter what I would do. But every time I step into an arena, I run to win. Not just for me, for my horse as well, because I want him to give a hundred and ten percent. Each time I ride, I think about ways I can telegraph to my horse that running is fun." Lorie looked at her watch and shrugged. "Enough. Let's get ready."

Thirty minutes later, I swung my leg over Piñata's saddle and stood at the end of the vast alley beside Lorie and a host of others, all of them preparing for their moment in the sun. Lorie had drawn number seventeen. I would be the twenty-fourth girl in the arena.

Lorie slipped out of her windbreaker and handed it to me. I glanced at her face, set in the same frozen mask as yesterday. Her eyes telegraphed the excitement she felt, and suddenly, I understood. Lorie didn't really do this to win, to be a star. She did it because she loved bursting into that arena to run like the wind, to be one with her horse, to feel the power and the driving speed. The crowd, the announcer, the noise—all were forgotten. I laughed, as the little brown horse danced up the alley, her excitement telegraphed through her body to him.

I was too far back in the mass of riders to see what happened in the arena, but I listened as the announcer chronicled Lorie's run. She went to the lead, and it would take a hard-running horse to knock her out of first place. She had nurtured a green colt, communicating to him how to be a winner. Sure, he had the breeding and ability, but Lorie had channeled that promise in record time.

I stroked Piñata's neck and talked softly to her. "You have more speed and talent than that colt. What your breeding is doesn't matter, because today we're going to do this—just because it's fun."

After Lorie had walked her horse to settle him down, she rode up and sat beside me. I handed her my jacket. I was next. My stomach flopped around like a landed catfish, and I was glad I hadn't eaten more. I squeezed the braided nylon rein with one hand and the horn with the other to keep from shaking.

"Go show them how champions run." Lorie's voice was belligerent, almost angry, and for a split second my eyes locked with hers. She smiled. "You can do it—together." She nodded at the mare under me.

The announcer called my name. My heels gently connected with Piñata's muscled ribcage, and we started up the long alley to the arena. Her ears pricked forward as she trotted toward the vast patch of sandy soil in the distance. Suddenly, the lights illuminated the red, white, and blue bunting. Thousands of red seats filled with faces rose above the manicured dirt of the arena floor. Then, far away, the first barrel filled my vision, and I squeezed until I felt that big talented mare explode under me. It was like we were up on the big sagebrush flat by the Bar O, running because that's what she loved, and I urged her on and talked to her as we scampered around the first, then dug hard toward the second barrel. Her body flexed, and I felt her drive into the turn with a power I'd never felt before. My eyes went to the third barrel at the end of the arena, and I leaned out over her neck. Somewhere in the back of my mind I knew I'd never trusted her enough to do that. She might buck or take one of her infamous sideways jumps. Then I'd be on the ground, but it was only a fleeting thought because we were running, we were one, and when we rounded the last barrel, I looked toward the gaping hole of the alley and whooped for joy when I felt the power of her stride as she sprinted toward home. I never touched her with the bat, or even thought of it because it wasn't about winning. This was about the thrill of the race.

Halfway down the alley I slowed her and moved to the side to let the next barrel racer run by me. Somewhere in the background I heard the cheering, and the announcer's excited voice heralding something about an arena record. But that wasn't important. What mattered was this mare, and that tonight, we had finally become partners.

# Chapter 43

Lorie reached over and hugged me as we walked our horses across the parking lot to the pickup. "How does it feel to be a winner?"

I felt a warm glow creep from my face right to my fingertips. "I didn't even think about winning. We just ran for the sheer fun of it—like up on the big sagebrush flat at home."

She nodded wisely. "If you do this for a very long time, there will be days where you forget the fun part. When you face those moments and you're in the dumps, think about tonight. Use today as a reference point in your career. If you always remember that you run because you love the sport, winning will take care of itself."

We unsaddled and watered the horses before walking back to the arena. Lorie and I sat on the fence and watched each run, but I fidgeted, unable to concentrate. If I were to carry out what I'd planned, it had to be now. Nervously, I touched Lorie's shoulder to get her attention. "Lorie, can I borrow your truck for a couple of hours?"

Perplexed, she dug the keys out of her jacket and handed them to me. "Sure. You need to go somewhere?"

"Well, I'd like to, if that's okay. My father was killed near here, and I'd just like to drive out and see where he died."

"Oh, I'm so sorry." Lorie turned away from watching the current barrel racer in the arena. "Do you want me to go with you?"

"No, I'll be okay, but thank you for offering."

"No problem. You've got your phone?"

"Yes." I glanced at my watch. "If I'm not back by seven, I'll call you."

Lorie gave me a long, appraising stare, and finally nodded.

As I slipped down the alley and out into the parking lot, I realized again how much I valued Lorie's friendship. She'd wanted to know more than what I'd been willing to disclose, but that hadn't mattered. She'd trusted my judgement, and I was grateful.

Google maps provided me with the shortest route northeast around the air force base. I wondered what I would find. How would I feel? I wasn't sure I would feel any sorrow or pain. Why couldn't my father have been different, a real parent instead of the vague, mousy little . . . what? Crook? Criminal? No other words came to mind. Memories of Papa brought a level of pain and embarrassment I could never talk about with Lorie, or anyone. But what about Lupita's assessment when she and I had walked out onto the porch in the early dawn and saw all the produce left by the *campesinos* for my Papa? She'd talked about how respected he was in the community. That hardly jibed with the Papa of my childhood. The father I had known hadn't commanded anyone's respect. And yet, several times his behavior had puzzled me, as if for a moment he was a different person. None of it made sense.

Carefully, I maneuvered Lorie's truck over the last mile of potholed dirt, hoping I'd correctly followed Frederick's directions. He'd said it was the old Red Bird mine. Perhaps visiting it would bring a sense of closure. Even if it didn't, I needed to see the place where he'd died for Mama's sake.

Halfway up the last spiny ridge, several ancient buildings huddled against the skyline. A weathered multi-story shed decked out in turn-of-the-century shiplap towered over the rest of the dilapidated structures. That must be what housed the headframe and shaft where Papa's body lay.

I parked and softly closed the door of Lorie's pickup. The late afternoon shadows had started to darken the building as I climbed the rocky hill to the paint-flaked door. I turned the knob and wrenched it open. Telltale signs of recent activity were everywhere. Scattered bits of paper, several empty beer bottles and pop cans littered the floor. The area inside was no larger than Mrs. Riddler's living room. The board floor, now mostly gone, had either rotted or been vandalized. A decrepit desk leaned toward me. A missing leg made it appear to be bowing to whoever entered. Perhaps it had housed a timekeeper who recorded the names of those lowered into the darkness for their dismal shift. Now, there was no machinery or cables, only a gaping hole in the ground. I peered over the edge. A murky light illumined the sides for the first twenty feet. After that, there was nothing but the eerie blackness of a thousand nights, and I peddled backward, horrified by the silent chasm below.

"*Hola*, Dina."

I whirled, my heart nearly jumping out of my chest. Panic constricted my throat. A man stood in the doorway, his face shadowed by the gloomy interior of the building, but after the initial distress, I recognized the voice. I should. In our living room, he had asked my parents for my hand in marriage.

Eduardo blocked the entrance, handsome as always in a blue short-sleeve polo shirt and slacks, but his bronze features might have been cast in stone. His full lips were parted, I suppose waiting for my joyous response. A lock of wavy black hair slipped over his high forehead. His dark, expressive eyes, unreadable in the gloom, searched for mine. "It's good to see you." He walked forward, reached over and hugged me. Nothing had changed with Eduardo.

I pushed away. "How did you . . . What are you doing here?"

"Dina, I work for a Mexican business organization. Presently, I am based here in Las Vegas. I saw you at the Futurity, so when you left the grounds I followed you. I know why you're here. We will punish those who killed your father. I will make sure of it."

"What do you mean?" I stepped further away from the gaping mine shaft behind me.

Eduardo's hands slipped into the pockets of his sharply creased slacks. With his right hand, he jingled a few coins. It was a nervous gesture I remembered well. A light turned on in my brain and I suddenly knew where the money had come from for the expensive BMW.

"You're working for a cartel, aren't you?" My accusation rang across the room, though I still didn't believe Eduardo would do that.

He shrugged, and his lips flattened. "We have to stick together in our country."

"Stick together?" I stepped toward the wall. "You sell drugs, Eduardo?"

He spread his hands. "It is the Americans who have created the demand. If we don't meet that need, someone else will. It's Business 101."

My shoulders slumped. "Which cartel do you pimp for, Eduardo? Those Sinaloa snakes, or is it Los Zetas?"

His face flushed with anger. "You do not understand, because you don't want to." His eyes smoldered with an instant disdain. "There is somebody else now?"

"Why shouldn't there be? You and I were never meant for each other. And besides, anyone is better than a drug cartel goon."

I backed further away, repulsed by his lack of morality. "Why, Eduardo? There is no excuse for you, because you didn't even need their money." By this time, I was shouting with anger. My back was now near the far wall, but still only a few feet from the mine shaft. I never could have loved him, but we'd been friends before he became a traitor to the country of our birth. Now, I only despised him and everything he stood for.

"Dina." He stepped forward and grabbed my shoulders. "I will fulfill all of your dreams. You will have the best horses that money can buy. Do you want a year-round arena? Perhaps a climate-controlled building in which to practice? A house with every convenience? An Olympic-sized pool? Tell me. I will provide it."

I jerked away in disgust as I stared at the cavernous opening to the shaft. Somewhere down there, my father rested, a man who sold out his family for money. "Eduardo, never would I marry anyone who had anything to do with the cartels. Your collaboration with them is a betrayal of everything I believe. You have spoken of the things you could give me—bought, I might add, with the blood of our people. You can't *buy* me. Months ago, my answer was no because I wanted to go to college first. Now, my answer is no because I do not love you, nor could I ever love you. You have become despicable to me."

Some say it is not possible for our dark Mexican faces to turn red, but Eduardo's turned bright crimson. His hand moved like lightning, and I staggered back as he slapped me. At the last moment, I grabbed at the broken cribbing behind me to avoid falling down the abandoned shaft. He followed me, his eyes now malevolent and deadly.

I slipped sideways, away from the hole, wanting to escape, but Eduardo stood between me and the door. He moved closer, every hint of friendliness gone. I shrank against the wall, now terrified. His arm shot out, his fingers searching for my throat.

"Stop." The voice came from the sun-streaked doorway. Eduardo whirled. My jaw dropped. Frederick stood in the opening, silhouetted against the bright sun outside. "If you touch her again, it will be your last move." He stalked toward Eduardo, his face grim.

"Frederick—don't." I circled toward him, away from Eduardo and the hole in the ground.

Eduardo's shoulders slumped. He ran a hand through his thick black hair and took a deep breath. "So, this is your American," he sneered.

"Yes. Unlike you, he has never hit me."

Eduardo nodded, but now his eyes held only hatred. Frederick stepped forward, and for a moment, I thought he would tear Eduardo to pieces. He stood, legs akimbo, his hands quiet and ready. The only sign of stress was a twitch in his left jaw muscle. I caught his eye and shook my head. I didn't want anyone hurt because of me.

The man who had asked Papa for my hand in marriage took two steps toward the entrance. "May I?" He glared at Frederick, his voice low and insolent. Frederick eyed him, then deliberately stepped aside. Eduardo left without a backward glance. Frederick and I watched him drive down the mountain. Then, we turned to each other and I fell into his arms. I didn't bother to analyze what that meant, other than I knew that when this man was close, I felt safe.

# Chapter 44

"How did you know I was here?" My cheek stung where Eduardo had slapped me, and my voice threatened to break.

Frederick's eyes still flashed with an icy anger and I felt his hands on my shoulders tremble.

"I found Lorie's trailer and recognized that wing-nut mare of yours. Lorie told me you'd borrowed her truck to visit the site where your father died. I knew exactly where you'd gone."

"Be careful. That *wing-nut* mare ran like a champion today." I buried my head in his chest. "Thanks for coming to find me."

His fingers stroked my hair. "I'm sorry I wasn't here sooner."

I looked up at him. "So, you followed me across three states for a reason?"

"Yes." He looked down into my eyes. "Mostly, because . . . because I love you, Dina Rodriguez."

In any credible romance story, a passionate kiss should have followed his words of love and fidelity. Not Frederick. He had to stir up other issues.

"Tailing you was for professional reasons as well. I suspected al-Qaida would show again, but I had no idea this old flame of yours would pop out of the woodwork."

I felt the rising red in my cheeks and pushed away. "Eduardo is not an old boyfriend. He never was more than a high school classmate—though I guess he didn't see it that way."

Frederick studied my face. Momentary doubt flickered in his eyes, quickly replaced by naked adoration. It was the first time I'd seen that look, and no matter what happened between us, I knew I would hold that moment in my heart forever. Then, just when I'd just about given him up as a romantic clod, everything stood still. Our lips met, and if there was any sound in that hot desert evening—I totally missed it. This was so right. If I hadn't known it before, I knew it now—I loved Frederick Roseman.

Our emotions eventually settled back to earth. Hand in hand, we stepped up to the gaping hole in the ground. Somewhere at the bottom of that shaft was my Papa's final resting place. Was he in Purgatory? Hell? Certainly, as much wrong as he had done, he wasn't in Heaven. I couldn't hold back the tears, and I wept for Papa, for what I'd missed, for what might have been. Frederick stood beside me, his arm wrapped tightly around my shoulders.

"I must call Mama. We have put off a memorial mass for too long. We need to have our time together. Perhaps she has found Alejandro."

"I would like to help wherever I can."

"Thank you. You have done so much."

"Would you like to fly home from here? I'm sure Lorie would understand. She could take the horses and go back to Miles City."

"No, I don't want to leave her with that long drive alone, and—"

"Do whatever you feel is right, but if you decide you should be with your family there will be a plane ready in the morning."

"A plane? Who's going to pay for that?"

"Dina, any cost associated with your father will be picked up by the government."

"Government? Why? He wasn't *that* bad." This was starting to sound like a repeat of Frederick's delusions that led to the Primrose Mall disaster.

His gentle eyes met mine. "Dina, your father worked for the CIA—since long before you were born. Any cost now is nothing compared to what he gave to his country."

I stepped back, for a moment unable to speak. "That's impossible. How could Papa have worked for . . . I mean, he was a smuggler. He wasn't even a good rancher. Mama had to make all the decisions, and sometimes even manage the hired help" My voice dropped nearly to a whisper. "Even when he was home, Papa just sat in his office."

The men with funny accents who had stayed at our ranch, the sudden change in Papa's demeanor when he'd caught me eavesdropping on the stairs. For a few seconds, the mask had slipped. It came to me in a rush. That mousy, incompetent, ne'er-do-well who lived in my father's clothes? That hadn't been my real father. Could he have spent most of his adult life playing a degrading, foppish role to serve the country he loved? I stared out into the twilight, hardly able to process the glaring revelation. "Did Mama know about him—what he did?"

Frederick shrugged. "You need to ask her that question."

I leaned over the mine shaft and slipped to my knees. Frederick reached down, touched my shoulder, then slipped outside to leave me alone with this new grief. I covered my face with my hands and whispered down into the midnight blackness.

"Papa, why didn't you tell us? I should have known, and I'm so sorry. It must have been hard for you to appear incompetent and uncaring to everyone around you. How I wish we could have had time together where you were your real self." I hunched forward, wiping my eyes, trying to understand a new grief I couldn't explain. Had duty to his country been that important? How could he have made this sacrifice that went on for years while Mama lost the man she married, and we, his children grew up, never knowing our real father?

Weary and drained, I pushed to my feet and stood as close as I dared to the gaping shaft in the middle of the room. "Goodbye, Papa. I wish . . . I wish you could have seen Piñata and me today in that huge arena. I think you would have been proud." At the door I looked back one last time, the sadness a Titanic-sized weight on my chest.

Frederick leaned against the hood of Lorie's pickup. "Are you okay?"

"I will be. I just wish this could have been different."

"I understand." He put his arm around my shoulder. "There was more to your father than either of us will ever know." He shook his head. "I had one glimpse of Ricardo, the CIA operative. It was the day I met him in Bisbee. We talked. Actually, it was more like a sparring match which he totally won, but when he walked away, I knew he was an agent, which I would have never known if he hadn't allowed me a brief glimpse. He was magnificent—one of the best."

"Why didn't you tell me?" Anger tinged my voice.

He pulled me closer. "Because he wouldn't have wanted that."

"Yes, of course." I pulled away and glared resentfully. "Old boys club. Stick together—zip the lip."

Frederick winced. "No, that's not it at all. He didn't want me to tell you—because he would have wished to do that himself. The plan was that it would be over soon. This operation was the culmination of many years infiltrating the al-Qaida network. In the end, he would come home. But . . . it didn't happen."

My shoulders slumped, and a huge wave of weariness smashed through my disappointment and anger. "Let's get out of here. Lorie and I traveled all last night, and I'm so tired."

"Would you like me to drive you back?"

"No, just follow me. I'll make it." A half-hour late, I parked in front of Lorie's trailer. Frederick pulled in behind me.

Lorie stepped outside and brushed off my apologies. "I'm glad you're here and safe." Her lips pursed together as the green Mustang pulled in beside the horse trailer. "How'd he get here?

I stuttered a few words about Frederick being in the area on business. Lorie stared at me as if I were one step removed from an idiot, so I mumbled about my father having died near here. That confused her even more. However, she graciously invited Frederick in for a cup of coffee. He declined, his excuse being that he had pressing business elsewhere, which I doubted. That left only me to tell Lorie a story that made little sense, even to me.

# Chapter 45

The sky dawned dark and blotchy, the purple and dark cream of a coming desert storm heavy on the gathering wind. Lorie made coffee while I fed the horses. As the flakes of hay from our last bale broke into my hands, I glanced out at the street entrance, hoping Frederick would arrive. It would be easier to further explain my dysfunctional family and my need to go home if he were here. Should I take his offer of a private plane to be with Mama in Agua Prieta, or should I return to Miles City and fly later in the week? And what about Trent and my job? How could I ever ask him for *more* time off?

As Piñata munched through her oats, I brushed her reddish-sorrel hide. She'd never run harder than she had yesterday, not even up on the sagebrush flat. Was her success in that huge coliseum a one-time event, or were her troubles like a bad dream—gone forever? It seemed yesterday's win was more encouraging than I had any right to expect. Nevertheless, in my heart it seemed we'd built a new level of trust.

"What are you smiling about?" Lorie walked out with two cups of steaming coffee.

I stood back from the mare and suddenly broke out laughing. "She is such a rags-to-riches success story. I still can't believe that a horse as messed up as she is could make a complete turnaround, even for a day. How can I ever thank you? Any success we have is due to you—and of course Merle."

Lorie handed me the cup of coffee and sat on the running board of the trailer. "Yes, he got you started on the right track with her. You and that mare will go far. This is only a beginning."

"Do you think so? I'm still in shock at the way it all came together yesterday. I would never have believed that Piñata would run like that."

Lorie chuckled. "If she keeps running like she did yesterday, you two will be unbeatable. More coffee?" Lorie asked.

"Sure, but let me get it." The sound of a vehicle interrupted our conversation. "We'll need a little tea as well." I nodded toward the familiar Mustang, waved to Frederick and walked inside.

When I returned, Lorie and Frederick were deep into a discussion, apparently about my immediate plans. I handed him the tea I'd made, then edged in beside him.

He laid his hand on my knee. "Thanks, and much appreciated. As you've just heard, Lorie and I have a good start on planning your future." Our eyes met, and he smiled at me over the rim of his cup. "Did you want a say, or shall we carry on?"

My face reddened. How well I remembered my accusation of him wanting to control my life, and my subsequent remorse. "I can't decide what to do. I would appreciate your help" I snuggled into Frederick's shoulder and listened.

"We think your family should have first priority," Lorie said.

"But what about my job? My absences there are already beyond ridiculous, and Trent—"

Frederick gestured with his cup. "You'll take less time off this way than if you go home, work for a day or two and then have to fly out of Miles City. Call him. He'll understand. Your father gave his life for this country. Trent can and will tough it out for a few more days."

How I wished I'd known the man Frederick had just praised. I scuffed at the pavement with the side of my boot, while inside, I wept. That man had been the father I never knew. A flash of anger replaced the grief. Serving his country meant he'd never been the dad I'd yearned for.

Lorie reached over and put an arm around my shoulder. "I can get the horses home. That's my contribution in this, and I'm glad to do that if it helps. Don't worry; I'll take good care of that futurity winner." She nodded her head toward Piñata.

I took a deep breath and pushed my grief and anger down into a hidden place in my chest. "Thanks, Lorie. But I feel bad sticking you with the long drive home. Are you sure this is the best option?"

"Absolutely." She stood. "Now, I need to go put on my face, at least enough to look presentable for the day, so I shall leave you two with the final decision."

Frederick smiled and tipped his cup at her. "Hey, thanks for the tea."

"Our pleasure." She gave me a sideways glance that was anything but guileless before she closed the door.

I scooted closer to Frederick. "Okay, I think it makes sense to go now. Will you come home with me—to the memorial?"

He eyed me like a frightened rabbit before he answered. "I suppose, if that's what you want."

I would like it if you would come. "I don't have much to pack. I suppose I'll have to buy some clothes. Oh, maybe not. I have closets full at home."

Frederick pulled a phone out of his jacket pocket and punched in a number. "I'll make the flight arrangements."

"Give me twenty minutes," I whispered.

He nodded as he stood and paced back and forth, the phone to his ear.

I slipped inside the trailer living quarters to pack the few items I would need. Fifteen minutes later, I was ready to go. Frederick reached for my bag, and after I hugged Lorie, we left for the airport.

Before we reached the main terminal, Frederick turned onto a side-road and parked in front of a small hangar. He locked the car, then led me through the building and out the other side. An efficient and new looking twin-engine plane seemed to be waiting just for us. I glanced sideways at him. "Who owns this?"

"The Feds."

"They sent it because of my father?" I pointed at the sleek nose of the aircraft in front of us.

Frederick nodded without further comment, as he guided me toward the steps.

Two hours later, the pilot began his descent into Douglas, Arizona. Before the wheels touched the ground, my stomach endured the first assault of predator-sized butterflies. What would Mama think? How would she react to my big blond American? She'd better not embarrass him or I would—no, I wouldn't borrow trouble. She might be reasonable, especially during this time of Papa's death.

At the airport, Frederick mysteriously produced a car, which likely came from the same people who had supplied the airplane. A half-hour later we idled onto the crushed, white rock driveway of our Sonora ranch. Lupita skipped down from the veranda to welcome us. I hugged her, then turned and put my hand on Frederick's arm as I introduced him. If I hadn't known better, I would have said he was trembling, but of course Frederick was afraid of nothing, so I shrugged it off. If there were some tremors, it must have been the long flight and the strain he'd been under for the last week.

Lupita slipped her arm through mine. "Dina, I am so glad you are here. Your mama needs you." With my other arm, I held onto the man beside me. He looked as if he wanted to run as we climbed the broad veranda steps.

At the top, Frederick's free hand straightened his already immaculate sports jacket. "Your mother . . . when will we meet her?" he croaked.

I giggled at his discomfort because it was so uncharacteristic. "Soon enough."

Lupita opened the tall wooden door that graced our front entry. We stepped into the spacious room some Americans call a vestibule. My mother appeared at the top of the stairs that led to the second story of our house. She descended the curved marble stairs, her face calmer than I would have expected.

"Sweetheart, I'm so glad you have come." Her voice broke, and for a few moments we held each other. Mama was uncharacteristically quiet, and I wondered why. What was going on? This was strange behavior from my melodramatic mother. When she stepped back, she glanced at Frederick. "Dina dear, you have brought company?"

"Yes, Mama, this is Frederick Roseman. He—he . . . well, I live at his grandmother's house, and we have become good friends, and he has helped me quite a lot, and he's a good friend, and I brought him home to meet . . ."

Why hadn't I thought this through? I sounded like . . . okay, I was nervous. It would have helped if I could have switched into Spanish, but with Frederick beside me, that wouldn't have been polite. "Yes," I finished. "So, I would like you to meet him, and—"

Mama rescued me in a fashion I never could have imagined. Graciously, she stepped forward and held out her slim hand. "Frederick, welcome to our home. I am Mariela, and I am so glad Dina brought you to be with us during this difficult time."

Frederick held my mother's hand in both of his, looking as if he didn't know whether to shake it, bow over it, or just drop it and retreat. He stuttered some inane remark about hoping he wasn't intruding, which I guess was the best anyone could have done under the circumstances.

Mama's control of the situation puzzled me. She was nothing like the mother I knew, and certainly not the woman I'd described to Frederick.

"Come." She touched Frederick's arm as she ushered him toward the stairs. "Dina, if you will show him to the blue room, I will help Lupita. *Comida* will be served as soon as you are ready to eat."

Frederick followed me up the curved staircase to the upper stories of our house. Though we had four guest bedrooms, we rarely used more than what we called *El cuarto azul*. The Blue Room isn't a very creative name, but the walls and even the ceiling were all a garish cobalt-indigo war, so that's what it was called—The Blue Room. Papa had cursed every time he had reason to see it. He tried to get my mother to repaint it. She refused. Mama said that company never overstayed their welcome if they had to stay in The Blue Room, because nobody could stand it for more than a few days. I couldn't help wondering if that was why she put Frederick there.

"Your mother is a gracious woman, not how I would have pictured her." His raised eyebrows told me my credibility had plummeted.

"Frederick." I spread my hands and rolled my eyes. "I swear, what you saw is not Mama. The façade will drop." I held the door open while he walked into the blue bedroom. "Sorry about the paint job, and no, you won't get used to it."

He grinned. "It doesn't matter. I've seen worse. You have a beautiful home. Umm . . . the Dina back there in Miles City—you know, that beautiful waitress at the Spur Bar. Is that the same girl as . . .?" he pointed at me with a glint of humor.

I looked at him uncertainly. "This ranch and house belong to my parents—my mother now. Whatever I accomplish in life will be on my own. It will have nothing to do with what *they* have accumulated. If you will recall, I've always viewed my father's money as tainted."

I walked to the window and stared out over the vast desert and the dry wash to the east. Now that Papa had died, had my view of our family changed? The evidence in the last few days had dramatically tipped in Papa's favor, which possibly meant Mama as well.

"It's difficult to switch how I've always thought about my father. Growing up, I was well aware he worked as a smuggler, though we avoided that subject." I reached for Frederick's hand and held it in both of mine. "Anyhow, I will leave you to get ready for *comida*. I took a deep breath. "And brace yourself for my *real* mother."

Ten minutes later, I waited for Frederick at the bottom of the stairs. When he appeared, he again looked positively ill. I took his hand. That seemed prudent so he didn't attempt an escape. We proceeded to the dining room to face what surely would be a disaster.

# Chapter 46

When Dina left the blue room, Frederick wiped the sweat from his forehead. Why had he agreed to come? Was this the punishment for falling in love? He could have handled her father. Both of them worked in intelligence. They at least had some common ground. But what would he say to her mother? She would be antagonistic, and before the sun set, the cold reserve Dina had warned him about would chill to an icy disdain. He wasn't Catholic—or Mexican. She would not approve.

He showered, changed clothes, and peered at the unsatisfactory image in the mirror. Every time he was around this girl, it felt like a first date. Tonight, it would be like the first date with her mother along. He combed his hair, squared his shoulders, and made his way down the stairs. Dina waited at the bottom. He gasped. She had changed into a soft, rose-colored gown. Her raven hair shimmered against the silk, and again he was completely mesmerized by her beauty. Then, his face fell. Why had he ever thought he would have a chance with a woman this lovely?

Dina's smile turned into a look of consternation. She glanced down at her dress, then at Frederick as he reached the bottom stair. "You don't like it? I'm sorry. Usually when we have company we dress for dinner. Wait, I will go change."

"No. It's not that. You are so beautiful. Don't change anything—ever."

She blushed with pleasure at the compliment, and demurely placed her arm in his as they made their way to the *comedor* to face her mother, and what Frederick was sure would be his last evening in the Rodriguez mansion.

When they walked into the dining room, Dina's mother stood, hands clasped in front of her, at the far end of the table. Completely in control, she graciously waved them to their places. Frederick pulled a chair out for Dina before he sat. Mariela immediately bowed her head. Frederick followed suit, though he had no clue how a Mexican Catholic family would say grace. Mariela's sincerity eclipsed the unfamiliar Spanish words. Dina intoned an "Amen," so he did as well. Both women made the sign of the cross. Frederick didn't feel comfortable doing that, so he mumbled another "Amen," hoping that would suffice.

Lupita stood in the doorway, and at a nod from Dina's mother she brought in bowls of a delicious looking tortilla soup.

As they sampled the first course, Mariella turned to their guest. "So, Frederick, you are not Catholic?"

Frederick's shoulders slumped as he set the ornate silver soup spoon on the edge of his plate. What a way to start. How should he answer what was the first and most damning question of the evening? "No, I'm sorry to say, I have never had much contact with the Catholic faith—until I met Dina."

"Then you are Protestant?"

Frederick took a swallow of water. "I am a Christian."

Mariela's eyebrow rose. "Which means . . .?"

"I'm a follower of Jesus."

"Oh—and Catholics aren't?"

Frederick picked up his spoon and toyed with his soup. This was deep water. He glanced desperately toward Dina, but she seemed intent on helping herself to the chicken dish Lupita had set out as a main course. He glared at her downcast, dark eyelashes. She sneaked a glance at him, and he instantly knew she was trying not to giggle at his discomfort. He'd better answer with great care.

"Perhaps I am not as familiar as I ought to be about Catholic beliefs."

Dina's mother laid down her spoon. "We Catholics have major issues with Protestants. Belief in the Savior is not one of them." Her voice was calm, almost distant.

Lupita scurried in from the kitchen and set another hot dish in the center of the table. Dina touched her arm. "Lupita, thank you for making this yummy chicken. It has always been my favorite." For a moment, they talked in rapid Spanish about the recipe, saving Frederick from further discomfort.

"Please, Frederick, have some chicken. I hope it is not too spicy for you. " Mariela picked up the platter and passed it to him. The rest of the meal, Dina steered the conversation toward less incendiary topics. She diligently avoided religion, and Frederick spoke little, happy to observe Dina's relationship with her mother. Several times, he noted her puzzled look as she watched Mariela speak. The reason needed no explanation. This thoughtful, intelligent woman bore little resemblance to the mother Dina had described.

At the end of the meal, Dina's mother placed her neatly folded *servietta* beside her plate. "Alejandro called this morning."

"He's coming home?" Dina asked.

Mariela nodded. "He will be here this evening."

"How thoughtful of him. It's been what—five years since any of us have seen him?"

Frederick winced at the underlying hurt behind the sarcasm. Why had Dina's brother apparently shunned not only his father, but his mother and sister as well? And yet Dina's mother had apparently been able to immediately reach him.

Mariela murmured a reply, her Spanish words obviously a gentle rebuke to her daughter.

In the cool of the evening, Frederick strolled toward the barn and corrals with Dina. In the large outdoor arena, Raul loped a colt around the perimeter. When they approached, he stepped off his horse and strode forward. Dina rushed to meet his open arms.

"*Bienvenido a casa*. Welcome home, little one."

"I'm so glad to be here. I missed you, Raul." Dina introduced Frederick, and later they leaned on the fence and watched as Raul again worked the dun colt in the arena.

"When I was home, this is where I spent most of my waking hours. We always had the best horses money could buy. I think I understand now. They weren't for the ranch. Papa bought them for me. But now the best one of all, my Chiquita is dying."

Frederick slid an arm around her shoulder. "It must be hard to come back and see her in that condition."

"Yes, though having Piñata helps."

He pulled her closer. "You took a useless renegade, dangerous to herself and everybody around her and turned her into a winner."

"There were so many days when I thought I'd made a mistake. She was so afraid."

They turned at the sound of a vehicle in the driveway. When the car stopped, Frederick's quick eyes appraised the tall, rangy driver as he stepped onto the gravel.

Dina stiffened. "That is Alejandro."

Frederick eyed the young man in dark slacks and a light-blue tieless shirt beside the black Lexus. "It seems he has done well."

Dina scoffed. "That is probably a rental car. Anyhow, I suppose we had better go meet him." They strolled up the worn path from the barn to the driveway.

Alejandro walked toward them. "Dina?" He stepped forward and switched into the language of their childhood. "My little sister has turned into a beautiful woman."

Dina submitted to his warm embrace. Frederick watched her closely, noting that her return hug had been less than genuine. She stepped away and motioned toward Frederick.

"Alejandro, I would like you to meet a good friend of mine. Frederick, this is my long-lost brother, Alejandro."

Pain flashed across the young man's face at Dina's sarcasm. Frederick stepped forward, nodded a greeting, and reached for Alejandro's outstretched hand.

"It's a pleasure to meet you, Frederick." Alejandro's grip was coolly polite. His sudden switch to English carried no accent. Obviously, in the Rodriguez household, everyday affairs had been conducted in American-style English.

The silence grew awkward, neither of the men able or willing to break the tension of the moment. Finally, Dina broke the uncomfortable lull in the conversation. "Well—shall we go find Mama?" Both men nodded, and she led the way up the stairs, but before they reached the veranda, Mariela rushed out and fell into Alejandro's waiting arms. "Finally, you have come."

"Yes, Mama," he whispered. "I will come often now. You understand, I think."

She wiped at the tears and nodded. "Yes, I know it was necessary."

"Necessary? Would one of you tell me what *that* means?" Dina asked.

Mariela turned to Dina. "Of course, this is all very confusing. For now, let's celebrate being a family. I so wish we could have done that with your father, but we will talk about that tomorrow. Tonight, let's enjoy being together, and discover all that is happening in each other's lives. Is that okay, my children?"

Alejandro patted his mother's shoulder. "That is fine with me, Mama. Whatever else there is to discuss can wait."

Dina shrugged and rolled her eyes. "Whatever."

Frederick stood to the side, wishing he'd not been present at this intimate but tense reunion. Why had he come? Certainly, to be a support to Dina, but honestly, wasn't he here to press for a greater commitment? With all these undercurrents of family tension, were either of them ready for that? And why had he thought this would be a good time to bring up *that* subject?

Dina saved Frederick from further self-recrimination. She grabbed his hand and followed Alejandro and Mariela through the spacious entry, past the locked door of what she'd indicated was her father's office and into the *sala*. She sat close to him on one of the elegant leather couches. Alejandro perched on a chair in the corner of the room. He looked uncomfortable, ready to ditch the whole gathering at the first opportunity. Mariela fired questions at a frantic pace, as if trying to make up for lost time. Some of the questions were directed at Dina, but Alejandro bore the brunt of her salvo. He talked of his townhouse outside Washington, and of course his job, one of a thousand paper-pushers for the State Department. However, his confident bearing and careful answers suggested to Frederick this brother of Dina's played a much larger role than he was willing to admit.

Later, Alejandro turned to Frederick. "Please forgive us. Our family has needed to make up for too many years we have spent apart, but enough. Tell me, Frederick, where do you live?"

Frederick leaned forward, his elbows perched on his knees. "Omaha, Nebraska has been home for the last few years."

"Ah, a bustling little city. I always think of Omaha as the brightest star in the Midwest. So many dynamic companies are headquartered there, which gives it a distinct flavor. And of course there's the king of cherry coke, not to mention a number of other significant people who make that city their home."

Frederick chuckled. "I presume you're referring to Mr. Buffet?"

"Who else? What do you do in Omaha?"

"I work for a government services contractor."

"Which one? In my profession we are in contact with many of those. Perhaps I have heard of your employer."

"Not likely. We're a small company, not at all well-known."

Silence greeted Frederick's evasive answer. Alejandro was not to be put off, and instantly Frederick knew this son of Ricardo's was a man to be respected and watched. "The company name is Stirling Associates. Most of what we do is off-shore—"

"I'm aware of Stirling's role." Alejandro leaned back and crossed one leg over the other. "So, you are *that* Frederick Roseman?" His voice, though still reserved, was filled with a new respect.

"I suppose." Frederick wiped his forehead. The room seemed stifling. He stole a quick glance at Dina. Her head was cocked toward him; her full lips turned upward in a quizzical smile. He scowled, simply because he could think of no other response to her brother's disturbing recognition of his role in the intelligence affairs of the nation.

# Chapter 47

Mama had been right to insist we wait to discuss family matters. Alejandro and I had been close. He was my big brother and as a little girl I adored him, so when he disappeared from my life, his seeming abandonment was a deep hurt. With time, the wounds closed, but the scars of bitterness made it difficult to pick up the relationship he had so callously abandoned.

At my parent's *casa*, our main meal, *la comida,* is about two o'clock in the afternoon, but we always have a light snack later in the evening. Tonight, Lupita had made quesadillas, probably because she knew Frederick, like most Americans, would be used to eating heartier fare than we were accustomed to at that time of day.

My brother and Frederick seemed to have much in common, both intelligent and intense men who would always create their own destinies.

During the meal, Mama managed the conversation—and her family. That wasn't new, but the quiet way she did it was something we had rarely seen in our growing-up years.

Conversation lagged at the end of the meal. Frederick and I bid good night to Mama and Alejandro, then slipped away together. At the front door, I held out my hand to him. "Come; there is a full moon, and the night is warm. Let's go to the barn and check on the horses.

He smiled and followed me out the door. "Can't think of anybody in the world I'd rather do that with than you." As he gathered my hand into his, I flushed with pleasure. Of late, that had happened with increasing frequency.

We tiptoed out of the house and down the stone steps. The desert night carried the well-remembered sounds from my childhood. A fox screeched in the upper pasture, and two Billy Owls argued somewhere in the mesquite below the barn.

Frederick slipped his arm around my shoulder as we picked our way down the well-worn trail to our horse-training facilities. "You have an interesting family."

"Meaning . . .?"

"Nothing negative. They're fascinating people, but I'm puzzled. Your mother is nothing like you described."

"Frederick." I threw up my hands in frustration. "I feel betrayed. I'm now convinced she was part of the whole charade with my father. She is so different I don't even know how to respond. One part of me is angry, but another part is relieved that she's not the calculating, hard woman I saw as a teenager. I feel as if I were adopted. I didn't know my real Papa, and now I have no connection with this new mother."

"But isn't this better? How would you feel tonight if everything were the same as when you left? And what if Alejandro had not returned, or worse, came home carrying only bitterness?"

"You're right, but I need time to digest it all. The only part of our home that's the same is Mama's faith. That part is good . . . and yet somehow, I want more."

We walked into the barn and strolled down the hoof-worn timbered floor of the alleyway. The familiar smells of sweet-smelling hay mixed with the occasional pungent odor of horse manure were a contrast to the warm, living scent of horse sweat and well-oiled leather. They were memories from my high-school years, aromas as important to me as the scented candle beside my rosary, and the Coco Chanel perfume on my dresser.

Hand in hand, Frederick and I strolled from the barn to one of the horse pastures, then back to the house. The cloudless night sky hung like a black quilt pinned to the earth's ceiling with a billion shimmering stars. I gazed at the glowing expanse and wondered how each one in its own peculiar way performed whatever duty the God of the universe had commanded. Was Papa up there? Was he now gathered together with my grandma and his childhood brother and parents? The stars seemed close and comforting, and though in my heart, anger and disappointment still rose up in rebellion, the first trickle of peace wet the parched desert in my soul. At the mine shaft, I'd given up the disdain and contempt I'd held for my father, but I still carried a deep resentment. He'd served his country well, but we his family had paid dearly. Tomorrow we would join friends, neighbors, and acquaintances with our shared grief, a formal goodbye to a father I would never know.

At the top of the stairs, I kissed Frederick, then snuggled into his arms. Suddenly, Mama appeared at the bottom of the steps, her visage dark and stern. "Dina, may I have a word with you in the office?" For a moment, I felt guilty. What was this about? Did Mama think Frederick and I were sleeping together? I hoped not. She would consider that disrespectful in *her* house.

"I'll be right there, Mama." I gave Frederick one last kiss, then resolutely made my way down to do battle. The door to Papa's office stood ajar.

"Come in, Dina."

Gently, I pushed at the solid oak door. Mama sat in the high-back chair behind Papa's desk, her glasses perched on the end of her nose. She beckoned me forward. I walked in with clenched fists and set jaw as I eased into one of the cane chairs. Mama's elbows rested on the same wine-red blotter from which I'd taken the documents the last time I'd been home. Momentarily, my stomach knotted. Papa might still be alive if I'd not stolen those papers.

My mother seemed not to notice my truculent antagonism. She picked up an envelope and extended it toward me. "This is for you. Your father wanted you to have this if anything happened to him."

I reached for the plain white envelope with my name printed neatly across the middle. "When did . . . when did he give this to you?" A lead ball careened from one side of my stomach to the other as I met my mother's eyes. "Do you know what's inside?"

"Not really. His only instructions were that it was especially for you."

My lips tightened with barely-controlled anger. "Apologies or money can never make up for what he did to us." I grabbed the envelope, turned, and swept through the door.

"Dina."

I stopped and glared back at Mama as I bit my lower lip to keep it from trembling. Her eyes, tinged with sadness held mine.

"Your father loved you dearly."

I opened my mouth, prepared to lash out with another bitter response, but Mama held up her hand.

"Read the letter. You have your whole life to be angry if that is what you wish." She rose and followed me to the bottom as I trudged up the stairs. I didn't fail to notice that she hadn't locked the door, to Papa's office, the one room in the house that had been barred to Alejandro and me since we were children.

Mama's voice stopped me at the landing. "Good night, daughter. I love you and thank you for coming home."

My face crumpled. I half-turned and nodded, too distraught to speak. The salty-hot tears threatened to spill over as I hurried to my room. I closed the door and stood with my back to it, breathing deeply. Why couldn't we have been an ordinary family? Ours was a good home. I had everything any girl could want, but we'd lived in a netherworld of deception.

I kicked off my shoes and arranged the pillows against the ornate headboard Papa had bought for me years ago in Guadalajara, then slit the envelope and stared at the single sheet of handwritten paper. My father's skills had clearly not included the use of a pen. I studied the cursive scrawl, wishing he'd typed the words, not that he did that well either.

"My dearest daughter." I reached for the box of tissues on my nightstand. I would need them if the first sentence was a bellwether of what lay ahead.

"If you are reading this, it means I made a dreadful mistake and am no longer around to watch you with a father's pride as you make your way through life. For that, I am sorry. I so would have liked to see you marry, to hold and love your children. I wanted to be a good enough grandfather that in a small way it would make up for what I wasn't able to be as a father. Please know that if God allows me to watch you read this, I will understand your anger and disappointment. In the days ahead, you will discover that you and Alejandro became part of the collateral damage of a career I chose more than three decades ago—long before you were born. By the time you came into our lives, quitting my journey was not an option, and to expose you or your brother to the truth would have been dangerous for you, our family, and many others as well. Was it a good decision? I often wonder. All I know is that as I write this, I wipe away tears at the thought that we will never have the opportunity to live a normal life. Often, I saw the hurt and loathing in your eyes at the parts I was forced to play. Your mother carried the daily burden of knowing all of my activities. I would never have had the strength to carry it all on my own. She is a woman of rare quality. You, my precious daughter will be the same.

"Bernardina, I love you and I pray that someday you will be able to forgive me and understand the duty and love of country I placed above all else. But if you can't, please forgive and love your mother. Take care of her. I will charge your brother with the same."

The stack of tissues was growing, but I couldn't stop weeping. Why? Why had our lives been warped in this . . . this cause my father called duty? I would never understand. Why were we the casualties of Papa's war against al-Qaida or some other weird Muslim offshoot? Now he was dead, and nothing he could say would make up for the years where there was no connection. I wiped at my eyes and continued to read.

"My daughter, I love you. I want to close this letter by telling you how proud I am for what you have accomplished. How I laughed with joy and pride when I watched you succeed with the mare I bought for you. Only God and your mother will know my deep disappointment when you had to leave her at the border and strike out on your own. I hope you understand how hard it was for me to not write a check for a new horse, and yet I am so proud of you for setting off with the pittance I gave you. You will reach the stars. I know this in my heart.

Be kind to Alejandro. He has been hurt, too.

Marry in the church. God has destined you for happiness.

With much love,

Papa."

I buried my head in the pillows and sobbed, trying to wash away the bitter disappointment of all those years. Later, I knelt in the corner of my room in front of the flickering candle. Somewhere in the midst of my grief, my prayers were directed to Him who is the author of grace and peace. He took all my anger and buried it. I'd carried it long enough.

# Chapter 48

After a breakfast devoid of any meaningful conversation, Mama deliberately set her cup of coffee in the saucer in front of her. "This morning, we need to have a family meeting." Her eyes met mine, then moved to Alejandro. "Could we meet in Papa's office?"

"That will be fine, Mama."

At the end of the table, Alejandro nodded wearily. Nobody seemed to have slept well, except perhaps Frederick.

"I hope that is okay, Frederick. We won't be long, but it is a necessary part of—"

"Señora Rodriguez, please . . ." Frederick held up his hand. "I understand. It will give me an opportunity to hike through that magnificent coulee I can see from my bedroom window. It appears there's an old creek bed with some unusual rock formations. Would I have your permission to do that this morning?"

"By all means." She raised her voice toward the retreating cook. "Lupita, would you be so kind as to fix something for Frederick, and of course, send a jug of water with him. He's going to hike up the coulee."

Lupita turned and flashed a smile at Frederick. She spoke English, as it was translated from the language of her heritage. "But, of course. We cannot have Dina's friend have hunger while he walks."

I smiled. Even though Lupita still mixed Spanish with English, she liked Frederick, and that meant a lot. She had always been perceptive when it came to people. How well I remembered the recent morning when we had walked out onto the veranda and seen the heaped-up vegetables and fruit left for my father. She had known what kind of man Papa was, whereas I his daughter had seen only what he'd wanted portrayed.

Frederick rested his hand on my shoulder while he thanked Mama for the meal, then slipped out of the room.

Mama held the door for us as Alejandro and I trooped into Papa's office. She immediately motioned my brother to the high-backed chair behind the desk. Nothing more needed to be said—at least not in our family. Alejandro was to take his place as the decision maker, the head of our clan. Mama and I took the two soft leather chairs facing him.

Though Alejandro was seated in Papa's chair, both of us looked to Mama to start the proceedings. She wasted no time.

"During breakfast, you both were distant. I presume that means you have read your father's letters." She clasped her hands tighter in her lap and stared at them. "There was little he didn't share with me during our years together, but those letters to you were something he wanted to do alone, a final private message to his two children. Whatever they said, he adored both of you. Alejandro, you can never know how hard it was for him when you left."

Alejandro sat stone-faced and silent, only moving enough to pass me the box of tissues on the desk, while I again shed tears of hurt, for Alejandro, for Papa, and our whole dysfunctional family.

"And you, Dina. I'll never forget the morning you drove away to pursue your dream in faraway Montana. When your father came back into the house, his eyes were red and swollen, and he was not an emotional person. It was so hard for him, because he understood why you both escaped as soon as you could." Mama stared at the floor. Her fingers twisted the white handkerchief in her hands, then nervously smoothed it, a slight tremble in her slim patrician fingers. She looked up. "Anyhow, we need to plan the memorial."

Alejandro picked up a pen and searched for a piece of paper in one of the desk drawers. "Would you like me to see Father Ramirez about the funeral mass?"

"If you would, my son. Second drawer on the left." Mama's voice was again quiet and controlled.

Alejandro dragged a tablet of lined white out of the second drawer and wrote on it. "We will need to put up notices in the town. Perhaps you could take care of that, Dina?" He glanced my way as I dried the last of the tears.

"Yes, and I will write up the announcement of Papa's memorial to put in *El Periódico*. Lupita can help me with some of the details. She will know what should go in the newspaper. Her experiences with Papa are more positive than mine."

Mama glanced over at me but made no response at my biting comment. "We will have a small reception after the service. Perhaps Dina, you and Lupita could plan the food as well?"

I knew what that would look like. When my grandmother had died, we had organized the same *small* reception. Hundreds of people had trooped through the food line. Papa's would be even larger, but between Lupita and I, we would see that every one of them was fed. We'd do our part to make sure Papa was ushered into the afterlife with love and respect. His friends would make sure it was accomplished with the proper mix of dignity and conviviality.

After we'd finished planning the details of Papa's wake, Mama wearily stood and wiped at a tear. Alejandro hugged her. Hesitantly, I put my arms around both of them. She was my mother, Alejandro, my long-lost brother. Today marked a step of forgiveness, a beginning.

# Chapter 49

After our family meeting, I trudged out to the big coulee, more intent on the coming funeral for my father then the beauty of the morning. A mile from the house, I saw him striding back toward me; his blond hair covered by one of those leather Australian bushman hats the Crocodile Dundee movies made popular.

I huddled under a mesquite with adequate shade and watched as Frederick picked his way through the flood-scattered debris of the old river bed. Even though he sometimes still made me angry, when he was close, I felt safe—and alive. Was that a part of starting to know and understand each other? But what about our faith differences? How would we deal with that? What had Papa said? Marry in the church. Frederick wouldn't have a problem—that is, if he even asked me to marry him. What if he didn't? Panic jolted through my chest, raced down my arms and into my trembling fingertips, but his broad grin as he approached eased my consternation.

"How was the family meeting?"

I scooted over so he could sit beside me. "The hardest part is getting reacquainted with Mama. Every time she speaks, I'm astonished because it is so different from what I have always known. On every level I like this mother better, but I feel cheated because all through childhood I never had this connection with her."

Frederick squinted against the bright sun while his fingers absently toyed with a strand of my hair. Either he chose not to respond or was unwilling to break the mood.

Nevertheless, my need for answers wouldn't let me leave it alone. I moved my hand to his leg, wanting his full attention. "How did you know about Papa—that he was someone entirely different than who he portrayed?"

Frederick picked up a dry stick and absently peeled at the bark. "As I told you before, it was when I met him in Bisbee. Your description of him was right on, until he talked about you. Then, for the briefest moment the mask slipped—enough that I suspected what he portrayed was all a carefully constructed façade."

"Me? How did my name come into the conversation?"

"Because you'd been kidnapped, and I was angry. I accused your father of being careless with your safety."

"And?"

"Well, I uh . . . asked him for permission to date you."

"Really." I jumped up and stood in front of him so I could see his face. "You asked my father . . .? Isn't that a little old fashioned?"

His face reddened, and he shrugged. "It seemed the right thing to do."

I laughed and hugged him. Asking my father for permission to date me might not be something most men did, but I loved him for it.

"And what did Papa say?"

Frederick picked up another twig and broke it in half before he answered. "Your father's exact words were: 'Dina has always had a mind of her own.' I didn't argue with him on that point." He snickered and ducked away from my playful punch. "Your father said, and again I quote, 'That likely won't change. You have my permission to date her if you're of strong enough character to interest her.'"

"Papa said *that*?" My voice faltered.

"Yes—every word."

With no warning, I choked up. Last night, I had cried for a Papa I'd never known. This morning, it was for a lost childhood. My home had revolved around a clandestine CIA operation, and though my parents had tried to shield us, they hadn't succeeded. Now I understood why Alejandro and I had lived with a tension we'd never understood, from the time we were in diapers. Frederick held me and just let the tears happen, and for that I was grateful. I would not cry again, but for my lost childhood and for Papa, I needed one last time to grieve.

Two days later, our family, Frederick, and a good part of the town trooped up the aisle of our shining white church in Agua Prieta. The building dominated the plaza—as it should. Every town in America would be well-served to have a religious center with the influence ours had, but when I articulated that view to Frederick, he shrugged and mumbled something about Catholic church control. We were already inside, so I couldn't tell him he was wrong, but I'd certainly remember to set him straight later.

Because we had no casket, the service was different from my grandma's, but the time afterward was the same. Hundreds of people gathered at our house, and I was glad Lupita was in charge. She had everything under control. Neighbors contributed so many platters of delicious food one would have thought it was a Cinco de Mayo celebration. As guests arrived, I stood on the veranda to greet friends of Papa's, some of whom I had never met. Each had a story of his generosity. Papa would have approved, because he loved people—or so Lupita said.

It was a good send-off, and none of us could have wished for more. After many hugs, toasts, and accolades, the last person exited the yard at two in the morning. According to the testimonies of those who had attended, Papa's concern for others had extended well beyond his family. For me, the day only left frustration, and more questions. Who was the man behind the mask of bumbling incompetence my father had so carefully cultivated? For that, I had no answer.

# Chapter 50

The day after Papa's memorial service, I said goodbye to Mama and Alejandro. Frederick and I caught a mid-morning flight out of Tucson with connections in Denver for Miles City. Alejandro and I had agreed that he would stay with Mama for a few more days. I'd already taken way too much time off work, and I needed to get back and resume my job at the Spur. Besides, I would need to start the classes I'd signed up for at the college, and, of course continue to train on that crazy, wonderful mare. That Las Vegas futurity was only the first step to even bigger wins.

Within fifteen minutes, Frederick fell asleep in the middle seat. My attention alternated between staring at his strong, chiseled face, and picking out the tiny roofs that identified scattered ranches below while I mulled over the time we'd spent together in my childhood home.

My father's friends had given the honor due him, for which I was happy. Sometime in the future, our family would travel to mourn alone at that remote mountain in Nevada where he'd died. And then there would be the agency. Two strangers had quietly ushered Mama, Alejandro and me into Papa's office. Mama and I were handed expense vouchers, plane tickets, and an invitation to Washington,

D.C. for the official ceremony for Papa where they would add his name to the memorial wall in the headquarters building. Their obvious respect and deferment to Alejandro's wishes, and the fact that they handed him nothing to cover any expenses told me more about who he was and his role in the intelligence community than anything he'd ever said about his employment. My brother had obviously risen high in the ranks of the CIA.

And what about Frederick? That wasn't so easy. The church issue remained. Maybe it was just something we had to talk about more. We couldn't end up like Lorie and Bud. I leaned against the headrest and tried to sleep, but Lorie's warning drummed an insistent message, poorly timed with the wing-mounted engines. Consequently, I never dozed until the pitch changed and we started the descent into Denver.

The sun had long set when we landed in Miles City. Frederick called a taxi, and twenty minutes later we pulled into his grandma's driveway. He reached for my hand before I navigated the stairs down to my suite. "How about dinner at the Spur? This will be our last night together."

"What do you mean?" I gasped. Panic clutched at every nerve end.

He gestured at his phone. "I got a text message from the boss. I have to leave for Omaha in the morning."

Suddenly, Frederick had never looked so appealing. I didn't want him to go. I couldn't face the thought of him not being here.

He reached over and pulled me close. I willingly snuggled into his muscular arms. "Let me say hello to Gram and make a couple phone calls. Dinner in an hour?"

"Sounds good. I'll be ready. However, not at the Spur. Some place where I don't work would be more romantic."

Frederick grinned. "Of course. It's a little soon for nostalgia, but can you go for Mexican?"

"Always. Great idea."

He kissed me tenderly, and I trudged down the stairs to my musty room. Everything was as I had left it before Lorie and I had left for Las Vegas, which seemed like a year ago. It still didn't look like the St. Regis in Mexico City, but at least al-Qaida hadn't returned to trash it.

I showered, then changed into a pair of form-fitting designer jeans and the red blouse Frederick liked. My hair and makeup took longer than usual, but as I daubed eyeliner on, the worry started. Would this be the night he asked the *big* question? Did I love him enough to spend my life with him? What would he look like in twenty-five years? I patted a hint of color onto my cheeks. He'd probably be a little overweight. Maybe not, if I spent some time with Lupita and learned how to cook more healthy dishes. Would we have kids? Certainly. Three or four? I made a mental note to talk to him about that—at the proper time. And of course, at their baptism and first communion . . . whoa! Those would be huge issues. What if he didn't want our children to be baptized into the church? But they had to be. How could they miss the wonder of that first meaningful sacrament of the faith? Suddenly, the makeup in front of me didn't seem important. I shoved the vials and jars into the flimsy old dresser, draped a white sweater over my arm, and walked up the steps. Frederick paced back and forth at the top.

When he saw me, his eyes widened. "Wow, you look wonderful."

I smiled at the compliment. "Hey, you look pretty good yourself." My stomach did a flip-flop and I forgot all about our church issues. He looked like the man with whom I wanted to spend my life.

He reached for my hand. "Shall we?"

I smiled and gladly slipped my fingers through his.

"You two behave yourselves." Mrs. Riddler stood in the doorway. "Don't be staying out too late." Then she chortled. "How are you, Dina? It's good to have you back."

"Thanks. It's great to be home. And how are you?"

"Oh, not bad for an old thing. Come upstairs and visit next week. I'll be lonesome after Frederick leaves."

"I will, Mrs. Riddler—for sure."

As we left the yard in Frederick's Mustang, I marveled at the change in the old woman's attitude toward me. Apparently, I was no longer a conniving migrant with questionable morals. For that, I was grateful.

Mexico Lindo was every bit as good as the first time I'd eaten there. Nevertheless, I picked at my food, every bite seasoned with nervous anticipation. Instead of broaching any subject common to our relationship, Frederick talked about his work. His company had ordered him to open their new office in Albuquerque. He would now be responsible for recruiting new agents, in addition to running their operations in Latin America.

I toyed with the tamales I'd ordered. They were Mexican perfection, but I couldn't finish them. Frederick had one of the combination plates with chicken enchiladas, an enormous burrito, and a shredded beef chimichanga. If he was distressed at our last night together, it didn't affect his appetite.

We both turned down desert, and Frederick asked for the bill. Hmm . . . I thought. This was a bit of a bust. Excellent dinner and a great time together. Romantic? Not so much.

After the waiter left the bill, Frederick stuck his elbows on the table and leaned toward me. "Dina, I've been thinking. Would you consider moving . . . well, like farther south?"

"I don't know. Depends." I would have added more caveats, but didn't have the courage.

His index finger now did weird patterns on the tablecloth. "We've spent a lot of time together, and I thought maybe . . . probably you wouldn't, but would you consider getting married?"

"And who would I marry?" I wasn't going to cut him any slack. He had to be more direct, even if I did want to marry him so bad I was now trembling with fear that he wouldn't ask me.

His eyes shot toward every hidden corner of the room. "I thought you might marry . . . well, what if I asked you?"

"Why would you want to marry me? We have a million differences."

He reached across the table and covered my hand. "I know we do, but my love for you is greater than those differences."

Once more I heard Lorie's voice, but I pushed it away. We wouldn't have those problems. We both had a vibrant faith. Our love would overcome the church issues. But what about your children? Lorie's voice piled up doubts like a serial car wreck as Frederick handed his credit card to the waiter.

Later, we strolled out of the restaurant, then drove across town to the cut banks on the far side of the meandering Yellowstone River. Stars twinkled in the heavens. We walked out to the edge of the bluff and he reached for me. Our lips met, bodies melded, and nothing else mattered. Finally, he purposefully dropped his hands and stepped back.

I nodded, respecting his resolve. This had never been harder. I wanted only to fall into his arms and surrender everything, every part of me to this vibrant man.

Arm in arm, we strolled along the high bank of the river, the dark ribbon of water below us silhouetted in the light of a rising moon. Far below, on the other side of the stream, the Miles City Fairgrounds jutted out from the park, the oval arena and pens distinct in the light of the September moon. A horse moved in a slow lope around a make-shift round pen. A figure in a battered straw hat urged the horse on, one way and then the other, gentle but persistent.

Frederick chuckled, his voice soft with wonder. "Down there is where you took a renegade horse and changed her life—you made her into a winner."

"I had a lot of help." I smiled as I watched the old man below. Merle hadn't been an angel in disguise, which was good, because I still needed him.

We followed the trail further along the bluff, the cool night air of a Montana autumn banking the fires of passion that threatened to explode out of control. On a jutting point of ancient granite, Frederick turned and reached for my hands. "I love you, Dina Rodriguez. I will always love you.

We have many differences, but somehow, we'll solve them. Will you marry me?"

How should I answer? My future together with this man flashed through my mind. He was bull-headed and stubborn—and so was I. We would argue over everything, yet I had come to respect him. I lifted my head and gazed into his eyes, or what I could see of them by the light of the moon. "Frederick Roseman, if I marry you, we will have so many problems. There will be little peace in our lives. Every day with you will be an argument, right down to the furniture and the icons in our house. The way we would worship? I don't even want to go there, but we share the risen Lord, you have been my protector, and—I trust you with my love and our future. So . . . my answer? YES! With the help of God, we will solve those other issues."

Frederick reached for my left hand. The diamond glinted in the moonlight, but maybe that's because of the tears of joy. There are special times to cry, and this seemed one of them.

The End

To you, my valued friends and readers: In our on-line world, authors live or die on book reviews. If you enjoyed *Free to Run*, please consider posting a review to whatever book site you enjoy.

With appreciation,

David Griffith